A WORLD GONE DARK: RAVAGED SKIES

A WORLD GONE DARK: RAVAGED SKIES

by Scott M. Baker

Also by Scott M. Baker

A Schattenseite Book

A World Gone Dark: Ravaged Skies
by Scott M. Baker.
Copyright © 2025. All Rights Reserved.
Print Edition
ISBN-13: 979-8-9884973-6-3

Cover Art © Christian Bentulan

DAY ONE

CHAPTER ONE

12 July

N OTHING SMELLS BETTER than the aroma of bacon sizzling in the frying pan.

Except for freshly brewed Dunkins' coffee.

Danielle Costner stood in front of the oven cooking the family's traditional Friday morning breakfast: scrambled eggs, bacon, home fries, and dark rye toast. They started every Friday with a good breakfast and ended it gathered around the big-screen TV in the living room watching a double feature. Tonight, Shawn got to pick, and her brother had chosen *Oppenheimer* and *Godzilla Minus One*, saying the two were related, though she could not figure out how.

As the food cooked, Danielle used the remote to turn on the TV mounted on the wall across from the counter. She hated the usual morning line-up, mostly biased newscasts or even more biased talk shows. She kept it on WMUR to watch the local news, partly to find out what was happening in southern New Hampshire, but mostly for the traffic update. Her morning commute took her into downtown Boston, and Danielle wanted to prepare herself for whatever circle of Hell the roads would be like today.

"...can expect it to happen anytime between this afternoon through Sunday evening," said the chief meteorologist. "Back to you, Jess."

"I thought solar flares were dangerous?" asked Jessica Waters, the morning co-anchor.

"Only the big ones."

"But you just said this was the largest flare ever recorded by NASA."

"It is, but you have to take into consideration the size of the flare, which is small compared to the solar system. The odds of it hitting Earth are greater than winning Mega Millions."

"Which is the perfect segue to our next story." David Perrine, the other co-anchor, steered the conversation back on track. "Thursday night's winner of the three hundred and fifty-six million Mega Millions jackpot is a local citizen from Laconia. Margaret—"

Danielle hit the mute button. She was not the winner, so she did not care. Maybe someday she would hit it big, then she could move out of her brother's house and get her own place. Not that she had anything to complain about.

When her husband threw out Danielle and her daughter Kirstie two years ago, Danielle had been terrified that they had nowhere to go. She was still one year from finishing her degree in accounting at Syracuse University, so her prospects of getting a job were slim and, with not enough money to pay rent, she feared her and Kirstie would wind up in a homeless shelter. Thank God for her older brother. Shawn owned a luxurious two-family house in Dunbarton and agreed to let the girls stay with him, so they moved up from New York. He lived in the smaller, twin bedroom portion and let Danielle and her daughter live rent-free in the main house. They had four bedrooms to themselves plus a huge dining room/kitchen. The only downside was that the property being pristine, Shawn would not let them have a dog, and she desperately wanted one.

A door opened upstairs, followed by the blaring of obnoxiously loud music. Kirstie, her sixteen-year-old, came down the stairs sounding like a herd of buffalo. As she entered the kitchen, Kirstie dropped her book bag on the floor before taking a seat at the counter.

Danielle was proud of her daughter. Kirstie did not have

the best grades, all Cs with one B in Social Studies, but she was a good girl who did not do drugs, drink, or get knocked up like so many of the others in her sophomore class. Probably because the girl lived on her cell phone. Kirstie stood taller than her mother by two inches and had a lean body maturing rapidly. Soon, she would have to deal with her little girl dating. Though that might take a while. Kirstie wore combat boots, expensive jeans shredded at the knees, and a sweatshirt with the logo of a band Danielle had never heard of. Her daughter had naturally brunette hair, like her mother, but with streaks of blue and pink on one side. Someday, Danielle would have to teach Kirstie how to use a comb.

"No electronics at the table."

"What?" Kirstie yelled over the music.

Danielle took the phone from her and turned off the music. "You know I don't like you playing with your cell phone while we eat."

Kirstie huffed as if her life had come to an end.

Danielle placed a plate in front of her daughter. "What do you want to drink?"

"Coffee." Kirstie stared at her mother. "Are you going to wear that to work?"

"Wear what?"

"Uncle's old denim shirt."

"No way." Danielle opened the shirt to reveal her red dress underneath and black heels. "I'm wearing it so I don't get grease splattered on me."

"Whatever."

Danielle poured a cup of coffee and placed it on the counter. "So, are we ready for movie night?"

"About that." Kirstie averted her gaze. "Me and the girls are going to Canobie Lake Park tonight for the grand opening of their new Ferris wheel."

"Can't you go tomorrow?"

"Abbey and Mikayla have to work tomorrow."

"At least they have jobs. You know we always reserve Friday night for the family."

"But they're debuting their new Ferris wheel today. Half off all tickets."

"I don't ask much of you."

Kirstie laughed.

"I don't. I want us to spend time together before you go to college."

"If I go to college."

Danielle's eyes widened. "What do you mean *if?*"

"What? Wrack up a huge student loan debt to get a job at Shaw's? I'm thinking of going to trade—"

The back door opened and Shawn stepped in, cutting off the discussion. Though twelve years older than his sister, he still looked in his late thirties. Of average height, with piercing blue eyes and a charming smile, Danielle could not understand why he did not have a steady girlfriend. Actually, she did understand. Shawn was devoted to his job as shift supervisor at Seabrook Nuclear Power Plant. He always said that with his good looks and his good job, he could have any woman he pleased, to which she always joked he never pleased any of them.

"Good morning, ladies. Breakfast smells good."

"Thanks." Danielle hugged her brother. "Want some?"

"I can't. Bob called in sick. His wife went into labor early. I'm taking over his shift."

"So that means you'll be missing movie night?"

"Sorry, sis."

Kirstie perked up. "You can't be mad at me if I miss it, too."

Shawn glanced over at his niece. "You won't be here?"

"She wants to go to Canobie Lake Park with her friends."

He smiled. "You girls want to be there for the opening of the new Ferris wheel."

"See. Uncle understands."

Shawn turned to his sister and flashed his pouty eyes. "We'll postpone movie night until tomorrow. I'll get Chinese food to make it special. What do you say?"

"I know when I'm outnumbered. Do you want a cup of coffee to go?"

"No, thanks. I prefer my coffee iced. I'll stop by Dunkins on the way to work." Then to Kirstie, "Do you want a ride?"

"No, thanks. Mikayla is picking me up. We're going to play video games at her house until Abbey and Regan join us later."

Kirstie had met Mikayla and Abbey when all three of them started middle school and, over the past five years, had become best friends. All three girls shared the same interests and were socially awkward, so they spent a lot of time together at each other's houses. Mikayla had a gentle soul and always maintained a positive attitude. Abbey was sweet but a little flighty.

"Who's Regan?"

"She's one of our friends. Smart and levelheaded. God knows why she hangs around with the rest of us." Kirstie chuckled.

"Why haven't I met Regan?"

"She transferred into our school right after the Christmas break. Her family in Texas sent her here to live with her aunt and uncle. And they ignore Regan but expect her to do all the chores around the house. We don't get to see her often outside of school."

A horn blared from the driveway.

"There's Mikayla." Kirstie jumped off the bar stool and headed for her pile of personal belongings.

"What about your breakfast?"

The teenager ran back, placed the three strips of bacon between her teeth, grabbed her stuff, and headed for the front door.

"Aren't you even going to say goodbye?"

Kirstie waved without looking back and left, slamming the door behind her.

Danielle shook her head. "You're lucky you don't have kids."

"I consider Kirstie my kid. I get all the love and don't have to deal with the bullshit."

Shawn left out the back door.

Danielle sighed. She made breakfast for three and now she had leftovers. If she had a dog, she could give it to him. Screw it. She would reheat the meal tonight for supper.

Putting the food on a plate, she placed it in the fridge and moved the dirty dishes and frying pan into the sink. She would worry about cleaning later.

Danielle paused to glance at herself in the mirror. She looked damn good for a thirty-seven-year-old divorcee. A beautiful face with deep brown eyes stared back at her. She kept her brunette hair longer than it should be for a woman her age but did not want to clip it since it made her look several years younger. Her lean body and long legs were accentuated by the red dress and black heels. When Danielle was ready to start dating, she would have no problem finding a good man.

She headed out for work before the traffic became too horrendous.

CHAPTER TWO

THINGS HAD TURNED out well for Danielle despite the bad start to her day. All the parking spaces were full at Oak Grove Station, so she had to drive around for twenty minutes until someone left. The Orange Line into downtown Boston ran on time, but her transfer to the Green Line at North Station got delayed by the police having to arrest a bunch of climate change protestors blocking the platform. By the time the authorities cleaned up that mess and the subway began running again, another fifteen minutes had been added to her commute. When she had entered the lobby elevator of the Prudential Tower and pressed the button for the eighteenth floor, Danielle had been forty-five minutes late.

On the plus side, the marketing campaign she had created for an expanding chain of sushi restaurants throughout New England had been a major success. Several executives had flown in from Tokyo for her presentation and were highly impressed, applauding loudly when she concluded. Even her boss, Brian Denton, sat at the opposite end of the conference table, a proud expression on his face. The executives spent over an hour asking questions, a good sign they liked what they had heard. Danielle then introduced them to the members of her staff, making sure they got credit for their role in the program. Following that, Brian gave the visitors a tour of the company.

At the end of the day, Danielle was preparing to leave when Carl Jenkins, her assistant, appeared outside her cubicle.

"I heard the presentation went well."

"You guys nailed it," said Danielle.

"You did. You're the boss."

"I oversaw your work and gave the presentation. The team's idea sold them."

"Thanks." Carl blushed. "Are you heading out?"

"Yes."

"I'll join you."

Danielle slipped off her black heels and was about to exchange them for the flats in her travel bag when Brian joined them.

"Excellent job. You and your team rocked it."

"Thanks."

"I have a favor to ask. The Japanese want to take us out tonight to show their appreciation for the great job you did. Can you make it?"

"Sure. I don't have any plans." *Thanks to my family*, she thought. "What time?"

Brian checked his watch. "It's about a quarter after five. We're meeting at six at their restaurant in Copley Square. And they're paying."

"Even better."

Danielle slid her heels back on and grabbed her travel bag. The three headed for the elevator, chatting about their plans for the weekend. Brian pressed the down button. A moment later, the bell rang, the red down arrow lit up, and the elevator doors opened. The three of them stepped inside. A young woman in a pink pantsuit moved to the rear.

"I have good news," said Brian.

"A raise?" Danielle said hopefully.

"Even better. You know how you wanted to work remotely from home but couldn't because Linda was doing that to take care of her kids."

"Yes."

"Linda's kids are starting daycare next week, and she'll be coming back full-time. How would you like to work remotely?"

Danielle could hardly contain her excitement. "Are you

serious?"

"You earned it. You'll have to come in once every two weeks, but that's better than doing it every day. And you'll save a ton of time and money not having to commute."

"That'll be a Godsend. I don't know how to thank you."

"You deserve it. You can start working remotely next—"

The elevator jerked to a halt, knocking everyone off balance.

The sudden stop bothered Danielle, but not as much as when the emergency lighting failed to switch on.

"THIS IS AWESOME," said Abbey.

"It's scary," added Kirstie.

Regan sighed. "It's only a Ferris wheel."

"Yeah, but I'm afraid of heights."

"Then why are you going on it?" asked Mikayla.

"And have you guys consider me a wimp? No way."

"Too late," kidded Regan as she elbowed Kirstie in the arm.

Kirstie ignored the ribbing, her gaze focused on the ride. When Canobie Lake Park announced they were building the largest Ferris wheel in New England, they were not kidding. It stood one hundred and fifty feet in diameter, as tall as the rollercoaster near the front entrance, another ride that terrified her to go on. The line for this one stretched halfway through the park, and they had been in it for over an hour. Kirstie did not mind the wait as much as listening to the screams from those reaching the top.

"What time is it?" asked Mikayla.

Kirstie checked her watch. "A little before five."

"I hope they hurry." Abbey pointed skyward. "Those clouds are wicked thick. It looks like it's going to rain."

Regan shook her head. "Don't worry. I checked the forecast. Today is supposed to be partly cloudy with no precipitation."

Mikayla ignored the conversation about the weather. "I'm getting hungry. After this, let's get a bite to eat. I know a stand that serves chili dogs."

Kirstie grimaced at the thought, grateful they had not eaten before going on the ride.

Abbey leaned closer. "Are you having second thoughts?"

"I've had second thoughts ever since we got into line."

"You can back out if you want. We won't tease you."

"Thanks, but I've spent too much time here to wimp out now."

The operator slowed the wheel's spinning, stopping each gondola one by one in front of the platform so those on the ride could exit and new passengers get on. The girls moved forward until the line stopped. Kirstie calculated they would be on the next round.

Kirstie stared up, for the first time getting an idea of its true size. The Ferris wheel towered above her. Each time a car reached the apex, it rocked slightly before beginning its descent. A cold pit formed in her stomach. Her anxiety spiked when the operator slowed it down to switch out passengers.

This was it.

Regan took Kirstie by the hand and dragged her into the gondola. "Come on. I want you with me."

The operator came over, closed the bar over their legs, and locked it. He stepped back to the control panel and called out, "Have fun."

The Ferris wheel rotated several feet before stopping to let the next people on. Kirstie glanced over the front. Abbey and Mikayla climbed onto the next gondola. Abbey waved.

"This is going to be fun," Regan squealed.

Kirstie forced a smile.

The next few stops were not that bad because the gondolas in front of her blocked the view. However, when their car paused at the top, Kirstie had all she could do not to vomit. They were one hundred and fifty feet in the air with nothing between her and the ground except the rod across her legs. She had to admit, though, the view was phenomenal. From up here, she could see most of the park and the throngs of people enjoying themselves. Lights from the various booths and rides spread as far as she could see. Off to her, right behind the trees, at the lake with the tourist ferry sailing across its surface.

Regan rocked the car back and forth.

"Stop that!" yelled Kirstie. "You know I'm scared of heights."

"I'm sorry."

"Let me get used to this."

Regan held Kirstie's hand to comfort her.

Kirstie felt relieved when the Ferris wheel moved forward, getting closer to the ground. That sense of easiness did not last long. Once the last car was loaded, the operator placed the ride into full cycle.

"This isn't too bad," said Kirstie, her mouth dry.

"I told you not to worry. Enjoy it."

The Ferris wheel began its second rotation, and Kirstie's car had reached the top, when the ride ground to a sudden halt. The bottom of the car swung back, giving them a view straight down to the ground below.

Kirstie screamed.

SHAWN SAT IN his office off the reactor's control room, finishing his paperwork. He had less than an hour to go until his shift ended. He did not mind filling in for Bob, and the extra eight hours of pay would be sweet. However, he had finished his iced coffee several hours ago and now only melted ice remained. He would stop by Dunkins' on his way home and pick up another cup.

Heading out into the control room, Shawn stood behind the panel, studying the gauges on the opposite wall.

Brad, the Operations Management Shift deputy supervisor. He and Shawn had become good friends despite Brad being ten years his junior. Like Shawn, Brad was single and had no family, so they spent several nights after work hanging out together. Brad wanted to learn the job, and Shawn enjoyed training him. Whenever he moved on, Brad would take over his position as shift supervisor.

"No chance of a China Syndrome."

Shawn rolled his eyes. Brad always used that reference to tell him things were okay. For some reason, Brad loved that movie. Shawn hated it for three reasons. One, it was bullshit. A runaway nuclear reactor would not burn its way through the Earth's core to China. The result would be a lot worse. Second, it starred Jane Fonda. And third, the release of the movie coincided with the incident at Three Mile Island, effectively turning the public against nuclear energy.

"How long have you worked here?" asked Brad. "Twenty-two years?"

"Twenty-three years next month."

"And never an incident?"

"Thank God, no."

"Don't you get bored?"

"All the time," Shawn admitted. "But the pay is good, and the benefits are even better. I'll put in my forty years and enjoy retirement."

"Lucky you. I have another twenty-nine years before I can hang up the towel."

"It'll go by faster than you can imagine."

Shawn looked at the clock on the control panel. It read 5:19.

"I'm going to finish up my paper—"

The lights in the control room, including those on the panels, went out, startling Shawn. Surprise morphed into concern when the hum of the machinery that regulated the reactor went silent.

The control room suddenly felt like a tomb.

CHAPTER THREE

"**W**HAT HAPPENED?" ASKED Danielle.

"We lost power," said Carl.

"Why didn't the emergency lights come on?" Brian's tone had an edge to it. "Does anyone have a cell phone flashlight?"

"I do." The young woman in the pink pantsuit reached into her jacket pocket, pulled out her phone, and pressed the light button. "It's not working,"

Danielle took out her cell phone. It did not work either. She pressed the button to restart it, but it failed to come back on.

A flicker flashed to Danielle's right. Brian held a Zippo lighter in his hand, the flame barely providing enough illumination to see.

Danielle raised an eyebrow. "I didn't know you smoked."

"Only cigars."

Brian reached over and pressed the OPEN button. Nothing happened. Opening the small door at the bottom of the panel, he removed the telephone and raised it to his ear. No connection. He jiggled the hook three times and tried again.

"It's dead."

The young woman grew nervous. "What do we do now?"

Brian handed the lighter to Danielle and stepped up to the doors. "Let's see if we can open them and get out of here."

Before he could try anything, an explosion echoed through the shaft. The building shook violently, bouncing the elevator off the wall. The young woman screamed. Danielle dropped the lighter, extinguishing the flame. She quickly picked it up and flicked it back on.

"We need to get out of here," said Brian, his tone even more urgent.

Fear gripped Danielle. "What's going on?"

Brian ignored her. He tried to wedge his fingers between the doors with no success. "Carl, help me."

Screams of terror and agony came from the floors above them. The young man hesitated.

"Now!"

Carl snapped out of his shock and rushed over to help. Both men managed to part the doors enough to slip their hands into the opening and pull them aside. The car sat halfway between floors. The corridors beyond were cast in total darkness.

The young woman sniffed the air. "Wh-what's that?"

Danielle detected the smell a second later. "Something's burning."

Brian jumped out into the corridor, turned around, and reached out to Danielle. "Come on. I'll help you."

Danielle crouched to make it through the opening and took Brian's hands. As she jumped out, the elevator shook and dropped a few inches, knocking her off balance. She tumbled into her boss and they fell against the opposite wall.

Another explosion ripped through the building. The elevator dropped a few more inches.

Brian jumped up and ran back to the open doors. "Come on, miss."

The young woman ran over to the opening, crouched down, and jumped. The heel of her left shoe snapped off when she landed. She fell over, but Brian caught her and moved her out of the way.

Carl made his way to the opening. He sat on the floor, his legs dangling over the side, about to exit.

A third explosion, smaller this time, shook the building. The noise of metal grinding against metal filled the shaft, followed by a snap. The elevator plunged down, ripping off

Carl's legs and splattering Brian in blood. The severed limbs dropped onto the rug, pools of blood staining it red as the legs bled out. Danielle noticed that flames covered the severed cables as they passed by. A few seconds later, a loud crash drifted from the shaft as the car smashed onto the basement level.

"Carl!"

Danielle rushed to the elevator shaft, but Brian pulled her back.

"We have to keep moving."

"But Carl...." Danielle could not bring herself to say it.

"We can't help him now." Brian spoke in a calm yet commanding voice. "All we can do is save ourselves."

Brian took the lighter from Danielle and led the way to an emergency stairwell at the opposite end of the corridor. The woman in the pink pantsuit hobbled behind him, in too much shock to remove the broken shoe. Three doors down, a middle-aged man in a Hugo Boss business suit stood by the office door of a law firm. Light came from the windows. Danielle looked out in time to see something on fire plummet by.

The middle-aged man saw Brian and nodded. "What's going on?"

"No idea. We were in the elevator when the power went out. Do your cell phones work?"

"Nothing works. Not even the emergency lights."

"What floor are we on?"

"The fourth."

"We're making our way to the lobby." Brian raised the lighter. "Your people are welcome to join us."

"Let me gather them."

As the businessman went back into his office and ordered his people to follow, Danielle took a moment to gather her thoughts. The screaming and explosions from the upper floor had stopped. All she could hear were panicked voices inside the law firm. Then it dawned on her. Not even the fire alarms were working.

Danielle had always considered herself a strong, independent woman, but what they were going through now was way out of her league. She could not think straight, her thoughts jumping from leaving these people behind and getting out as quickly as possible to waiting here until someone came to rescue them. Thank God Brian had his shit together. Danielle told herself to stay close to him.

Once everyone from the law firm had gathered, eleven people in total, Brian led the way to the emergency exit. He opened the door. It bumped into something.

A man in a janitor's uniform peered around the door. "Watch it."

"Sorry."

"Hey," a female voice from farther up the stairs called out. "He has a lighter."

"Would you mind leading us?" the janitor asked in an apologetic voice. "We can't see a thing in here."

"No problem. Follow me."

Brian led the way, with Danielle close behind. She glanced over the railing. A dozen or so people were two floors below them, being led by a woman holding a candle.

The descent was excruciatingly slow. The lighter barely provided illumination for a few feet, so those at the rear of the column still had to feel their way down the stairs. Brian paused every few steps and held up the Zippo, a desperate gesture to provide light for those in the rear. What should have taken a few minutes stretched into more than half an hour, and they were only halfway down.

On the second-floor landing, they passed an extremely overweight black woman sitting on the stairs trying to catch her breath.

"Are you okay?" asked Danielle.

"I'm not used to this much exercise." The woman smiled at Danielle. "Thanks for asking, though."

Danielle reached out her hand. "Come on. I'll help you."

"You're a dear, but I don't want to hold up everyone. I'll wait for the fire department."

Brian paused on the landing. "I doubt the fire department will be coming for a while. You'd be better off with us."

Danielle helped the woman to her feet.

The businessman in the Hugo Boss suit stepped forward. "I'll help her."

"Are you sure?"

"Yes."

The overweight woman slowed their progress even further, generating complaints from those at the rear of the line. At the next landing, Brian stopped.

"Let the others go by us."

"They can wait," said the businessman.

"Let them go," said the overweight woman. "I need a moment to catch my breath."

The businessman and woman leaned against the wall, making room for the rest of the line to get by. Brian stood by the stairs, holding the lighter so the others could see. Danielle positioned herself in the corner, not wanting to abandon Brian. His demeanor calmed her.

Once everyone had passed, they continued their descent.

The door leading into the lobby had been locked open, allowing sunlight to filter in. Brian pocketed his lighter and helped the businessman bring the woman down the last flight of stairs. Once in the lobby, the woman pointed to a cushioned bench near the door. Brian and the businessman escorted her over and helped her sit. The businessman then disappeared into the lobby.

"I'm fine," she gasped. "Leave me to rest up. I can make it on my own from here."

"Are you sure?" asked Danielle.

She nodded. "God bless all three of you for being so kind."

"Good luck," said Brian. "I'll let the security guards know

you're here."

"Thank you."

When Danielle and Brian entered the lobby, chaos greeted them. The only illumination came from outside. A crowd of people stood by the pane-glass windows, staring onto Boylston Street and chattering excitedly amongst themselves. As Danielle got closer, she noticed the charred wing of an airliner lying in front of the building. Papers fluttered down from the upper floors, some of them on fire.

Brian led them over to a security guard in the center of the lobby.

"What happened?" asked Brian.

The guard turned to them, fear in his eyes. "A 747 crashed into the 42nd and 43rd floors."

Danielle gasped. "Was it a terrorist attack?"

"I don't think so. Whatever knocked out all the power in the building stopped all the cars and buses. Apparently, aircraft are also affected. I've heard that planes are dropping out of the sky all over the city. One of them happened to hit us."

"Is the fire department on their way?"

"I have no idea. No one has cell phone connections. Even the landlines aren't working."

Brian motioned to the crowds by the window. "If the building is on fire, you should get these people out of here."

"I've tried, but they're too scared to move." Another security officer from the reception desk called his colleague. Before the guard left, he said, "Good luck out there."

Brian led Danielle to the exit. Shattered glass and other debris littered the sidewalk. Stalled traffic jammed the street. Scores of people stood around, gawking at the flames that engulfed the upper floors. Others ran away as fast as they could. Danielle wanted to join them.

As Danielle stepped out of the doorway, Brian grabbed her arm and pulled her back. A body slammed onto the cement directly in front of her with a loud, sharp crack. The body deformed as its bones fractured and its organs ruptured. The impact broke open its skull, spewing out brain matter and blood.

"Oh my God." Danielle turned to Brian. "What's going on?"

"People are jumping to get away from the fire." He looked up, then placed a hand on Danielle's shoulder and nudged her along. "Let's go."

The two raced across the square to the opposite side of Boylston Street, avoiding the debris scattered around the area. Shards of glass and paper littered the cement, intermixed with chunks from the plane. They maneuvered their way around one of the landing gear. The tires still burned, and the jagged metal of the struts indicated how hard the airliner had struck. Once around that obstacle, Danielle stopped and gasped. One of the seats from the plane had broken loose and fallen into the square, its passenger still strapped to the charred cushions, the body hanging loosely to one side, its limbs at obscene angles from having been broken in the fall, its skin and clothes burned.

A loud thud from behind distracted Danielle. She turned around to see the corpse of another person who had preferred to jump to their death rather than burn alive.

Brian clutched her arm and pulled her along. "Hurry up before something falls on us!"

The shout broke Danielle out of her shock. Moving around the seat, she followed Brian to the other side of the street.

They paused to study the Prudential Tower from a safe distance. The 42nd and 43rd floors were engulfed in flames, which slowly spread to the next floor. Dense black smoke billowed from the holes ripped through the structure by the airliner. People stood by shattered windows, trapped in their offices by the flames, or gathered on the roof, screaming and waving their arms for help that would not be coming. A young woman on the 43rd floor leaned against the broken glass to escape the inferno. The glass shattered. Danielle watched as the woman plummeted through the air, her body careening twice before splattering on the cement. Danielle stared at the bloodied corpse, wondering if she would soon end up dead like her.

"We need to get out of Boston as quickly as possible," said Brian.

"The metro station is this way."

Brian stopped her. "The subway isn't working either. And the last thing you want is to be trapped down there with all those terrified people."

"How are we going to get out of here?"

Brian pointed down Boylston Street in the direction of The Commons. "We walk."

CHAPTER FOUR

R EGAN LEANED OVER the side of the car and yelled down to
the operator.

"Hey, asshole! Try making the stops a little less rough!"

Kirstie nudged her friend. "It's not his fault."

The entire park had lost power. Every ride had come to a halt. The lights had gone out and the music that played from dozens of speakers had stopped. An unsettling silence fell over Canobie Lake Park, followed a few seconds later by fearful voices coming from those below.

"Can you believe it? A power outage." Regan leaned over the side of the car again and yelled, "Sorry!"

"I think it's more than an electrical outage." Kirstie tried to dampen down the panic rising inside her.

"Why do you say that?"

Kirstie pointed to the lake. "Because the ferry's dead in the water."

Regan followed her friend's finger. Sure enough, the ferry had shut down and now drifted across the lake's surface. She turned back to Kirstie.

"How are you doing?"

"Scared as shit. But other than that, I'm okay."

"Don't worry. I'm with you. Besides, they must have procedures for such incidents."

As if on cue, they heard a bullhorn squeak, followed by the voice of the operator.

"Please remain calm. We're experiencing an electrical outage. The power should be back on momentarily."

Others on the Ferris wheel began shouting questions. Kirstie did not listen, concentrating instead on calming her fear of heights.

"What do you think of Billy?" asked Regan.

Kirstie stared at her friend as if she had two heads. "Who?"

"Billy. You know. The kid who sits behind me in Algebra."

"What about him?"

"He asked me to the junior prom."

"Why are you bringing this up now?"

Regan ignored the question. "I want your opinion. I told Billy I'd get back to him. What do you think of him?"

"I don't know. Whatever."

"That's not an answer."

A gust of wind blew, slightly rocking the car. Kirstie gasped.

"So, what do you think?"

"He's a math geek."

"I know. He's been tutoring me in Algebra. He's really sweet, and he's good-looking."

Kirstie forced a chuckle. "You think every guy is good-looking."

"I'm not into looks. I prefer a decent guy."

"Ha," Kirstie said sarcastically. "You like the brainy ones."

"Of course, I do." Regan winked. "They'll get better jobs. That means I can stay home and—"

The blare of the bullhorn interrupted Regan. "Ladies and gentlemen, this power outage may last indefinitely, so we're going to get you down manually."

"You mean with ladders?" Mikayla yelled.

"No. We'll move the wheel by hand. But it'll take a while, so please be patient."

"See?" Regan gently nudged Kirstie. "We'll be fine."

Kirstie inhaled deeply. "I hope so."

She closed her eyes and tried not to think about her situation. Kirstie's mind wandered to more pleasant thoughts. The girls and all the fun they had up until now. The upcoming prom, though she had not decided whether she wanted to go. No one had asked her yet. That morning's banter with her moth—

Mom! Jesus, she was still at work. What if the power outage had affected Boston? How would her mother get home?

The Ferris wheel jerked, causing Kirstie to cry out.

"It's okay." Regan placed a comforting hand on her friend's shoulder. "They're starting to bring us down."

Kirstie leaned sideways and peered over the side of the gondola, more afraid of not knowing what was going on than the height.

Seven men stood on either side of the Ferris wheel—the operator, a park employee, and five guys who looked like high school or college students. They manually pulled on the frame, turning the wheel clockwise until the first gondola reached the platform, then stopped. The operator detached the support bar and helped the riders out, then the process resumed.

"We'll be on the ground in a minute," Regan reassured her.

The minute stretched to fifteen. Every movement was jerky, rocking their gondola. Kirstie closed her eyes, straining her eyelids because they were shut so tightly. She imagined the worst scenario: the gondola tipping so much she plummeted to her death. She knew the chances of that were slim. But then, so were the chances of being stuck on a Ferris wheel during a power outage.

"We're almost there," Regan whispered.

Kirstie slowly opened her eyes. They were only three gondolas away from the platform and eye level with the roofs of the concession stands. Her irrational fear dissolved into nervousness. Looking around to check on the situation in the park, her gaze fell upon the roller coaster. Those stranded were being evacuated along the narrow wooden catwalk with the low railing. Maybe being stuck on the Ferris wheel was not that bad after all.

When it was their turn to disembark, the operator un-latched the bar and helped them out.

"Make your way out of the park, please. There are staff along the way to guide you."

"Thanks," said Regan.

Kirstie breathed a sigh of relief when her feet touched solid ground.

They waited for Abbey and Mikayla, then the four girls silently followed the flow of people. Park employees stood at two-hundred-foot intervals on either side of the crowd, guiding them along. An increasing number of people merged in from other areas of the park until the crowd devolved into a massive horde with little room between people, slowly making their way out.

Kirstie sensed the anxiety amongst the others, all of whom were as bewildered as her by what had occurred. Children cried. Parents and couples quietly talked amongst themselves about what to do next. To make matters worse, the sun had started to set. Soon it would be night. As more people came to that realization, the atmosphere reeked of borderline panic. Kirstie had only experienced such fear once, a year ago when there was a false report of an active shooter at their high school. Thankfully, that turned out to be a hoax.

This was real and would get much worse.

As they passed through the main gate, Regan chuckled. "Getting out of the parking lot is going to be a nightmare."

"I doubt it," Abbey replied and gestured toward the lot.

None of the cars would start. Hundreds of people milled around the lot, several cursing at or kicking their vehicles, anger mixing with fear. Most of the others had given up and made their way along the road leading to Route 28, having no idea what they would do from there.

"What now?" asked Kirstie.

"We'll have to walk home," answered Regan.

"To Dunbarton? Are you crazy? Do you know how far that is?"

"My grandmother lives in Atkinson," offered Mikayla. "We could go there and hang out until this blows over."

Abbey shook her head. "That's still pretty far."

"It's a lot closer than Dunbarton." Kirstie had a gut feeling they needed to get off the streets as quickly as possible.

"Then it's settled. We'll head to my grandmother's house. Let's stop by my car first. I have a flashlight in the trunk."

The four girls made their way through the lot until they reached Mikayla's car, an eleven-year-old Nissan Altima that had been given to Mikayla by her brother when he bought a new Audi. The car remained in good condition despite having close to a hundred and fifty thousand miles on it but had seen better days. Mikayla unlocked the doors and slid into the driver's seat.

"You know it won't start," said Kirstie.

"I have to try." Mikayla pushed her foot on the gas pedal and pressed the START button. Nothing.

Kirstie nudged her. "I told you so."

Leaning to the right, Mikayla rummaged through the glove compartment, throwing onto the passenger seat a pile of napkins, straws, two opened packs of gum, and the owner's manual.

"There it is." She removed an LED flashlight from the bottom of the compartment and pressed the ON button. The bulbs remained dark.

"Shit."

"Maybe the batteries are dead," suggested Abbey.

"They shouldn't be. I bought this a few weeks ago." Mikayla tossed the flashlight on the seat with the rest of the stuff and pulled the lever to open the trunk. "I have another flashlight in back."

The four girls moved around to the Nissan's rear. An old, rusty toolbox, a folded blanket, and a raincoat were pushed up against the rear wall. A cardboard box sat over the tire well. Inside were a pair of gloves, a dirty baseball cap, jumper cables, and a combination flashlight/yellow light warning system. Mikayla removed the flashlight and turned it on. It did not work.

"Damn it."

"Maybe the batteries are dead." It was the only explanation Abbey had.

"It shouldn't be. I bought this one at the same time as the one in the glove compartment."

"What's in the toolbox?" asked Regan.

"I don't know. My brother left it in the car." Mikayla reached in, pulled it forward, and opened the lid. Inside sat a road flare, a screwdriver, and a flashlight that had to be at least twenty years old. She picked up the latter and examined it. "The 90s called. They want their stuff back."

"That's because they can't text," joked Abbey.

Mikayla pushed up the switch. A beam of light lit up the trunk.

"Damn. It works."

"Thank God," said Abbey. "Now we won't have to make our way to Atkinson in the dark."

Regan motioned to the LED flashlight. "Take those batteries with us."

"Why?" asked Abbey. "They don't work."

"Maybe it's not the batteries that are bad but the flashlights. In any case, it can't hurt."

Mikayla emptied the batteries from the flashlight/warning light and slid them into her pocket. Kirstie removed the flare and screwdriver from the toolbox and slid them between her slacks and her back.

Mikayla opened the flashlight in the front seat, removed the batteries, then tossed them onto the pile of stuff. "These won't work. They're double AA. This old thing takes D batteries."

Mikayla closed the car door and locked it. "Let's go."

The four girls joined the crowd making their way to Route 28.

CHAPTER FIVE

S HAWN WAITED FOR the emergency diesel generators to switch on. The seconds slowly ticked by and nothing changed. The overhead lights and the monitors on the control panels did not come back on. Combined with the air conditioning not working, which generated background noise, the lack of power plunged the control room into an eerie, silent darkness. Libby, the youngest member of the shift who had worked at Seabrook for two years, broke the stillness. "What the fuck is going on?"

"Why haven't the emergency lights come on?" chimed in Kevin, the newest member of the team with less than six months on the job. Concern tinged his voice.

"Maybe it was a space-detonated nuke?" suggested Wilson as he pushed his eyeglasses up his nose. The third oldest employee on the shift, he also happened to have the most experience next to Shawn and Brad. "You know. An EMP that cut off all electricity."

"The news said a massive solar flare—"

"Calm down." Shawn attempted to conceal his anxiety. "It's irrelevant what happened. We have a Station Black Out and need to get the situation under control. Does anyone have a lighter?"

"Just a minute," answered Andy, the deputy shift supervisor after Brad. A few seconds later, a small flame came on, providing enough light to see within a few feet. The expressions of concern on the faces of his team were obvious.

"Let's get the flashlights from the cabinet so we can see

what we're doing."

The shift crew made their way into Shawn's office. He opened the metal cabinet, pulled out the nearest spotlight, and moved the button into the ON position. The bulb did not illuminate.

"Just our luck," huffed Kevin. "The batteries are dead."

"They can't be." Shawn placed it back on the shelf and removed another one. "I changed out all of them less than a month ago."

This one did not come on either. Putting it back, Shawn tried the remaining spotlights and flashlights, none of which worked.

"Fuck!"

"Let me try something." Brad stepped over, crouched down, and pulled out a metal footlocker resting on the bottom shelf. A padlock with an inserted key kept the footlocker closed tight. He unlocked it and lifted the lid. Andy moved closer, placing the lighter over the opening so they could see inside.

Three layers of tinfoil lined the interior. Numerous items filled the interior, each individually wrapped in the same material. Brad removed one and pulled off the tinfoil, revealing a worker's helmet with a light attached to the front. The light came on at the first try.

"God damn, Preppie was right." Brad handed the helmet to Shawn.

"Who's Preppie?"

"The supervisor before you. He was super cautious—"

"More like paranoid," Wilson interrupted.

"Maybe, but the son of a bitch was right."

Shawn placed the helmet on his head, still confused. "I don't understand?"

"Preppie always talked about how screwed we'd be if an EMP struck." Brad removed the other items as he spoke. "He made this Faraday cage to absorb any electronic pulses and keep the stuff inside safe. We joked about it amongst ourselves but never said anything to him. The shift gave him the nickname Preppie. You know, like a prepper. We meant it as insult, though it seems events proved him right."

No one spoke as Brad unwrapped and passed out each item. Inside the Faraday cage were twelve spotlights and an equal number of safety helmets with headlamps, as well as a dozen dosimeters, enough for the entire crew. The last six items were long range two-way radios. Once everyone had been properly equipped, they moved back into the control room.

To Shawn's chagrin, none of the control panel monitors had switched back on.

"Did Preppie have any thoughts about correcting this situation?"

Libby chuckled. "If he did, he never shared them with us. He knew we all considered him weird."

I wish he was here now, thought Shawn.

"Brad, you and Wilson go to the basement and check the diesel generators. See if you can start them manually."

"Sure thing." The two men each grabbed a helmet and headed out.

Shawn assessed the situation.

SCRAM rods were electronically held in place above the atomic pile and were designed to automatically drop into the reactor in the event of a power outage. The material in the rods absorbed the fission neutrons inside the core and ended the chain reaction. The control panel contained a row of lights arranged in eight columns of seven lights, each representing a rod. When they glowed red, it meant the control rods had successfully dropped. With no power, none of the lights shone, so he had to assume they had deployed.

That did not concern Shawn. Without power, he had no means to lower the built-up heat inside the reactor. Because Seabrook had been holding a constant power level for one hundred and fifty-nine hours, it meant that despite the SCRAM at least seven percent of the reactor's power remained, the result of fission product decay, a process the SCRAM rods could not prevent. As the fission products continued to decay, they would generate heat that would quickly evaporate the water currently in the cooling system. The diesel generators powered the Emergency Cooling System and, with no power to work the pumps, they had no way to circulate water to cool the reactor. As the decay heat dried up what water remained in the system, the heat generated by the core would rise to dangerous levels. In two hours, the current water level inside the reactor would evaporate enough to expose the top of core. An hour after that, the core would begin to meltdown. When that happened, the melting fuel rods would break through the suppression chamber into the surrounding containment vessel, the leaking radiation from such a breach exposing the entire crew. Not only did they face the possibility of suffering from radiation poisoning, Shawn also needed to confront the reality that they now had to deal with a potential nuclear incident that in all probability would contaminate much of northern New England.

On top of that, without electricity they had no way to monitor the pressure inside the reactor, the water level in the cooling system, and the temperature of the reactor core.

The word FUBAR came to mind.

Brad and Wilson returned.

"It's no use," said Brad. "We couldn't start the diesel generators or get the switchboards to work. Whatever hit us wiped out all power."

"What now?" asked Libby.

Shawn thought for a moment. "We need to proceed based on the assumption that the core cooling safety functions are inoperable and go from there. First, we need to figure out a way to pump water into the cooling system. Andy, call the fire control unit and have them bring over one of the engines. They can pump water from the tributary into the reactor."

"Roger that." Andy headed over to the control panel and

picked up the phone. "The line is dead."

"Great. What else can go wrong?" Kevin immediately regretted making that joke given the current situation.

Shawn ignored it. "Run over to the fire unit and tell them what's going on. They'll know what to do."

Andy grabbed a spotlight and raced out of the control room.

Brad stepped up to Shawn. "I have an idea. I have a car battery in my trunk. I planned to replace the one in my pick-up this weekend. If we can hook it up to the control panel, we might be able to get some of the monitors working. At least that way we'd know what we're dealing with."

"Do you think it'll work?"

"We can at least give it a try."

Shawn turned to Wilson. "Help Brad bring in the battery and set it up. I'm going to call Local Emergency Response Headquarters and let them know what the situation is."

As the two men left the control room, Shawn went into his office and sat at his desk. He picked up the phone's handset and held it to his ear. No dial tone. He pushed the hook several times but still got no connection. Replacing the handset in its cradle, he took his cell phone from his desk. It had no power. Shawn went back out into the control room.

"Are any of your cell phones working?"

Everyone checked their phones, but none were.

Fuck. They were cut off from the outside. He had no way to call for help or warn state and local officials.

For a second, Shawn wondered where Danielle and Kirstie were and whether they were safe. He could not worry about them now. Their priority was to keep the cooling system filled with water to prevent a meltdown.

Kevin removed his helmet and wiped the sweat off his forehead with his palm. "It's getting warm in here."

"That's because the air conditioning is out," answered Shawn.

"Shit." Libby sighed. "This place is going to be a sauna in a few hours."

"Don't worry." Kevin patted Libby on the shoulder. "The electric company will have the power back by then."

Shawn realized some of his team had not yet comprehended the extent of the situation. "Don't count on it. If a solar flare caused this, then everyone is affected. All transformers have blown out, and there are no utility vehicles available to repair them. Face it, we're on our own for quite a while."

The mood in the room became as dark as the lighting.

CHAPTER SIX

D ANIELLE AND BRIAN made their way down Boylston Street. Brian walked briskly and with determination, not making eye contact with anyone or responding to those who called out to him. He ignored the chaos around him and only glanced over his shoulder at each street corner to make sure Danielle was still with him before continuing. She had diligently followed Brian since leaving the Prudential Tower although, unlike him, she could not as easily dismiss what went on around them.

Stalled vehicles filled every street, blocking traffic. Danielle chastised herself. Like there was any traffic to block. The only forms of transportation still operable were bicycles and skateboards, their riders maneuvering through the maze of cars, vans, and trucks as if it were an obstacle course. Drivers stood around, either questioning each other what had happened or offering their theory about why the power went out.

Mass confusion reigned through the streets. The sidewalks were crowded with people, most gawking at the burning Prudential Tower. Others stood around dumbfounded, frozen in place by shock and fear. Scores of people angrily tried to turn on their cell phones, having become completely disoriented without their technology. A tall man in a business suit screamed the F word and smashed his phone onto the sidewalk, breaking it into dozens of pieces. He then stomped on the device repeatedly, cursing loudly with every blow.

As they approached Copley Station, an MBTA employee argued with five Boston cops at the station's stairwell.

"You gotta help me get those people out. They're stuck down there in the dark."

"I told you, we can't help," the older of the five policemen replied angrily. "We don't have flashlights that work. Besides, we're needed up here. Once it gets dark, this place is going to become a madhouse."

"Can you call for backup?"

"Are you friggin' deaf? Nothing works. Our flashlights. Our radios. Not even our cell phones."

"But they're only two hundred feet from the station. They're terrified. I can hear them screaming."

"What about the rest of your staff?" asked a tall, black officer.

"They all took off when the electricity went out. I'm the only one left."

The tall officer turned to the commander. "Sarge, we can't leave them down there. Let me go help them. I'll be back soon."

The older officer sighed and focused on the MBTA employee. "Denning will help you get them out and lead them topside. Once he's done, I need him back here. Understand?"

"Thank you."

The MBTA employee led Denning back into the station, both men keeping one hand on the wall to guide them through the darkness.

Danielle wondered how many thousands of riders were stranded throughout the city's subways, then quickly pushed that terrifying thought from her mind. Thank God she had listened to Brian.

At the end of Boylston Street, Brian paused to get his bearings. The Boston Common stood across from them.

"Where are we going?"

"I'm heading for Bunker Hill Community College."

"Why there?"

Before Brian could reply, sadistic laughing came from the

Commons followed by a woman shouting, "Leave me alone! Someone, help!"

A cold shiver shot down ran down Danielle's spine. She pushed from her mind the image of what that poor woman must be enduring.

Brian took her hand and headed north along Arlington Street. "Stay close to me."

They continued to Storrow Drive which, like everywhere else in the city, contained hundreds of vehicles that had stalled during rush hour. Brian made his way between the cars and groups of people milling around with no idea what to do. Ahead of them sat an ambulance with its rear doors open. A blanket covered the body and face of the patient laying on a gurney. A female paramedic sat on the bumper, her head in her hands, sobbing. Her partner stood three feet away, smoking a cigarette and staring off at nothing.

A quarter of a mile later, they passed beneath Longfellow Bridge. A Green Line subway train had come to a stop on the tracks, the passengers having disembarked and broken into two groups. One headed north into Boston, and the other crossed the bridge back to Cambridge.

Brian glanced over his shoulder. "We're making good time. Mass General is off to the right."

Mass General? Danielle had not even considered that hospitals would also be affected. She glanced over at the building. The main hospital as well as the outlying structures had no lights shining through the windows. Weren't they supposed to have back-up generators? Without power, those on life support would die. Most were more than likely dead already. Nurses would be unable to monitor their patients' vital signs. And once the sun set, patients and staff would be trapped in total darkness. Danielle closed her eyes and said a silent prayer for those inside.

By the time they reached the end of Storrow Drive, the sun had crested the horizon. However, rather than the city being plunged into a pitch-black nightmare, ribbons of red, yellow, and green lights danced across the sky, lighting the surrounding area like a full moon.

"Is that what I think it is?" she asked out loud.

Brian glanced up. "It's an aurora."

"I didn't think we got them this far south."

"We usually don't. That's a result of the ionized air from the solar flare."

"What solar flare?"

"The one they've been talking about on the news all day That's what caused the power outage."

Danielle suddenly felt stupid for not knowing.

"It's a good thing." Brian forced a smile to make her feel better. "At least it gives us light to see by."

Turning left off Storrow Drive, they picked up the Charles River Dam Road.

Danielle's legs ached. She had no idea how far they had walked. Nor did it help that she still wore high heels. She had left her book bag with her flats in the elevator and now paid the price for that oversight.

"Can we stop and rest for a few minutes?"

"Sure." Brian motioned ahead of them. "We'll take a break at the corner."

When they reached the corner, Brian checked the area and paused. "Rest up for a few minutes."

Danielle leaned against a streetlamp, raised her right leg, removed the shoe, and massaged her foot. God, how long had they been walking? It seemed like hours. She glanced at her Smart Watch. Not surprisingly, it did not work.

"Any chance you have the time?"

"Sure." Brain pulled up his sleeve and checked his watch. "It's 8:58."

"Jesus, we've been walking for two hours." Dainelle slipped on her shoe and removed the left one to massage her other foot. "How come your watch works?"

"It's a Rolex. It doesn't run on batteries."

Made sense.

Dainelle replaced her shoe and rested against the street-lamp, using her hand to wipe sweat from her brow. After a few minutes, her breathing returned to normal, and she felt a little better.

"Ready?" asked Brian.

Not really, she thought. *But we can't stay here all night.*

Brian turned right and led the way across Gilmore Bridge, which spanned the railroad tracks. Ten minutes later, they reached the intersection with New Rutherford Avenue. Bunker Hill Community College stood to their left. Ahead of them sat Charlestown, completely enshrouded in darkness. As with every other street in the city, these were also clogged with stalled vehicles that had been stranded when the power went out. At least here the people were better organized. They had broken off into groups, some heading north toward Somerville, some toward Charlestown, and a majority heading into Boston.

"I need another break."

"That's fine." Brian checked the area to make certain it was safe. "We'll rest here. It's not far to go."

"What's not far?"

"My house." Brian motioned with his head toward the neighborhood behind him. "I live in Charlestown. We'll be there in less than half an hour."

"We?"

"Yes. You can spend the night with my family. You'll be safe there."

"I appreciate the offer, but I can't stay with you. I have to get home."

Brian scrunched his eyes, a gesture barely visible in light from the aurora. "Don't you live in Concord?"

"Dunbarton, outside of Concord."

"That's a four- or five-day walk. You'll be safer with us."

Brian's tone made Danielle nervous. "I have a teenage

daughter. I can't leave her alone."

"Isn't there anyone at home who can look after her?"

"Only my brother, but he works at Seabrook and is more than likely stuck there."

Brian resigned himself to her decision. "I can't blame you. I have a seven-year-old and an eleven-year-old. I'd do anything to get to them and make sure they're protected. Just make sure you stay safe."

"I will." Danielle answered in a nonchalant tone.

"You don't understand. Today everyone is in shock over what happened. Within the next forty-eight hours, when people realize the power is never coming back, fear is going to take over. With the police out of commission, the criminals are going to take advantage of the situation and run rampant. Even decent folk like us will do anything to keep themselves and their loved ones alive. Within five days, every place affected by the power outage will become a warzone with no rules and no mercy. Do you think you can handle that?"

Danielle swallowed hard, unsuccessfully tamping down the fear rising inside her. She watched apocalypse movies with Kirstie, enjoying them because they were fiction. Now that scenario had become a frightening reality. It was bad enough she would have to endure it, but Kirstie would be going through the same thing by herself. As if to add to her anxiety, she recalled the cries for help from the woman in the Commons. Danielle would never be able to live with herself if she did not at least attempt to get home.

"I have to try."

"Good luck." Brian pointed north along New Rutherford Avenue. "Follow this road for about a mile then get onto Mystic Avenue beyond the rotary. It'll eventually take you to an on ramp for I-93. Whatever you do, don't travel alone. Try to stay near groups heading north, but don't join up with them. And trust your gut. If something feels threatening, it probably is."

"Thanks." Danielle forced a smile. "Who knows. I might be lucky."

"Sure." Brian's expression told Danielle he knew better than her what she would go through over the next few days. He gave her a supportive hug then left, heading toward Charlestown.

Okay, girl, Danielle told herself. *You've always thought of yourself as a strong, independent woman. Now it's time to nut up or shut up.*

Taking a deep breath to calm her nerves, Danielle headed north.

CHAPTER SEVEN

"SHIT," SAID KIRSTIE. "It's even worse out here."

The girls had exited onto Route 28, the main road that ran through Salem from Massachusetts to northern New Hampshire. All four lanes were jammed with stalled traffic and people standing around, confused and afraid. Every building along Route 28 as far as they could see had no power.

"I hoped the outage was confined only to Canobie Lake," said Abbey, a tone of fear in her voice.

"I'm afraid not." Regan reached over and squeezed Abbey's hand to comfort her. "The outage is widespread."

Kirstie had not noticed it before. The usual glow emanating from the commercial stores stretching along the road was gone. How extensive was this blackout?

Mikayla pointed north. "Look."

A Salem Police squad car sat among the traffic a quarter of a mile ahead of them. The officer had pulled a metal trash can near the vehicle and lit the contents, creating a fire that provided the only source of illumination. A dozen or so people had gathered around it.

"Come on." Regan made her way to the fire. "Maybe he knows something."

As they approached, Kirstie noticed the police officer had set up his fire can in front of the parking lot of a Super Walmart. The streetlamps throughout the lot and the lights inside the building were extinguished. A crowd stood around the building's entrance, confused and uncertain about what to do.

Several more people had gathered around the barrel by the time the girls reached the squad car.

A young woman stood close to the officer, hugging a frightened child against her leg. "How long before the power comes back on?"

"I don't know."

"What do you mean you don't know? Can't you call someone on the radio and ask?"

"Ma'am, the radio's not working. I can't reach headquarters."

"Will they be sending back up?" asked a middle-aged man in a Patriot t-shirt.

"I doubt it." Several of those around the trash can bombarded the officer with questions. He held up his hands to silence them. "This power outage has affected the entire area. I assume the rest of the force is stranded like me. I understand you're scared. If you stay by the fire, I'll protect you."

"What happened?" Kirstie asked the police officer.

"Your guess is as good as mine, ma'am. I have no clue."

"It's a God damn war." A heavy-set man with a beard and an America #1 baseball cap pushed his way through the crowd. "The damn Chinese set off a nuke so the EMP would knock out all our electronics. I bet they're invading as we speak."

"We're at war?" asked the mother clutching her child.

"Hang on." The officer tried to calm the crowd and regain control of the situation, a task becoming increasingly difficult. "It wasn't a nuclear explosion. We would have seen it go off."

"Not if they did it in space," responded the heavy-set man.

The officer glared at him. "Stop speculating. You're getting everyone upset. It's a failure of the power grid."

"Then why are our cars not working?" asked an elderly lady in the back.

"I don't know." The officer took a deep breath. "Everyone, remain calm. We'll figure this out soon—"

"Maybe a terrorist attack," offered a college-age guy behind the officer.

A young woman in a skirt and tank top gasped. "Was it the
Iranians?"

"I told you. It was the Goddamn Chinese." The heavy-set
man sighed. "Haven't you been listening?"

"That's enough!" yelled the police officer. The crowd quieted down. "I have no idea what's going on. There's no
indication that we're at war or that this is a terrorist attack.
You're safe so long as you stay by the fire."

A murmur of discontent flowed through the crowd, but
everyone stopped talking. A Chinese couple off to the side
stared at the heavy-set man, whispered between themselves,
then nervously but quickly disappeared down Route 28.

Kirstie motioned for the girls to join her. They moved
twenty feet from the fire.

"How far is your grandmother's house from here?" she
asked Mikayla.

"About six miles."

"We should head there now. It'll only take a couple of
hours."

"Maybe we should stay here with the cop," suggested Abbey.

Regan shook her head. "No way. These people are too
unstable."

"And I'm not?" asked Abbey. "I'm scared as hell."

"We all are." Kirstie glanced over at Mikayla. "What's the
quickest way to her house?"

Mikayla pointed north. "Lake Street is a few hundred feet
that way. It'll take us right there."

"No." Abbey's voice wavered. "It's a back road. We'll be by
ourselves."

"That's a good thing," said Regan.

Abbey motioned to the north. "Route 111 is only a quarter
of a mile beyond Lake Street. It'll take us to within a few miles

of your grandmother's house. There's a lot of traffic on that road. We'll be safer."

Kirstie stared at her friend. "Are you serious?"

"I'm scared. I want to be around people."

Regan motioned with her head back toward the fire. "Do you really think you'll be safe around people like them?"

"Yes. There's safety in—"

A scream coming from the Super Walmart parking lot cut off Abbey in mid-sentence.

A woman raced out of the store with a shopping cart filled with bottled water and canned goods. Two employees tried to stop her, the smallest of the two standing in the way of the cart. The woman slammed it into the employee, shoving her out of the way. When the second employee grabbed the woman's arm, she pushed the employee to the ground. Several people rushed over to the melee. Rather than help the employees, they began looting the items from the cart, grabbing as much as they could before disappearing into the dusk. When the woman tried to stop a large guy who had grabbed four bottles of water, he punched her in the face, knocking her out, then took the cart and ran off.

Others used the melee to rush into Super Walmart, using lighters to guide them. They emerged a few minutes later, but rather than carrying food, they carried large screen TVs and computers. One woman ran out, her arms filled with clothes. She tripped, falling face-first on the pavement. With barely a pause, she climbed to her feet, picked up as many clothes as she could carry, and raced toward the street.

The heavy-set man by the fire turned to the police officer. "Aren't you going to do something?"

"What? Arrest them? How would I get them to the station?"

"Shoot them."

"We haven't reached that point yet."

The word "yet" terrified Kirstie.

"That settles it," said Regan. "We're taking Lake Street."

Mikayla headed north along Route 28, following the flow of people. The other girls stayed close, with Kirstie and Regan bringing up the rear. Abbey walked with Mikayla.

"I'm worried about my mom," Kirstie confided.

"That's right. She works in Boston."

"I don't know how she'll get home."

"She'll probably stay at the office until this blows over."

"That's the problem," said Kirstie. "What if it doesn't blow over?"

Regan struggled to respond. "Let's take it one day at a time. First things first. Once we get to Mikayla's grandmother's we—"

"Leave me alone!" yelled Mikayla.

A burly man wearing a baseball cap stood in front of Mikayla, struggling to take the flashlight from her. "Give it to me."

"No!"

Without warning, the burly man punched Mikayla in the face. The blow knocked her off her feet. She stumbled backward, hit the side of a car, and slid to the pavement. He bent down and ripped the flashlight out of her hands.

Abbey slowly backed away. Regan ran over to help Mikayla.

Kirstie confronted the burly man. "That belongs to us."

"Fuck off."

"Give it back." Kirstie stepped closer, ready to block the asshole's punch if he tried to hit her.

He withdrew a Glock 23 from under his jacket and aimed it at her head. "Fuck off, bitch."

Kirstie stopped arguing but did not back down.

He moved forward and placed the barrel near her forehead. "I'm not screwing around."

"Let him go," Mikayla mumbled.

"Listen to her." The burly man slowly backed up. When

ten feet away, he turned and ran, merging into the crowd.

Kirstie helped Regan raise Mikayla to her feet. When they let her go, Mikayla swayed and fell back against the car.

Regan steadied her hand. "Are you okay?"

"Just a little dizzy. I'll be fine." She forced a laugh. "I've never been punched before."

"You'll be fine." Regan turned Mikayla's face but could not see anything in the dark. "You'll have one hell of a bruise in the morning."

Kirstie spun around to face Abbey. "You weren't of any help."

"I was scared."

"We have to stick together through this. Understand?"

Abbey lowered her gaze. "Yes."

"Don't be too hard on her." Mikayla pushed herself off the car and stumbled down the road. "Let's go."

Kirstie and Regan stayed in the rear again, only this time keeping a cautious eye on everyone around them. The blackout only happened a few hours ago and already people were looting and robbing each other. Kirstie had seen enough end-of-the-world movies to know things were going to get worse. She only hoped they would not become as terrible as Hollywood predicted. In any case, in a few hours they should be at the grandmother's house in a safe neighborhood. Thank God they were miles away from any major cities.

Kirstie thought about her mother trapped in Boston. With all the cell phone towers offline, they had no way of communicating with each other. It was bad enough being stuck in the middle of this nightmare, but at least she had friends with her who would help her see this through. Kirstie had no idea where her mother was, whether she was safe, and what she might be going through.

The girls reached Lake Street and turned right, cutting between the two strip malls on either side of the road before entering into the residential area. After they passed a few houses, Kirstie stopped and checked behind her. The setting sun provided limited light, but as far as she could tell no one followed them, which made her feel relieved.

Overhanging trees over the road leading through the neighborhood made the area even darker. Kirstie did not mind. The farther away they moved from Route 28, the quieter it became. The frenzied sounds soon gave way to crickets, dogs parking, and small groups of neighbors standing around in their driveways. She felt infinitely safer here. These people were already home and, though they might be scared, they were far from a state of panic. Kirstie kept telling herself that in a few hours they would be at a safe haven themselves and would not have anything to worry about.

Assuming their luck held out.

CHAPTER EIGHT

BRAD AND WILSON returned to the control room with the car battery, each man sweating heavily. As Brad placed it on the floor by the wall panel, Shawn walked up to the two men.

"Do you think this will work?"

"It better. We tried starting our cars but they didn't start. I don't know if the flare fried the electronics, the battery, or both. This is the only chance we have." Brad knelt in front of the panel. "Wilson, can you get the toolbox from the office?"

"Sure."

Shawn crouched beside Brad. "What's it like out there?"

"Bad. The power is out everywhere. When you look across the tributary, there's not a single light on in Hampton. We ran into one of the security guards who said Seabrook is the same way."

Shawn sighed. "It's that bad?"

Brad nodded. "On the plus side, it's not completely dark. There's a brilliant aurora across the sky. It's beautiful. Too bad we can't enjoy it."

Shawn motioned toward the battery. "How long will it take to hook up?"

Brad shrugged and placed on his head one of the helmets with a flashlight. "Ten minutes, fifteen at most. Though I'm not a hundred percent sure it'll even work."

Wilson returned with the toolbox and placed it by Brad. Shawn watched as his friend removed the panel to the electric circuits, examined the wires until he found the one connected to the pressure gauge, and detached it. Using a wire stripper, he used it to cut the insulation and remove enough of it to expose enough wire to wrap around the terminals. Shawn stood nearby. his gaze switching every few seconds from Brad to the monitor and back again. As much as he wanted to ask Brad if he was almost finished, he did not want to be like an annoying child on a long car ride blurting out "are we there yet?" every few minutes. After what seemed like an eternity, Brad stood.

"Done."

The monitor on the wall lit up and the gauge rolled into position. Shawn moved closer and muttered one word.

"Fuck."

The others joined him, staring at the monitor. Brad summed it up best when he said, "We're screwed."

The pressure inside the containment vessel registered six hundred and seven kilopascals, dangerously above the safety limit of four hundred and twenty-seven.

Seabrook had entered the early stages of a nuclear accident.

"What now?" asked Kevin.

Shawn thought for a moment. "We need to pump water into the cooling system so the reactor doesn't melt down. That'll also decrease the pressure inside the containment vessel before it ruptures."

"How can we do that without power?" asked Wilson.

Shawn turned to Andy. "Take a flashlight and head over to the fire unit. Tell them we need one of their engines over here to pump water into the cooling system."

Andy nodded, grabbed a flashlight, and headed out of the control room.

"Wilson, grab a Geiger counter. Go down to the doors leading into the containment vessel and get a reading."

The man's eyes widened. "You want me to go inside?"

"No. Get a reading on the outside. It's our only way of knowing if the reactor is entering meltdown mode."

"Thank God."

As Wilson exited the control room, Brad asked, "What do we do now?"

"The only thing we can. Monitor the situation and wait."

CHAPTER NINE

B RIAN HAD BEEN right about the aurora being a Godsend. Okay, he did not use that word, but it fit because it provided enough light for Danielle to see. Without it, she would have stumbled around in the dark. Being able to see her surroundings gave her a sense of security, which she desperately needed after parting ways with Brian.

The walk from Bunker Hill Community College to the entry ramp onto I-93 had been uneventful, with only a dozen abandoned vehicles and even fewer pedestrians. For a few minutes, Danielle foolishly thought this might continue now that she had left downtown, an assumption that slapped her in the face when she reached the rotary funneling in traffic from Everett and Somerville, the road congested with stalled traffic. Lines of people walked back to the relative safety of the smaller cities. Danielle made her way between the cars, detouring around an eighteen-wheeler, and followed Mystic Avenue. According to the road signs, this should take her to the on-ramp to I-93.

She ran into few pedestrians, most still in shock over what had transpired in the last few hours. The number of stalled vehicles increased the farther she walked. When she reached the intersection with Revolution Drive, she found it gridlocked yet eerily lacking people. Ironically, an hour ago, having crowds around her made Danielle nervous. Now their absence creeped her out.

Danielle crossed the intersection, wondering how—

"Watch out!"

A bicycle rushed between the row of cars, traveling reck-
lessly fast. Danielle jumped back against the rear fender of an
SUV. The cycle blew past her, the handlebars missing her by
inches. The driver, a young man in his early twenties wearing
an orange cycling jersey, stuck out his middle finger and shoved
it into Danielle's face as he raced past.

"Watch where you're going, asshole!"

"Fuck you, bitch!"

Danielle watched the bicyclist, hoping the shithead would
crash into an open car door. Unfortunately, he did not and
disappeared into the dark. She looked in both directions before
continuing across the intersection.

A few yards later, a sign pointed left to the on-ramp leading
to I-93. Halfway up, she ran into a group moving in the
opposite direction. The man she supposed as the leader nodded
as he passed.

"How are you doing?"

"Scared as hell," Danielle replied.

"Join the club. You want to come with us?"

Danielle shook her head. "I need to get back to Concord.
My daughter's waiting for me."

A woman in the center of the group laughed derisively.
"Good fucking luck."

"What do you mean?"

"I-93 is a traffic jam." The group leader shook his head in
despair. "Nothing's moving up there. And people are starting
to panic."

Brian had warned her about this.

"Why don't you join us. We're going to find a safe place to
stay for the night and figure out what we'll do in the morning."

"I have to get home to my daughter."

The group leader nodded. "I understand. Good luck."

"You're going to need it," someone else called from the
back.

Danielle waited until the group had passed then continued.

When she reached I-93, Danielle realized the others had not been exaggerating. Traffic blocked all lanes of the interstate, both north and southbound, stretching as far as she could see in the limited light provided by the aurora. Most of the drivers gathered in groups of a few people to several dozen. Others hovered near their cars. She could feel the tension and fear and knew it would only get worse so long as this crisis lasted. If what Brian said was true, this situation would last for months at best.

A part of Danielle wanted to turn around and join the group seeking shelter, but she quickly pushed away that thought. She could not succumb to her fears. Now more than ever she needed to tamp down her anxiety, pull herself together, and get back to Kirstie as quickly as possible before those around her switched into panic mode, making her travel north difficult if not impossible. Danielle was scared, but Kirstie must he going through worse. Kirstie had never spent the night alone because either her mother or Shawn were always at home. This would be Kirstie's first night alone, and under terrifying conditions. Danielle had to get back to her daughter no matter what it took.

Pulling the cell phone from her jacket pocket, Danielle checked it one final time in the vain hope service had been restored. It had not.

Taking a deep breath to steady her already frayed nerves, Danielle headed north.

She maneuvered from lane to lane, avoiding any groups of people she came across. The farther she traveled, the fewer people she encountered, most of the stranded motorists having left the highway to find safe haven in the surrounding cities. Which suited Danielle fine. The less people around, the less the chance of running into trouble.

After twenty minutes of walking, a voice called out, "Miss, can you help me?"

It was not a cry of terror from someone being attacked, like back at Boston Common, but of someone paralyzed by distress.

Danielle glanced around but could not find the source of the voice.

"Over here." The slapping of a hand on a car roof accompanied the call.

A young woman in her early twenties, attractive and casually dressed, stood by the open door of a Prius, waving frantically to attract Danielle's attention. A crying infant sat strapped into a car seat in the rear. A boy no more than seven sat beside the infant, trying to comfort his sibling while staring through the side window at Danielle, obviously worried about her being so close.

Danielle approached slowly, trying not to make any moves that might send the frightened mother over the edge.

"How can I help?"

"My car won't start."

"A power outage has affected the entire area."

"Can you help me get it going? I need to get my kids home."

"No one's car will start."

"But… how am I going to get home?"

The woman bordered on irrational. Danielle reached the car but stayed five feet distant to be on the safe side.

"I have to get my kids home. Tracy will miss her feeding time."

"What's your name?"

The woman stared at Danielle with a deer-in-the-headlights look.

"You do have a name, right?"

"I'm Joanne."

"Hi, Joanne. Where do you live?"

"Woburn."

Danielle tried to keep her tone as soothing as possible. "There is no power anywhere in the area. The only way you'll be able to get home is to walk and—"

"I'll never make it that far." Joanne bordered on a complete breakdown.

"I know that."

"So, how am I—"

"Listen to me carefully," Danielle interrupted, her tone forceful but calm. "You must get yourself and your kids to a safe place. The Somerville Mall is not far from here. There will be of others there, so you'll be safe."

"Where's the mall?"

Danielle motioned in the direction of the onramp she had ascended earlier. Other groups were moving toward it, having come to the same conclusion. "Those people are heading there. Follow them and you'll be safe."

"No, no, no, no, no." Joanne backed into the door, her head lowered and shaking. "I can't do it."

"You have to if you want to be safe."

Joanne's eyes widened as if she had thought of something brilliant. She rushed toward Danielle. Danielle prepared to defend herself, but the distraught woman only grabbed her hands, squeezed tightly, and focused her gaze on her supposed savior.

"Come with me to the mall. I can't do it on my own."

"I need to get home to my daughter."

"I need your help. Please!" Joanne practically yelled the last word, her voice filled with so much trauma it nearly broke Danielle's heart.

Joanne clearly did not have the emotional capacity to take care of herself and her kids. Under normal circumstances, Danielle would help. But these were not normal circumstances. Social norms died along with the power. Helping Joanne would be a nightmare, at best. If she agreed to assist the woman, she would wind up taking responsibility for her kids, something she refused to do. Danielle's priority was to get home and take care of Kirstie. It would take several days to do that and, if the situation kept devolving as it had been today, she would be traveling through a war zone.

"Joanne, I can't help you. Sorry."

Joanne released Danielle's hands and shoved her away, her fear morphing into anger.

"Fuck you!"

The gesture caught Danielle off guard. "What?"

"You're a selfish bitch!"

Danielle took a few steps backward and continued walking, putting a row of stalled cars between herself and Joanne. She had gone twenty feet when Joanne called to her, this time her tone reverting to fear and helplessness.

"I'm sorry. Please, come back. Don't leave me alone."

Danielle ignored her and continued walking.

"Fuck you, bitch! I hope you can live with yourself!"

The words pierced Danielle's soul because Joanne was right. It would be hard for Danielle to deal with the decision she had made. She knew the next few days would be disastrous for Joanne, and especially the kids. Chances were good they would not survive.

As Danielle hurried away, she heard Joanne's voice echoing through the stillness.

"Will somebody *please* help me!"

AFTER AN HOUR of walking, exhaustion began to overtake Danielle. Her legs were sore and her feet ached. Now she understood why every woman in apocalypse movies did not wear high-heeled shoes. She regretted leaving her book bag with her flats behind in the elevator. Nothing she could do about that now.

Off to the right, a green sign read:

Concord   65 miles

Shit!

Pace yourself, Danielle thought. You need to find a safe place to rest, though that would be next to impossible out here. On the plus side, there were not as many people on the interstate compared to when she first set out. Most had wandered off seeking a place to hold up for the night. Those that lingered seemed in a state of shock, uncertain what to do next. This seemed as safe a location as any to get some rest.

Half a mile ahead of her loomed an eighteen-wheeler with the Shaw's supermarket logo on the sides and back. A few cars behind it sat an Audi Q3 with the driver's door open. Danielle paused by the door and peered inside. The owner had abandoned the SUV. Since no one yelled at her to get away from there, she took the chance and slid into the driver's seat, then closed and locked the doors.

Danielle noticed a pink book bag resting on the passenger's seat, opened it, and rummaged through the contents for anything useful. A laptop. A pack of Marlboro cigarettes. A lighter. Paperwork held together with a clip. A small bag of cosmetics.

Jackpot. A pair of Dolce Vita plain black flats.

Danielle removed them, kicked off her heels, and slid on the flats. She almost squealed with joy. They fit perfectly. Thank God. Now she wouldn't have to deal with the long walk home with blistered feet.

She settled into the seat. Once she had recharged a bit, she would continue heading north.

Rest did not come as easy as she had hoped, though. Kirstie was with her friends, so at least she was not alone. Still, they were teenagers and were more than likely scared. If only she could text Kirstie, find out where she was, if she was safe, and let her know she was on her way home and would be there in a few days.

We had become too reliant on technology, and now were paying the price.

Before she realized it, Danielle lapsed into a deep sleep, oblivious to everything around her.

CHAPTER TEN

"**A**NY IDEA WHERE we are?" Regan whispered.

"I have no clue." Kirstie replied. "But Mikayla knows the area. I trust her."

Since leaving Route 28, the girls had settled down, being away from the panicked throngs having eased their tension. The only people they came across were neighbors standing in the street discussing what had happened and one guy who had taken advantage of the power outage to take his two Boxers for a walk. Everyone treated them in a friendly manner. A far cry from what they had endured earlier.

With their eyes having adjusted to the darkness, the girls were able to see their surroundings better despite the cloud cover, which made them feel at ease. Kirstie noticed the eerie darkness coming from the homes. No lamps. No glare from televisions. No porch lights. Only the soft glow of candles emanating from a few houses. As if everyone had gone on vacation and left the neighborhood deserted. It made Kirstie uneasy. What she would not give at this moment to hear an annoyingly loud radio blaring from someone's backyard.

After a two-hour walk, Mikayla stopped at an intersection and pointed to the opposite corner.

"That's my grandmother's house."

A two-story house stood in the center of five acres of land surrounded on two sides by trees. A driveway stretched from one street across the property to the other one, both sides lined with LED pagoda-style landscape lights that had gone dark. A soft glow came from every window.

"How does your mother have electricity?" asked Abbey.

"She doesn't." Mikayla looked embarrassed. "They're candles."

"How many candles does your grandmother own?" asked Regan.

"Don't ask. If she stopped buying them, Yankee Candle would go bankrupt."

"I thought she might be a survivalist," joked Kirstie.

"That would be Mark Dignam." Mikayla frowned and motioned toward the dwelling on the other side of the street. In comparison to the grandmother's pristine property, this house looked like the season premiere of a hoarder series. Saplings had taken root and bloomed in the rain gutters. The front and back yards had not been raked of leaves in God only knew how long. Piles of discarded furniture and empty water cooler bottles sat in disorganized mounds around the rotting shed by the driveway. Something white surrounded the property.

"Is that snow?" asked Regan.

Mikayla shook her head. "Cigarette butts. Dignam smokes two packs a day and tosses the butts into the yard when he's through with them."

Kirstie stared at the mess, dumbfounded. "You can't be serious."

Mikayla nodded. "If Dignam spent as much time cleaning up his property as he did collecting guns, the place wouldn't be an embarrassment to the neighborhood."

"How many guns does he have?"

"According to him, he has close to eighty and—"

"Eighty?" exclaimed Regan.

"And ten thousand rounds of ammunition."

"Who needs that many guns and that much ammo?" asked Regan.

Mikayla shrugged. "He thinks he does."

As the girls went on about the gun nut living across the street, Kirstie told herself to make friends with this guy. Those weapons would come in handy if the shit hit the fan.

When the shit hits the fan.

"Who's that?" Abbey pointed to the grandmother's house.

A figure walked up the driveway and peered through the front windows. The girls raced over to stop him. Kirstie removed the screwdriver from the small of her back in case they needed it.

Mikayla reached the house first. "What do you want?"

The figure turned around. In his thirties, he sported trimmed hair and beard and wore jeans and a tan t-shirt.

"Mikayla, is that you?"

"Mr. Williams?"

"I came over to check on Lori. What are you doing here?"

"We were in Canobie Lake Park when the power went out. We came here to ride out this... event." Mikayla hugged him. "Thank you for checking on my grandmother."

"My pleasure. Do you mind if I wait around to make sure she's okay?"

"Of course."

Kirstie slid the screwdriver back into her pants.

Mikayla rang the doorbell, then made a frustrated grunt. She knocked.

"Coming." A minute later, an elderly lady with snow white hair opened the door. She was small, barely five feet in height, hunched over and using a walker. "What's all the commotion out here?"

Mikayla ran in and hugged her. "I'm glad you're all right."

"Of course, I am. It's just a power outage."

Mikayla broke the hug and gestured toward the girls. "Grandma, you remember Abbey. These are my other friends, Kirstie and Regan."

"How sweet of you to come by and check on me."

"We were at Canobie Lake when the power went out. My car wouldn't start, so we walked here."

"Oh dear, you must be exhausted."

"We are. Can we stay here for the night?"

"Of course. Come on in. My name is Lori." She glanced up. "Andrew, what are you doing here?"

"I came over to check on you. I arrived at the same time as the girls."

"How are Jeanette and the kids?"

"Scared, but they'll be okay."

"You're welcome to come here if you want company."

"Thanks, but we're good so far." Andrew touched Mikayla on the arm to get her attention. "Come get me if you need anything."

"I will, Mr. Williams. Thanks."

Andrew headed back to his home as the girls entered Lori's house.

Each room had three lit candles in it, with ten more laid beside them. They would have lights for several nights, which made Kirstie feel comfortable.

Lori closed the door, secured the three bolt locks, and made her way into the parlor on the right.

"Come in, girls. Have a seat."

Lori moved over to an electric recliner. She picked up the remote and pressed the rise button, but to no effect. She mumbled a swear word under her breath, maneuvered her back toward the seat, and dropped into it with a groan.

"I made some coffee earlier this afternoon. You're welcome to it, but it's cold by now."

"I don't drink caffeine," said Regan. "But can I have a glass of water?"

"I wish you could, but the faucets run on pumps and don't work without electricity. Sorry, dear." Lori butt walked back into the recliner. "What's going on out there?"

Mikayla spent the next half an hour relating what they had gone through, from being stuck on the Ferris wheel until they arrived here, leaving out the part about the looting at Super Walmart and her being punched for the flashlight, not wanting to upset her grandmother. When finished, Lori shook her head.

"It sounds horrible. At least the lights will come back on soon."

None of the girls popped the woman's optimistic bubble.

"I have bread and peanut butter in the kitchen. Feel free to make yourselves sandwiches. There are two guest bedrooms upstairs. You're welcome to spend the night there."

"Thank you," said Kirstie.

"Now, if you girls will excuse me, I'm going to bed. Help yourselves to whatever I have."

Lori tried to stand but could not because the recliner would not elevate. Kirstie and Mikayla helped the woman out, waiting for her to gain her balance and grasp the walker.

"Thank you, dears. I'll see you in the morning."

They waited until Lori had left the room before Abbey asked, "What do we do now?"

"Not much we can do," answered Kirstie. "We'll grab a bite to eat and go to bed. Hopefully, we'll have a better understanding of what's going on in the morning."

CHAPTER ELEVEN

ANDY RAN ACROSS the compound, a task made more difficult by the heat and humidity. Sweat poured off his forehead and ran down his body, pasting the shirt against his back. He finally reached the fire unit. Like everything else in the area, the building was pitch black. One of the bay doors had been raised and anxious voices came from inside.

As he entered, Andy noticed the same level of chaos in the fire unit as in the control room. Wally, the fire chief, a middle-aged man with a slight beer belly, stood in front of his team, his well-known temper at its peak. He did not yell at them, though his tone dripped with disappointment.

"You're telling me none of the God damn fire engines will start?"

"Yes, sir," replied a younger man with a blonde crew cut.

"Why?"

"A solar flare," huffed Andy as he walked over, trying to catch his breath.

Wally faced him. "A what?"

"A massive solar flare. It knocked out anything in the area dependent on electricity. We have no power at the reactor building."

"What about the emergency generators?"

"The electronics on them were fried. They didn't turn on."

Wally's demeanor went from surly to professional. "What's the situation at the reactor?"

"Not good. Most of our instruments are down, so we don't know what's going on inside the containment vessel. We were able to get one working, though. The pressure inside the vessel is over six hundred kPa. We have no way to pump water into the cooling system and were hoping you could do that with one of your fire engines."

"It won't work," said the younger man with the blonde crew cut. "None of them are operable."

"We'll make it work," said Wally.

"How?" asked Andy.

"We'll push one of the God damn things over there." When his crew complained, Wally shut them down. "Quit your bitching. There's six of us. We can do it. I'm not letting that God damn reactor melt down on my watch."

The grumbling stopped.

Wally turned to Andy. "Who's the shift supervisor to-night?"

"Shawn."

"Tell Shawn we're on it. Let him know it might take a while for us to get over there."

"I will. Thanks."

As Andy ran out of the bay, he heard Wally shouting commands to his team.

"Grab all the radiation suits we have and throw them onto Pumper One, then load up all the bottled water we have. We're going to need them."

SHAWN CHECKED THE pressure monitor again for the tenth time in as many minutes. The pressure inside the containment vessel had risen from six hundred and seven kPa to six hundred and thirty-one. If it went over seven hundred, he would have a difficult decision to make.

On the plus side, the radiation level outside the doors to the containment vessel was slightly elevated but nothing that posed a threat to his team. He assumed the coolant water inside the reactor was evaporating, which caused the increase in radiation levels, but had not yet evaporated enough to expose the top of the reactor core, though that would be inevitable without an additional supply of water. Once that happened, the reactor would start melting down and, without power, they would have no way to stop the process. With luck, Wally would have the fire engine over here by then and would start pumping water into the cooling system.

They might be able to reverse the situation, but they only had a few hours left to do so.

Andy arrived a few minutes later. Shawn could tell by his expression he did not bring good news.

"Are they on their way?"

"Eventually," Andy huffed, catching his breath.

"What do you mean eventually?"

"Like everything else around here, their fire engines won't start."

"Fuck."

"The chief said they'll push one of them over and figure out a way to get the pump working."

It's better than nothing, thought Shawn. "How long will that take?"

Andy shrugged. "He couldn't give an estimate. It's not going to be easy pushing a fire engine over here."

Shawn must have let his anxiety shown because Andy added, "Don't worry. I know the chief. He's a neighbor of mine. He's a determined son of a bitch. If anyone can do it, he can."

Libby came over to Shawn. "Can I talk to you for a minute?"

"What's up?"

Andy joined the others at the control panel. Libby looked at the others uncomfortably, then turned his attention back to Shawn.

"I've had no word from my family since this began. I'd like your permission to go check on them."

"Denied."

"But...." Libby was at a loss for words.

"How do you plan on getting there without a car?"

"I have to at least try," answered Libby defiantly. "They could be in danger."

"I empathize with you. I have no idea where my sister and niece are and whether they're safe. But you're needed here."

"My family is my priority."

Shawn needed to end this discussion. He stepped up to Libby, who immediately lost his defiance. "Where do you live?"

"Kensington."

"We're facing a catastrophic nuclear incident. The pressure inside the containment vessel is building. If we can't release it, the vessel will explode. That'll contaminate everything within a ten-mile radius, which includes all of Kensington. If the reactor melts down, the contamination will spread as far north as Saco and Concord, as far south as Boston, and as far west as Manchester and Nashua. You'll be dead before you reach your family. And so will over four million people who have no idea what's going on here and no way to evacuate even if they did. To prevent that, I need all hands on deck. Stop whining and get back to work."

Libby lowered his head. "You're right. Sorry for being selfish."

"No need to apologize. I understand. But the best way to protect your family is to stay here and prevent an incident."

Libby forced a smile. "Thank you."

As Libby rushed off, Shawn went back to checking the pressure gauge, which had climbed to six hundred and thirty-two.

Where the Hell is the fire engine?

DAY TWO

CHAPTER TWELVE

DANIELLE MADE HER way along Route 77. Limped would have been a better word. Her legs ached from all the walking, and every step she took was agonizing due to the blisters covering her feet, both the new ones and those that had burst open on the trek. She had found a t-shirt draped over the guardrail along I-93 and tore it into strips, using the pieces to pad the inside of her flats. It eased the pain slightly, but the sweat from her feet soaked the strips which irritated her open-sored skin. Thankfully, she had been smart enough to keep the rest of the shirt so she could swap out the old strips when they became unbearable and had picked up a few other abandoned pieces of clothing along the way.

What did not ache was disgustingly dirty. Danielle had left Boston seven days ago and hiked over seventy miles in the summer heat and humidity. Her body and dress were constantly drenched in sweat, and both had a nauseating stench about them which she could not get used to. Even worse, her crotch had become sore, making each step painful. She dried it occasionally with the discarded clothes, but rashes had developed where her legs met her crotch. And her vagina and ass stank even worse than her body. She had not defecated or urinated for days because she had not eaten or drank anything. No one would give up any of their supplies to help her, though she could not blame them. She had detoured off a few exits along I-93 to see if she could find anything at service stations, but by now they had been raided of everything. She had given up on that effort after the fifth try.

She had considered sleeping during the day and traveling at night when the temperature would be cooler, but quickly thought otherwise. The farther north she traveled, the fewer vehicles were on the road, which meant fewer people around to provide safety. Gunshots and screams penetrated the night, the number of incidents increasing with each passing day. While the highway remained relatively safe, the surrounding areas had become a warzone. She reasoned it would be safer to hold up at night in an abandoned truck or van with the doors locked and move during the day.

Dainelle felt relieved when she saw the turnoff to her street up ahead. She would be home in a few minutes. Once she hugged Kirstie, she could clean up. There would be no running water since the electric pump would be dead, but a stream flowed through the woods behind the house. She would bathe in it, put ointment on her sores, change her clothes, and sleep for the next twelve hours.

Turning onto her street, Danielle noticed an Amazon delivery truck on the left side of the road. Torn open boxes littered the pavement, the wind blowing the packing material into the woods. She paused to examine the remains. Whoever had raided the truck had done a thorough job. Clothes, food, medicine, and anything considered a necessity had been looted, the only items left behind being books, electronics, and sundry other things that a week ago would be considered valuable but were now nothing more than useless luxuries.

It suddenly dawned on Danielle that this truck had been raided by her neighbors, people she had known and trusted for years. What had the world become?

Reaching her driveway, Danielle turned up it and stopped. The front door to the house stood open and some of her personal belongings littered the front yard. Panic overwhelmed her. Ignoring the pain in her feet, Danielle raced up to the house and ran inside. Shawn lay on the floor, two gunshot wounds to his chest and one to his head. He had died defending his home.

She maneuvered around the body and ran into the kitchen, which had been ransacked. Cabinet doors had been torn from their hinges and anything edible stolen. The three packages of bottled water she had left on the counter were gone. Rushing over to the pantry, she found the same. Everything of value had been looted. Who would do—

Kirstie!

Dainelle ran upstairs. Clothes and toiletries lay scattered across the hall floor. She paused at the door to Kirstie's bedroom. It had been ransacked, but she saw no signs of her daughter.

"Kirstie!"

A moan came from the master bedroom. Danielle rushed down the hall and entered, screaming at the sight before her.

The room had been looted like the rest of the house. Kirstie lay at an angle on the bed, her arms tied to the headboard with belts, pieces of tattered clothes hanging off her limbs, her breasts and lower half exposed. Bruises and blood covered her face. Kirstie glanced over at her mother, staring through eyes partially closed from swollen skin. She opened her mouth and uttered a single phrase.

"Please, you have to help us."

Danielle awoke with a start, her heart pounding inside her chest. Dear God, it was only a nightmare. Slowly, her thoughts gathered. She sat in the driver's seat of the Audi Q3 she had held up in the night before. The interior felt like a sauna. The sun sat high in the sky. Shit, it must be almost noon. She had slept longer than planned.

A female voice pleaded, "Please, you have to help us."

A crowd had gathered around the rear of the Shaw's truck, arguing with the driver, the situation becoming tense.

A middle-aged man menacingly pointed his finger at the driver. "We're hungry and thirsty. Open those fucking doors now."

The driver, a young man in his mid-twenties, scared and outnumbered, unsuccessfully attempted to calm the mob.

"Try to understand. I'm responsible for what's inside this truck. It'll be my ass if you rob it."

A black man in business slacks and shirt stepped forward, raising his hands to quiet down the others, then turned to the driver.

"I understand your position. Listen to me for a minute. That truck is going nowhere. What's inside is no longer your responsibility. We all need to survive, including you. Please, open the doors and let us have what we need."

An expression of resignation washed over the driver's face. He sighed and stepped to the side.

"Go ahead. Take what you need."

Danielle expected the crowd to behave rationally. Instead, they acted like an angry lynch mob. The man in the business slacks opened the doors and pushed them aside, which started the riot.

Three young men shoved him out of the way and climbed into the back of the truck, two of them tearing open the packages while the third prevented anyone else from getting in. After the young woman who had been pleading with the driver got kicked in the face, three men grabbed the attacker by the legs and yanked him out of the trailer. His head struck the metal floor. Dainelle heard his skull crack even from this distance. They tossed aside the asshole, crawled up in back, and pummeled the two men ripping through the packages, beating them unconscious and tossing the bodies out onto the highway. The crowd surged into the trailer, fighting for anything useful.

Someone tossed a box of canned soup out the back. The cardboard ruptured, spilling tin cans across the highway. Other boxes soon followed, some empty, most containing items no longer of value to a normal society. The driver looked on in shock at the melee, then turned and ran away.

The middle-aged man who had threatened the driver earlier jumped off the back of the trailer, clutching two one-gallon bottles of water in each hand. The young woman who had been pleading for help stepped in front of him.

"I have three kids in my car. Please give me one of those."

"Fuck off."

She grabbed the bottle from his right hand and yanked it away. Rather than let her have it, the middle-aged man released the second, which dropped to the highway and broke open, then punched the woman in the face. She fell onto the highway, still clutching the bottle. He kicked her in the stomach. When she released the bottle, he picked it up and ran off.

Danielle checked to make certain the car doors were locked and slid down in the seat, hiding from the others. Several looters jumped off the back of the truck carrying water and food. Some got away. Others were overpowered by the rest of the mob and beaten senseless for their supplies, then left battered on the pavement.

The carnage lasted only a few minutes. A burly guy jumped out of the trailer carrying a package of bottled water under each arm. As he raced by the Q3, he stumbled and fell into the driver's door, tearing off the side mirror. He yelped and stared at Dainelle.

"What are you looking at, cunt?"

Danielle's crotch became wet as she pissed herself.

When everyone had left, she climbed out of the car, ignoring her soaked panties. Those who had been beaten slowly got to their feet and staggered off except for the young woman who had tried to grab the water bottle. She had crawled into a kneeling position and stayed there, sobbing uncontrollably.

Danielle cautiously approached. "Are you okay?"

The woman stayed focus on the ground. "Fuck off."

"I'm only trying to help."

"Help?" She raised her head. Dried blood from her broken

nose covered her mouth and chin, some having dripped onto her t-shirt. "You sat in your fucking car while they beat me and took the water bottle. How will my kids survive?"

"I was scared."

"We all are, bitch."

Danielle ignored her, headed for the truck, pushed aside the discarded cardboard boxes, and climbed into the trailer. Everything had been thoroughly ransacked. She rummaged through the remnants, quickly losing hope of finding anything useful. A package of bottled water had been broken open and trampled during the chaos, most of the bottles empty, the wasted water leaving a wet spot on the boards covering the floor. One bottle that lay on its side against the wall had some water remaining. Danielle gently picked it up and gulped down the contents. It did little to satisfy her thirst but was better than nothing.

Danielle made her way to the end of the trailer. The young woman had left. She could empathize. Protecting your children during a crisis was a mother's number one priority. At least the woman knew where her kids were, a luxury Danielle wish she had. As she recalled her dream, Danielle wondered if it had merely been a nightmare or an omen.

Get your shit together, Danielle chastised herself. If she wanted to survive, if she wanted to get home and check on Kirstie and protect her, she had to grow a pair. Civility died along with the electricity. The idea of being a sweet, single mom no longer played well. She would have to become as bad ass as those around her, would have to do things she never thought possible, and would have to stop caring about others. Everything that was against her nature.

Climbing down from the trailer, Danielle made her way around the truck and continued north toward Concord.

CHAPTER THIRTEEN

K IRSTIE AWOKE WITH a start and sat upright in her bed. For a brief moment, she thought everything that had happened had been nothing more than a bad dream. That fantasy crashed around her when Kirstie realized she was not in her bedroom but the guest room of Lori's house. Damn it. She still lived the nightmare.

Regan stood by the window, leaning out and staring up. A weird light shone through the panes.

"Is it morning?" asked Kirstie.

"No. But you have to see this."

Kirstie swung her legs out of bed and joined her friend.

Bands of red, yellow, and green lights streaked across the sky, creating a spectacular kaleidoscopic view.

"Is that an aurora?"

Regan nodded. "Isn't it beautiful?"

"What caused it?" Kirstie asked.

"My science teacher told us it's created when energized particles ejected from the sun hit our atmosphere. The Earth's magnetism directs the particles toward the poles and, as they travel, they glow and light up the sky."

"Do you think that's what caused the power outage?"

Regan shrugged. "We won't know for sure until the power comes back on."

If the power comes back on, thought Kirstie.

Regan closed the window. "Let's check on Abbey and Mikayla."

Finding the other bedroom empty, Kirstie and Regan made

their way downstairs. Lori and Abbey sat at the kitchen table drinking bottled water, the glow from a candle lighting up their faces.

"Good morning," Lori greeted the girls with a smile. "Did you sleep well?"

"Like a rock," admitted Kirstie.

"Good. You girls needed a good sleep."

"Where's Mikayla?" asked Regan.

"She's over at Andrew's house." Lori took a drink from the bottle. "She's asking if we can borrow his outdoor grill."

"For what?"

"I have bacon and eggs in my fridge, but without electricity they'll go bad. I figured we could make a big breakfast for us and Andrew's family. You know, make the most of a bad situation."

"I thought it was a great idea," said Abbey.

The back door opened and Mikayla entered. "Mr. Williams says thank you. He loves the idea, but the grill is too big to move. If we bring the food over, he'll cook breakfast for all of us. Will you help me?"

Mikayla opened the fridge and pulled out the eggs and bacon, handing them to Abbey and Regan. Opening the freezer, she rummaged around among the partially frozen dinners and containers of melting ice cream. She removed three packages of chicken microwave breasts and two packages of ground meat, which she passed to Kirstie.

"What are you going to do with those?" asked Lori.

"Mr. Williams told me to bring over any frozen meat we have, and he'll also make dinner for us."

Lori smiled. "He's so sweet."

Mikayla opened the back door. "Are you coming, Grand-ma?"

Lori tapped the walker. "It's too far for me to walk. Bring me back a plate when it's ready, please."

"Of course. Do you want one of us to stay with you?"

"I'm used to being by myself. You girls go and have fun."

"Okay, Grandma. We'll check in on you."

The sun had crested the horizon, its beams filtering through the trees. Kirstie looked both ways before crossing the street, chastising herself. No sense looking out for traffic if none of the cars worked.

They found Andrew in the backyard setting up the four-burner propane gas barbecue grill. A young girl about fourteen years old, tall and with an athletic build, with her long blonde hair tied into a ponytail, stood by her father, holding a candle that she hovered near where Andrew worked. He checked the gauge on the propane tank nestled beneath the grill, turned the knob to get the gas flowing, then stood and withdrew a wand candle lighter. Flicking it on, he moved the flame closer to the grill until the propane ignited. Andrew stepped over and hugged the young girl.

Mikayla approached. "We're here, Mr. Williams."

"Good. And please, call me Andrew."

"Are you sure? Grandma said that'd be impolite."

"Considering the situation, it'll be okay."

"Thanks." Mikayla turned to her friends and motioned toward the young girl holding the candle. "This is Stephanie, Andrew's youngest daughter."

Stephanie blew out the candle. "Wish we met under better circumstances."

"Stephanie is a freshman at Timberlane High School," added Mikayla. "She's on their track team."

"Good thing, too." Stephanie chuckled. "We'll be walking everywhere for a while."

"Girls, put the food on the table there and unwrap them so I can start cooking."

As they prepared the food, the back door to the house opened and two women exited. The first was exceptionally attractive, with auburn hair that flowed over her shoulders. She wore shorts and a tank top that accentuated her buxom chest and well-toned legs. The second was a teenager, also with auburn hair cut down to her neckline and a physique that matched her mother. The older of the two carried a box filled with Tupperware containers. The younger held several packages of frozen meat in her arms.

The older woman placed the box of containers on the table. "Oh, good. You got the grill working."

"There's less than a quarter of a tank left, but it should be enough to cook what we have." Andrew turned to the girls. "This is my wife, Jeanette, and my oldest daughter, Sarah. These are Mikayla's friends, Kirstie and Regan."

Jeanette came over and gave the two girls a hug. "Welcome to the cookout."

"Thanks," both girls replied.

Jeanette stepped over to say hello to Mikayla and Abbey. When she saw the bruise on the former's face, her eyes widened. "What happened?"

"I had a flashlight, but some asshole punched me and stole it. When we tried to take it back, he pulled a gun on me."

Jeanette hugged her. "It's already started."

"What has started?" Kirstie asked.

Before Jeanette could respond, Andrew called out to her.

"Hon, I need some help here, if you don't mind."

Sarah stepped over. "Are you from around here?"

Kirstie shook her head. "We're from Dunbarton, outside of Concord."

"You're far from home. Where were you when the lights went out?"

"In the dark." Regan laughed at her bad joke.

Kirstie rolled her eyes. "We were at Canobie Lake Park when the power went out. We're staying at Lori's place."

"I'm sure she'll enjoy the company. If you'll excuse me."

Sarah returned to the table and began dicing an onion and a green pepper.

Andrew placed the bacon on the grill then cracked the eggs

and poured them into a large frying pan, making scrambled eggs and adding the diced onions and peppers. Jeanette went back into the house and returned a few minutes later with paper plates, cups, and utensils as well as a gallon of orange juice and a gallon of apple juice. Andrew finished cooking then divided the food into nine plates, two of which he handed to Mikayla.

"This plate is for your grandmother."

"Thank you so much."

The six girls sat at the table, eating breakfast and chatting about school, boys, and anything to keep their minds off the current situation. Andrew and Jeanette ate theirs at the grill, with Andrew cooking the meat and Jeanette dividing it up into plastic containers. She placed half of them in one box and the rest in another. By the time they were done with breakfast, the sun had risen above the trees. Kirstie could tell it would be a hot day. Thankfully, the humidity would be low today.

As the girls prepared to leave, Jeanette handed Mikayla a box of containers.

"Here. This is for you. I divided up the meat equally. Be sure to eat it before it spoils."

Mikayla smiled. "You didn't have to do that, Mrs. Williams."

"Yes, I did. We're all in this together. If you girls or your grandmother need anything, just ask."

"Thank you."

"I'll check on you later," added Andrew.

As the girls made their way back to Lori's house, Kirstie noticed a crowd of people gathered in Dignam's driveway arguing with a man in his late forties or early fifties with a long, greying beard. He wore jeans, military-style boots, a white t-shirt stained with sweat, and an NRA baseball cap. A dog barked menacingly from inside the house.

"What's going on?" she asked.

Mikayla glanced over. "Those are some of our neighbors.

The grizzly looking guy is Mr. Dignam."

"The prepper?"

Mikayla nodded.

Kirstie stopped and listened to the conversation.

"You have three generators," one man yelled at Dignam. "You don't need that many. Why can't you lend the others to us?"

"I told you they don't work. The solar flare ruined them."

"Bullshit," yelled a pudgy, middle-aged woman in the back. "You don't want to share."

"Do you hear any of my generators working?"

That quieted down the crowd, but only for a few seconds. An older man with a cane yelled at Dignam.

"What about all the food and water you hoarded? You can share those, can't you?"

"I warned you all this would happen, and you all scoffed at me. It's not my fault you didn't prepare."

"That's selfish," said an attractive blonde at the front of the crowd.

"No, that's life."

"You're always boasting about how many guns you have. You don't need them all. We need some for self-defense."

"Really?" Dignam exploded in anger. "You've been complaining about me owning weapons ever since you moved in. You reported me to the police a couple of times. Now you want me to hand them over? Fuck off!"

"Come on," pleaded the pudgy woman. "We're all in the same boat."

"No, we're all in the same storm. My boat is better prepared."

A tall man in the back yelled, "Let's take them. He can't stop us all."

Dignam took several steps back and removed a .357 Magnum from the holster behind his back. "Go ahead and try."

The crowd hesitated. Dignam raised the revolver and fired

a shot above their heads. The crowd panicked and ran away, each heading back to their homes.

The gunshot brought Kirstie back to reality. She ran off to join her friends.

CHAPTER FOURTEEN

"PUSH, GOD DAMN it," ordered Wally in his usual gruff tone.

"Can we rest a minute?" asked Eric, the young man with the blonde crew cut. "We're exhausted."

Carlson, the deputy fire chief, who stood beside Wally as they pushed the pumper from the rear, leaned over to his boss.

"We need take a break. We've been pushing this thing for close to half an hour."

Wally cast his friend a disapproving glare that quickly softened.

"Take five."

Katherine, who had been steering, applied the brake and shifted the vehicle into PARK.

"Secured."

An audible sigh of relief came from the team as they took a break. They stretched, twisted their torsos from side to side, or crouched against the pumper. Even Carlson sat on the rear bumper and exhaled deeply.

Wally did not blame any of them. He felt the same way, even worse since he was in his late fifties. However, being the chief, he could not show weakness among the team, especially with what lay ahead.

Unfortunately, pushing the pumper across the compound was the only way to get it to the reactor. Despite doing so non-stop for thirty minutes, they were barely halfway to their destination. If pushing a fifteen-ton vehicle was not enough, they did so in the heat and humidity, and with the distinct threat of having to work in the wake of a nuclear accident. The only saving grace so far had been that flat ground lay between the station and the reactor building. Wally could not imagine how difficult it would have been having to push this thing uphill.

Before leaving, the team had loaded everything necessary onto the back of the pumper, including their armor-like silver fire protection suits. Since the truck's pumps were run by the engine, which would not start, Carlson had the forethought to check on an old diesel generator they had stored at the station. Luckily, it worked, which meant they would have the ability to pump water through the hoses, albeit at a significantly lower rate than if the engine's system worked. But it was better than nothing and would hopefully deter a meltdown.

Yet none of this would happen unless they got the God damn pumper to the reactor.

Wally checked his watch. They had been resting for seven minutes.

"Back to work, people. Katherine, you come and help us push and let Eric steer for a while. We'll switch out every five minutes so we all get a chance to rest. Let's move it. We need to prevent that God damn reactor from melting down."

SHAWN PACED BACK and forth in the control room, carefully weighing his next options, none of which were good.

He had sent Kevin out a few minutes ago to check on the fire unit, and he came back to say they were almost at the reactor building. Thank God. Now they could get the fuel rods under control.

That left the issue of the pressure building up inside the containment vessel. So long as the heat turned what little water remained into steam, the pressure increase would continue until—

"Shawn," Libby called out. "You wanted me to let you when the pressure reached seven hundred and fifty kPa. We're there."

Shawn stepped over to the control panel and checked the gauge. Not because he mistrusted Libby. He needed to see it for himself, a balm for his next decision.

"That settles it. We need to manually open the valves to reduce the pressure."

The rest of his team stared at him silently.

"Only the governor or the local Nuclear Regulatory Commission rep can authorize that," said Wilson. "Did you get permission?"

Shawn shook his head. "I didn't. All forms of communication are down and I have no way of contacting anyone outside this building. We're on our own, which means I have to take the course of action I think is best."

"What about the surrounding communities?" asked Libby. "We have no way to warn them to evacuate."

"I know this sounds brash, but it's a risk I'm willing to take. Venting the air inside the containment vessel will release radiation into the atmosphere that, at worst, will expose a few thousand people. If the containment vessel explodes, over a hundred thousand people risk being contaminated. And then we won't have a hope of cooling the reactor, which will lead to a meltdown."

Brad supported his friend. "Besides, the pressure valves would automatically open at eight hundred kPa. We're only doing manually what the system would perform if functional."

"Are we all on board?" asked Shawn.

The rest of the team begrudgingly nodded in approval.

"One thing," asked Wilson. "How do we manually open the valves?"

"We have to go down to the containment vessel and open them from there."

CHAPTER FIFTEEN

THIS WAS FUCKING unbearable.

Danielle had never considered herself athletic, but neither was she overweight or out of shape. She used to walk around the neighborhood for half an hour most nights after dinner unless it snowed. She enjoyed it. It gave her a chance to clear her thoughts before returning home to relax and read. Even in extreme weather, she would dress appropriately. The fact that trees lined the road where she lived made it pleasant, blocking out the cold wind or the hot summer sun.

This was anything but a pleasant stroll through her neighborhood.

Danielle trudged along a major highway. There was no cover from the sun. No shaded areas to rest. No place to sit down and relax other than the hood of a car or the guardrail which, after sitting in the sun for so long, were unbearable to touch. Even the asphalt proved too much to handle. Being exposed to the sun all day, it heated up to over one hundred degrees, radiating heat like a hotplate.

The trip would not have been so bad had it happened in the spring or fall but, being mid-July, the heat and humidity turned it into a nightmare. She had discarded her urine-soaked panties hours ago because they irritated her already chafed thighs. Not that it helped. Sweltering in the weather, her body became a massive ball of sweat. Her soaked dress clung to her skin, adding to the discomfort. At least the nightmare had given her the idea of using t-shirts to pad her flats. She had found one in an abandoned pick-up and stopped every two hours to tear off more strips to replace the drenched ones. Blisters were forming on her soles, which would only add to the discomfort she already endured. On top of all that, her body began to stink from all the sweat and exercise, the foul odor bothering her sinuses.

Even worse, she had not urinated since yesterday and, even then, it came out dark orange, which indicated severe dehydration. And she had not taken a shit since leaving the Prudential Center. At this rate, by the time she arrived home she would have major kidney and intestinal issues which, considering the lack of medical care, would be a death sentence.

Assuming she made it home.

Danielle heard people up ahead. She stopped and listened. Unlike the usual arguing or threats she had grown used to, these people were carrying on normal conversations. Still, after what she had been through the past few days, caution prevailed.

An Irving Oil tanker sat on the highway ahead of Danielle. She made her way to it, using the vehicle as a shield, and peered around its side.

Half a mile ahead, a Walmart tractor-trailer sat on the exit ramp surrounded by other stalled vehicles. The trailer had been emptied. A dozen or so college-aged students surrounded the truck, talking to motorists who had been stranded. The longer she watched, Danielle realized the college students were bartering with others, trading the goods from the truck to those who had something to offer. She reached into the dress pocket and pulled out what little cash she had. It amounted to twenty-seven dollars. God, she hoped they had bottled water.

Danielle moved forward, slowly approaching the Walmart truck and observing how the transactions were carried out. Most of those trading occurred around the tractor trailer. However, two boys stood by a plumber's van a hundred feet away, open boxes of clothes surrounding them. They appeared clean-shaven, friendly, and bored. Rather than deal with the crowd, she walked over to the van.

The shorter of the two, a boy with blonde hair and wearing a UNH t-shirt, greeted her with a smile.

"What do you need?"

"Water." Danielle practically croaked the words her throat was so dry.

"What do you have to trade?"

She pulled the wad of bills out of her pocket. "Twenty-seven dollars. How much water will that get me?"

"Sorry, ma'am. The only thing money is good for now is toilet paper. What else do you have?"

Danielle slid the money back into her pocket and removed the watch. "How about this? It's a Tissot PRX. I paid over four hundred dollars for it. That should be worth something."

"It's electronic and doesn't work anymore." The blonde boy held out his hand. "May I?"

"Sure." Danielle handed it to him.

He looked it over. "Is this solid gold?"

Kirstie shook her head. "Gold plated stainless steel."

"It has no value now." He handed it back. "Do you have anything else, like a lighter or maybe cigarettes?"

"This is it." Danielle's hopes sank. She needed water desperately.

The other college student, a boy four inches taller than his friend and muscular, leaned over and whispered in the blonde boy's ear. The blonde boy turned to his friend and said, "Shut up."

"What did he say?" asked Danielle.

"Nothing."

"Tell me."

The blonde boy sighed. "He said if you give him a blowjob he'll give you two bottles of water. Five if you do both of us."

At first, the idea shocked Danielle. She had not been with another man since her husband left two years ago. Then she reconsidered. It was not like they were forcing her to have sex with them. The blonde student seemed embarrassed by the idea. And without the water, she would never make it home to check on Kirstie.

"It's a deal."

The blonde boy seemed stunned. "Are you serious?"

"Yes. But I need to see the five bottles first."

"Be right back." He ran over to the truck and chatted with a female student with pink hair. She nodded. A minute later he returned with a plastic bag and the pink-haired student.

"Lisa is going to mind the store." He held up the bag. "Follow me."

"Where?"

The blonde seemed taken aback by the question, but then he replied, "Behind the van."

The three of them went around the van so they were out of sight from the others.

"Let me see the water."

The blonde opened the bag and showed it to her. Five bottles of Dasani rested inside. Danielle reached in and removed one.

"What are you doing?"

"My mouth is dry. I need to wet it if you want me to do a good job."

Danielle opened the bottle, swigged down half of it, then put the cap back on and placed it in the bag.

"Ready."

The blonde leaned against the van and unzipped his pants. His length was about the same size as her former husband, though a little wider in girth. Danielle dropped to her knees, opened her mouth, and slid him between her lips.

Danielle could not believe she was doing this. Sure, she had a few lovers before meeting her husband, but had never been with two men at once, and never had sex outside the bedroom let alone in public. However, if this is what she had to do to survive, so be it. Kirstie meant more than her dignity. God knows what else she would have to do in the coming days.

The blonde must not have been with another woman for a while. After only a few minutes, he moaned and finished. Danielle swallowed, released him, and wiped her lips.

The muscular student took the blonde's place and lowered his pants. Dear God, he was three times the size of his friend. What had she gotten herself into?

"Come on."

He placed his hand behind Danielle's head and pushed her toward him. She opened her mouth and slid her lips around him. Unlike the blonde, this boy took control, holding her head between his hands as he pumped in and out of her mouth. Several times she gagged at the size, which only turned him on even more, making him pump harder and faster. After five minutes that seemed like an eternity, he grabbed her hair and pulled Danielle deep down his length, releasing down her throat for a good ten seconds. When finished, Danielle pulled away, fighting back the urge to vomit.

Danielle stood, grabbed the bag, and gulped down the remainder of the opened bottle.

"Thank you," said the blonde student.

"Thank you," she replied with a smile, trying to hide her embarrassment.

The muscular student pulled up his pants. "You're welcome."

As they came around the van, the pink-haired girl gave her two friends a glare of disapproval. "Happy now?"

"Very," said the muscular student.

The blonde student turned red. He removed a sixth bottle of water from his pants' pocket and slipped it into the bag.

"What's that for?"

"A tip," replied the muscular student with a laugh.

"Jesus Christ." The pink-haired girl stormed off.

The blonde escorted Danielle back out onto the highway then stopped.

"Where are you heading?"

"Dunbarton, outside of Concord."

"Don't stay on I-93."

"I know. Gangs from Manchester have taken over that part of the highway."

"Even worse, they're moving north to Concord. And rumor has it that the mall area on I-293 is a war zone. Once you reach New Hampshire, get off at Exit Five and take the back roads. It's your best chance."

Danielle appreciated the gesture of kindness. "Thanks."

"Good luck. You'll need it." The blonde hugged her and then went back to the van.

Danielle continued north, worried about what she would face next.

CHAPTER SIXTEEN

KIRSTIE AND THE other girls played Uno while Lori returned to her bedroom to take a nap. They had pulled the dining room table near the window to have light to see by and been playing for hours. At the end of the current round, Abbey banged her head on the table, enough to make a noise but not cause any damage.

"Mad because you lost?" asked Mikayla.

"No. I'm sick and tired of this game. Doesn't your grandmother have any other board games?"

Mikayla shook her head. "This is the only one she plays."

"Not even a deck of cards?"

"Nope."

Abbey sighed dramatically. "I'm so fucking bored."

"There's a shelf with books in the living room."

She grunted, took her cell phone out of her pocket, and tried to turn it on without success. "Why won't this damn thing work?"

"Nothing electrical works," said Kirstie.

"But I want to check out TikTok."

"You should be more interested in contacting your parents," huffed Regan. "I'm sure they're worried sick about you."

"I know mine are," Abbey replied dejectedly. "My mother gets nervous when I'm at school. She must be losing her mind right now."

"What about your dad?" asked Regan.

"I'm sure he's worried, too. But he never shows his emotions. He's probably spending all his time calming mom down."

Abbey glanced over at Mikayla. "What about you?"

"I'm more worried about my little brother Nate. Mom and dad fight all the time and it stresses him out. He spends a lot of time with me to calm down. God knows what's going on at my house right now."

"Maybe they put aside their differences to get through this," suggested Regan.

"I hope so." Mikayla added under her breath, "But I doubt it."

"What about you?" Abbey asked Regan.

"I could give a shit about what happens to my parents. They pawned me off on my aunt and uncle, and those two won't miss me until they need someone to do the chores around the house."

In all the excitement of the last few hours, Kirstie had forgotten about her mother. She didn't even know where her mother was. Remembering that asshole who beat up Mikayla for the flashlight last night, Kirstie hoped her mom had found a safe place in Boston to hold out in until this blew over, assuming it would, which seemed doubtful. Knowing her mother, she was more than likely trying to get home to check on her and Shawn. Mikayla finished shuffling the deck. "Do we want to play another round?"

The table responded with an unenthusiastic yes.

Half-way through the round, gunfire erupted nearby, followed by screaming.

Abbey jumped out of her chair. "Wh-what's that?"

More gunfire and screaming.

Regan jumped up and ran for the front door. "It sounds like it's coming from Mr. Dignam's house."

The rest of the girls followed. Regan had already pulled aside the curtain in the living room window. A bunch of people swarmed through the front door of the house across the street where the stand-off had occurred earlier that morning.

"Who are they?" asked Kirstie.

"They're our neighbors." Mikayla's tone had a tinge of sadness to it.

More gunshots came from inside the house, followed by a cheer. Several minutes passed before the crowd exited carrying rifles, semi-automatic weapons, and pillowcases filled with food and bottled water. The girls watched in amazement as everyone rushed down the street and disappeared into their homes.

"How many guns did he have?" asked Abbey.

"He claimed he had over seventy," answered Mikayla. "I always thought he was boosting. I guess I was wrong. I can't believe they stole his stuff."

"Well, he was an asshole," answered Kirstie.

"Still, you don't do that to a neighbor."

An awkward pause followed before Mikayla broke the silence. "Let's go back and finish the game."

"No." Kirstie turned to Regan. "Let's check out the place. They may have left something useful behind."

Regan nodded.

"You can't do that," protested Mikayla. "That's stealing."

"You're neighbors already did that. We need to look out for ourselves and your grandmother."

"I don't know." Mikayla's voice hesitated as she weighed taking care of her grandmother and doing something totally against her nature.

"Besides, you heard the gunfire. Someone may be hurt and need our help."

"Okay," Mikayla gave in. "Just be careful."

"We will. Get us a pair of candles and some matches." She turned to Abbey. "Go upstairs and get us some pillowcases."

As the two girls went about their tasks, Regan kept a watch on the house across the street. Kirstie took the screwdriver and flare she had left on the table, sliding them between her pants and the small of her back.

Mikayla and Abbey returned with the candles, matches,

and four pillowcases and handed them out to Kirstie and Regan.

"Are you ready?" asked Kirstie.

"Let's do this."

Kirstie turned to the other two. "Stay by this door until we get back in case we run into trouble."

"Okay."

Stepping out into the driveway, Kirstie and Regan scanned the area for any more looters then raced across the street onto Dignam's property.

As they circled around the front yard, they spotted two bodies by the front door—a middle-aged woman prone on the grass and the man who had challenged Dignam earlier curled up at the base of the steps. The former had a gunshot wound to the abdomen and another to her face, which blew away half her head. The other had taken several bullets to the gut. His intestines lay in a bloody heap on the ground in front of him. Flies already fed on the remains.

"Let's go back," suggested Kirstie.

"If there's anything left in here that we can use, we need to get it now before someone else loots it."

Both girls stepped inside.

The small hallway had two stairwells, one leading to the main floor and one to the basement.

"I'll take the basement," said Kirstie. "You check out the top floor."

"Gotcha."

Kirstie stopped her friend and handed her the screwdriver she had brought along. "Take this, just in case."

Regan took the screwdriver and two of the pillowcases and headed up to the main floor.

Kirstie lit her candle and descended the stairs.

Two bodies lay on the bottom landing, filling the small hallway. One had taken several rounds to the gut with a high-caliber weapon since little remained of his abdomen other than dangling pieces of flesh. His intestines and several organs lay on the stairs, his spine visible through the wound. The second victim was Dignam. At least Kirstie thought so since the body wore the same clothes he had on earlier. Someone had fired several rounds into his face, turning the head into a mush of blood, brains, and skull fragments.

The two doors on either end of the hall were open. Stepping over the body on the stairs, the blood-soaked rug squished under Kirstie's foot. She entered the room off to the left, entering the master bedroom, and immediately became overwhelmed by the smell of cigarette smoke, making her gag. An unmade bed sat in the center of the room along the front wall with an ashtray on each nightstand filled with cigarette butts. Piles of clothes were stacked on the furniture on the opposite side of the room. Blackout curtains covered the two windows, plunging the room into darkness. The owner definitely had no concept of cleanliness.

A bureau with an HDTV stood against the wall opposite the end of the bed. A pile of DVDs filled the rest of the bureau top. Kirstie rummaged through them. All of them were porno films and cheaply-made action movies she had never heard of. Beside the bureau stood a gun safe seven feet tall and three feet wide. It had a combination lock that had been hammered at with something, the looters obviously trying to open it without success. She could not help but wonder what he kept inside that was so valuable. Pushing that thought aside, Kirstie checked out the bureau drawers, the closet, and under the bed for anything useful, finding nothing of value.

Making her way across the hall and carefully maneuvering around the tattered corpses, Kirstie entered the other room and realized she had hit the jackpot. This room was the same size as the bedroom across the hall, only Dignam used it as his storeroom/arsenal. The walls to the left and right were lined with metal shelves that at one time had been well stocked with supplies to last several months, if not longer. The crowd had looted most of it, ignoring items that were of no use in their present situation. However, in their haste to get away, they had left behind such essentials as a few boxes of canned chili and corned beef hash, one thirty-six-roll pack of toilet paper, and six gallons of spring water.

Across from the door stood three metal gun cases, their padlocks hammered off and the doors left open. As with the supplies, the mob had taken everything, leaving only a handful of items behind. All the long guns had been confiscated except for a double barrel shotgun and a hunting rifle with a scope, two pistols, a machete, a Bowie knife, and dozens of boxes of ammunition. Kirstie knew she should be excited about the cache, and she would have been if she knew anything about firearms. Not that it mattered. The looters had left enough stuff behind to allow the girls and Lori to stay alive for several weeks, and that's what's mattered.

Kirstie started packing the food supplies into one of the pillowcases when she heard the scuffling of feet followed by Regan screaming. She grabbed one of the pistols out of the locker and ran upstairs. The sound of a struggle came from the kitchen off to the right at the rear of the house. Kirstie raced in and stopped at the entrance, shocked by the sight that greeted her.

A teenage boy, well-groomed and well dressed, had Regan pinned face down on the counter. He must have caught her by surprise because the screwdriver lay in the center of the floor. The teenager's legs spread Regan's apart, preventing her from moving. His left hand clutched Regan's hair and kept her head pinned to the counter while his right hand fumbled unsuccess-fully to pull down her jeans. Regan struggled to break free. When she did, the teenager lifted Regan's head by the hair and slammed it against the counter.

"Leave her alone!"

The teenager ignored Kirstie.

"I said, leave her alone!"

"Fuck off, bitch, unless you want to be next."

Kirstie aimed the pistol at his back and pulled the trigger.

Rather than the roar of a bullet exiting the barrel, the chamber clicked. Fuck! It was not loaded.

Hearing the failed attack on him, the teenager glanced over his shoulder, a malicious smile on his face. He slammed Regan's head against the counter again, rendering her dazed, then threw her on the floor before turning to Kirstie.

"I'm going to fuck you first, then beat the shit out of you."

He walked toward Kirstie. If she ran, she might make it to safety before he caught her, but then Regan would be left alone with him. Instead, Kirstie threw the pistol at his head. The teenager ducked and the weapon slammed into the cabinet above the sink. He lunged at Kirstie, his left hand grabbing her by the neck and slamming her head against the wall. He pushed against Kirstie, his erection rubbing against her groin. She wanted to puke.

"I like a bitch who plays rough. It turns me on." He reached up with his free hand and slid it under her t-shirt, squeezing her breast until it hurt. "I'm going to fuck you so hard you'll walk funny for a week."

The teenager pushed his hand under Kirstie's bra and pinched her nipple.

Kirstie reached behind her back, removed the flare from the back of her pants, and lit it. The sparks burned her skin. With her right hand, Kirstie brought the flare around and shoved it into the attacker's left eye. The orb sizzled as it ruptured and burned. The teenager released her and stepped back a few feet.

"You fucking cunt! I'm going to fuck you up bad!"

"Not without a dick you won't."

Kirstie stepped forward and shoved the burning flare against the bulge in his pants, pushing with all her might.

The teenager howled in agony for several seconds before dropping to his knees. Tears flowed down his cheeks and his face grimaced. Only then did Kirstie notice the smell of burnt flesh.

Movement from the other side of the kitchen caught Kirstie's attention. Regan stepped up behind the attacker, holding a carving knife. She lifted his chin in her left hand, and with her right ran the blade along his neck, slashing two inches deep. The wound opened and blood flowed out, staining his shirt crimson. As the blade moved along the side, it severed his artery. Blood spurted out, covering the floor and cabinets. Regan stepped back and watched. The teenager tried to shout an insult at them, which only came out as an anguished gurgle. After a few seconds, his body collapsed at Kirstie's feet, the blood pooling across the tiled floor.

The front of Kirstie's pants was soaked. She had pissed herself out of fear.

Regan seemed unnaturally calm given the situation. "Thanks. God knows what he would have done to me if you didn't show up."

"What happened?"

"The bastard snuck up on me while I was rummaging through the cabinets. I didn't hear him until he attacked me."

Kirstie glanced down at the corpse. She still could not believe she had been capable of doing that to someone.

"Don't worry about him. The son of a bitch got what he deserved. There's going to be a lot more of that in the days ahead. Oh, and next time, don't shoot a firearm at someone if one of us is in front of him. If that had gone off, I'd be dead, too."

Kirstie remained stunned at her friend's calm and level-headedness.

"Did you find anything downstairs?" asked Regan.

"Uh, yeah." Common sense suddenly returned to Kirstie. "Some food and water, several weapons, and lots of ammo. What did you find?"

"A lot. Nobody bothered to loot up here. There's plenty of

food." Regan held up the pillowcases. "These won't be enough to carry it all back."

"Let's take what we can back to Lori's house. We'll get Mikayla and Abbey to come back with us and pick up the rest."

CHAPTER SEVENTEEN

"WE'RE HERE," ERIC called from the cab as the rest of the group pushed the pumper parallel to the reactor building.

"Thank fucking God," Carlson gasped, exhausted.

Wally ignored him. "Put it into PARK."

Eric applied the brake and shifted the gears. "Done."

The rest of the team practically collapsed in a collective sigh. Wally wanted to order them to set up the hoses and diesel generator. However, one look at his team told him they needed a break. He would give them a few minutes to rest. God damn, they would be working their butts off for the next few days.

"Take five." Wally headed for the reactor building. "I want to check things out."

As he approached the exterior wall, the thought crossed his mind concerning the radiation level outside. He doubted it represented a health threat to his team, assuming it was elevated at all. They were only a few hours into the outage, so the situation inside the containment vessel, while dangerous, was more than likely not critical. They had been able to get the pumper here in enough time to initiate the feed and bleed, the non-technical term for feeding water into the reactor's coolant system to prevent a meltdown then bleed into the air the steam inside the containment vessel. Hopefully, they could get the situation under control quickly and head back to the station because, when the control room performed the bleed, it would expose his team to the vented radiation.

The engine sat twenty-five feet from the Low-Pressure

Coolant Injection pump on the outside of the reactor building where they would add water into the Emergency Core Cooling System. That part would be a cinch. They had enough water in the engine's tank to pump four hours of fresh water into the system. The hard part would be feeding water once the tank ran dry. Without being able to access the facility's water reserves, the only source of available water came from one of the seawater tributaries from the ocean a quarter of a mile away. Getting the water would be relatively easy. However, when the seawater evaporated, it would leave behind salt in the cooling system. Best case scenario, the salt would corrode the pipes in the cooling system, rendering the reactor inoperable. Although, under the current conditions, he seriously doubted Seabrook would ever go back online.

Worst case scenario, the build-up of salt in the cooling system would cause a hydrogen explosion, a steam explosion, or a re-criticality of the reactor. No one had a way of controlling that. Like his drill instructor in the Marines used to say, hope for the best but plan for the worst.

Wally returned to the others and began issuing orders.

"Break time's over. Katherine, hook up a hose from the engine to the LCPI pump. Carlson, set up the diesel generator to the pumper. I want to start injecting water into the cooling system the minute the hoses are laid. The rest of you lay out the remaining hoses to the closest tributary. I want to be ready in ten minutes. I'm heading inside to check on the situation."

Wally grabbed one of the older flashlights that still worked and entered the building. He had been to the control room numerous times and knew how to get there. Still, the pitch-black corridors and eerie silence broken only by his footsteps gave him a sense of foreboding.

When he eventually reached the control room, Wally was relieved to see that the situation there remained tense but calm. Good. So long as everyone maintained their wits about them, they had a chance of keeping things under control. He was happy to see Shawn on duty. He had known him for several years and considered him to be the most experienced and level-headed of all the shift supervisors.

"The cavalry is here," Wally announced with a forced sense of humor.

"Thank God you're here." Shawn stepped over and shook Wally's hand.

"My team is outside setting up. We should be able to start pumping water into the cooling system within thirty minutes."

Shawn looked surprised. "The pumper works?"

"No. Like everything else, it has no power. We have an old diesel generator we'll use to feed the water."

"How did you get it here?"

"We pushed it."

The control room crew looked shocked. Brad asked, "You gotta be fucking kidding?"

"We're tough SOBs." Wally chuckled, then became serious. "What's the situation with the reactor?"

"Not too bad at the moment." Shawn pointed to the one working monitor on the control panel. "We attached a car battery to the pressure gauge. The last reading was seven hundred fifty-nine kPa."

"God damn."

"Exactly. Now that you're here, we're hoping to pump water into the coolant system and get the pressure under control. Though I have to warn you, a team is prepping to go down to the containment vessel to vent some of the valves, so you're people outside run the risk of being exposed."

"What's the radiation level at the moment?"

"Earlier, I sent a team down to the outer doors of the containment vessel to take a reading. So far, no radiation has leaked from the reactor. At least inside the building."

"What about outside?"

"We haven't checked." Shawn turned to Wilson. "Give Wally one of the Geiger counters so he can keep track of the radiation levels outside. And get him one of the radios so we can keep in touch."

Wally was taken aback. "They work?"

"The only reason they're operable is because the supervisor before me built a Faraday cage in the office and kept equipment in there."

"Good ole Preppie. I guess he wasn't as paranoid as everyone thought."

Wilson came over and handed Wally a Geiger counter and radio. "Do you need any flashlights?"

"I'm good, thanks. The aurora is giving us enough light to work by." Wally turned to Shawn. "What's your next step?"

"We'll monitor the pressure inside the containment vessel and keep you posted. I'll be sending some of my men down every hour to check on the radiation levels."

"What do you have for protection?"

"We have several Tyvek suits."

"I have a few fire protection suits on the engine. I'll have one of my men bring four up to you."

"Thanks."

"Don't mention it. I'm heading back out to see how things are progressing. I'll let you know when we start pumping water."

"Thanks." Shawn placed a hand on his friend's shoulder. "Good luck and stay safe."

"I hope to."

Wally left the control room and made his way outside, thankful to finally be out of the building and where the aurora provided some semblance of normalcy. As he approached the pumper, he noticed Katherine had attached the hose from the LCPI pump to the engine. Carlson saw Wally and waved him over.

"We're all set to go once you give us the go ahead."

"How are the others doing?"

As if on cue, Eric ran up to the two men. "We have a problem."

"What?"

"We don't have enough hoses to reach the tributaries. We're three short."

Wally handed him the flashlight. "Go inside and grab whatever you need from the fire stations there."

"Roger that." Eric turned to the others and shouted. "Come on."

As the others ran off, Carlson asked, "What's the situation inside?"

"The kPa is at seven hundred and fifty-nine. So far, no radiation has leaked inside the building. Shawn's on duty. He gave me this."

Wally switched on the Geiger counter and slowly swung the sealed chamber in an arc. The readings were normal.

"Thank God for that," said Carlson.

"Tell me about it. With luck, we'll get this God damn reactor under control in no time."

CHAPTER EIGHTEEN

Danielle felt much better physically now that she had water. She had swigged down one full bottle a few minutes after leaving the trading truck. It revitalized her. Her throat was no longer dry and scratchy, her thinking had cleared a bit, and she did not feel as tired as before. She considered drinking another one but decided against it, saving the last three for when she desperately needed a drink. God knows when she would be able to resupply.

Though the water perked Danielle up, it did nothing to ease her aching muscles after walking so many miles. The pain had not fully set in yet because she used them every day. She knew if she ever made it home, she would have to binge on Tylenol and spend a day or two in bed.

If?

Stop being negative. *When* you get home.

Danielle concentrated on positive thoughts. She had been making better time than she had anticipated and, so far, had not encountered any serious threats.

So far?

There you go with them negative waves again.

Danielle chuckled. She remembered the line from an old war movie Shawn had made the family watch one night. She did not enjoy the movie and could not remember most of it other than that line one of the characters kept repeating throughout the film.

Thoughts of Shawn pushed their way into Danielle's mind. She tried to ignore them. Her brother was the smarter and more responsible of the two. Whereas he studied hard and graduated with a 3.5 GPA, she tended to be more of a party girl. Their mother used to joke that Danielle's grades were underwater—below C level. Unlike her, Shawn was safe at work. Even if he did decide to go home, he worked closer than her and was better suited for traveling on foot. She would not be surprised if he greeted her at the front door of their house, teasing her about not being around to make him a sandwich.

Danielle focused on the task at hand, trying to keep track of how far she had traveled, anything that might be of use, and searching for a safe place to hold up for the night.

She had passed Exit 42 when she spotted something on the asphalt. She bent down and picked it up. Someone had discarded a cell phone. It appeared in good condition, so the owner must have thrown it aside in frustration over not being able to use it. For the Hell of it, Danielle pressed the ON button and held it for several seconds. As expected, it did not switch turn on.

Suddenly, a tidal wave of negative thoughts flooded her mind, all of them about Kirstie. God, she wished she could find one operable cell phone to call her daughter. Not knowing her whereabouts and her situation was maddening.

Danielle did know her daughter's location. Kirstie and her friends had gone to Canobie Lake Park. That was near Exit 3 in New Hampshire. If Danielle stopped by there, she could find Kirstie and accompany her home.

Stop being an asshole, Danielle mentally chastised herself. That was a day ago. The chances of the girls hanging around the park were zero. Figuring out where they had gone would be impossible. She knew Mikayla had a grandmother who lived in the area and that they probably had gone there, but she did not know the address or even the town where the grandmother resided. And that's assuming they were at the park when the solar flare hit. Being teenagers, they could have left early for the mall or gone somewhere for dinner. Without a means of communication, trying to track down Kirstie would be a waste of time.

Danielle had only one viable option—to assume Kirstie had also decided to head home and would be there when Danielle arrived. That was the best-case scenario.

Danielle did not even want to consider the alternatives.

CHAPTER NINETEEN

KIRSTIE AND REGAN spread out across the dining room table the items they had taken from Dignam's house while Mikayla and Abbey rummaged through Lori's house for supplies. When finished, the girls counted what they had: a double barrel shotgun, a hunting rifle with a scope, a .38 caliber revolver, a .357 magnum revolver, a machete, a Bowie knife, and dozens of boxes of .38, .357, and hunting rifle ammunition as well as shotgun shells. When the cans of chili and corned beef hash were added to those Lori had in storage, they had enough food to last them two weeks if they each consumed only one can of food per day. Lori enjoyed baking, so her pantry included several dozen boxes of cake, cookie, and bread mixes. Not the healthiest meals to eat, not that it mattered. Even if they could find eggs and milk that had not gone bad, they had no way to bake them.

Unfortunately, they came up short on drinks. The grandmother had two one-gallon plastic jugs of water, one of them half-empty, as well as the six one-gallon bottles of spring water left behind during the Dignam raid. Rationed to only one glass a day, they would run out within four weeks, and Kirstie and Regan both knew this crisis would last longer than a month. Lori's refrigerator contained an unopened case of Diet Coke for when the girls visited and two plastic bottles of iced tea, none of which would hydrate them.

The four girls stood around the table staring at the stash. Regan had a concerned expression on her face.

"What's wrong?" asked Abbey.

"This is not going to last long."

Mikayla disagreed. "It'll last long enough for the National Guard to bring in supplies to keep us going like they do in every natural disaster."

"Don't count on it." Regan's voice sounded desperate. "This isn't a localized event. It's worldwide. Even if the guard had the resources, all their vehicles are inoperable, so they have no way of getting them to us. We're on our own."

"You're optimistic," chided Mikayla.

"I'm realistic." Regan turned to her friend. "And that's assuming no one tries to steal what we have."

Mikayla scoffed. "They wouldn't do that."

"I bet Dignam thought the same thing," added Kirstie.

Mikayla stepped away from the table.

Regan picked up the Magnum and examined it. "At least we have a means to defend ourselves if that happens."

"No way." Abbey raised her hands. "I hate guns."

"You're going to have to learn to use them if you want to survive."

"I don't know how to use one," added Kirstie.

"Me neither," said Mikayla from across the room.

"I can teach you. It's not difficult."

Abbey shook her head. "I'd rather get killed then become a killer."

Regan stared her down. "What about protecting the rest of us, or your grandmother?"

Abbey's eyes widened as the realization suddenly hit her.

A knock on the front door interrupted the awkward silence.

Abbey jumped. "Don't answer it. It might be the same people who attacked Dignam."

"I doubt that."

"I'll answer it." Kirstie headed for the hall, noticing out of the corner of her eye Regan checking the Magnum to make sure the magazine was full.

Andrew greeted her with a forced smile. "Hey, I wanted to

let you know we're gathering tonight at my place. We're having a community meeting to figure out a way for us to survive. We're not going to make it through this unless we work together as a team."

"Thank God. We were getting nervous, especially after what happened to Dignam."

"That's one of the reasons we're doing this. We're meeting at five o'clock. Will you be there?"

"Yes."

"Good." This time, Andrew's smile was genuine. He waved and walked down the street to the next house.

As Kirstie closed the door, Regan stepped out of the dining room clutching the Magnum.

"Thank God someone in this neighborhood has common sense. We might make it through this after all."

"Agreed." Kirstie knew that even if the entire neighborhood pulled together, their chances of making it through until winter were not good.

CHAPTER TWENTY

S HAWN HAD WANTED to lead the two-man team into the containment vessel but, after a long debate, Brad convinced Shawn his expertise and experience were needed in the control room.

Shawn watched as Brad and Wilson donned their Tyvek radiation suits. Those would not be enough to protect the two men from the increasing levels of radiation but, thankfully, Wally had brought armor-like silver fire protection suits, air tanks, and heavy rubber boots. The downside was the two suits would severely limit the men's maneuverability. Also, the tanks had limited air supplies of only twenty minutes, so they could only turn them on at the last moment before entering the containment vessel, and the mouthpiece of the breathing apparatus had two layers, making it impossible to speak normally.

As the two suited up, Shawn retrieved the reactor's operating manuals from his office and thumbed through them to find the exact location of the valves. When ready, they joined Shawn at the control panel.

"You two study this."

"What is it?" asked Brad.

"It's a diagram of the containment vessel. Try to familiarize yourself with it." Shawn pointed to a spot inside the vessel. "Here is the location of the motor-operated valve. Write it down on your gloves. You're responsible for opening the MO Valve. We'll send in another crew later to close the pneumatic air-operated valve. Your dosimeter alarms are set for eighty milliSieverts. If they go off, come back here immediately so you don't get radiation poisoning."

"Gotcha."

"One more thing. We have no way to communicate with you while you're down there. If you're not back in thirty minutes, I'll send a team in after you. Understood?"

Wilson nodded.

Brad replied, "Yes."

"Good luck."

The two men pulled the hoods of their radiation suits over their heads and exited the control room.

Shawn said a silent prayer for them. Nobody had any idea what type of Hell they were entering.

BRAD AND WILSON made their way through the building, the only light provided being from their spotlights.

It took only a few minutes to reach the reactor building. The exterior appeared normal enough. On the opposite side sat of the wall the containment vessel that housed the reactor.

Both men paused, staring at the first of two doors leading inside.

"Ready?" asked Brad.

"No. But let's do this."

Brad undid the door latch, opened it, and stepped inside. Wilson followed, closing and securing the door behind them. Then Brad opened the interior door and both men entered.

It was an entirely different world down here. Unlike the pristine hallways and rooms of the main building, the area around the containment vessel consisted of an array of pipes, metal stairwells, and valves, all immersed in darkness. The temperature felt worse than a sauna, making both men sweat inside their radiation suits. Due to the intense heat, steam wafted off the exterior of the vessel, further decreasing visibility and preventing the beams from their spotlights to reach far, adding to the eeriness. Somewhere ahead of them sat the containment vessel.

"Follow me."

The two men crossed the open space. After a few seconds, the beams of light fell on the containment vessel, a flask-shaped structure, wide at the bottom and thin on the top, two hundred feet in height, sixty feet in width, and with a concrete wall twenty feet thick.

Brad headed for a set of metal stairs and ascended until he reached the second level then, with Wilson close behind, ascended a second set of stairs next to the heat exchangers. Once on the third level, they made their way to a ladder that led to the MO Valve and shone the flashlight up.

"Shit," Brad mumbled to himself.

After six feet, a circular covering like those used on fire escapes enclosed the ladder. Brad started to climb but, after a few feet, the top of his air tank hit the covering. He leaned closer to the rungs and tried to climb again, and again the tank banged into the covering. Shifting his torso to the right, he finally pushed through on the third attempt, though the position made it more difficult to climb. At the top of the ladder sat a cramped walkway, barely shoulder width, leading in both directions along the vessel. Thankfully, the walkway had an exterior railing, so he did not have to worry about falling off. He moved to the valve and checked its number with the one written on his glove.

"Valve 365!" He screamed to be heard through his mask and the noise inside the vessel.

"Valve 365!" Wilson yelled back in confirmation.

Grabbing the latch-lever off to the side, Brad tried to pull it from automatic to manual mode, a task made more cumbersome between the restrictions of the radiation suits and the fact it had never been used before. After a few seconds, it shifted into manual mode. Brad sighed, his strained arm muscles and the sweat pouring down his face wearing him down quickly.

Wilson stood by him and shone his flashlight on the gauge. Brad grabbed the handwheel and turned it. Like the lever, it was difficult to move due to lack of use. It finally gave way but moved slowly, taking thirty seconds to turn. The needle in the valve-opening gauge moved in five percent intervals, taking close to a minute for it to reach twenty-five percent.

"We're at twenty-five percent!" Wilson yelled. "Valve 365, open!"

"Valve 365, open!"

"Let's get out of here!"

Both men moved as quickly as the heat and restricted suits would allow. After a few minutes that seemed like an eternity, they reached the double doors leading out of the containment vessel. Brad opened one, ushered Wilson through, closed it behind them, then opened the exterior door. The temperature in the building here was much lower than in the vessel. Brad removed his hood and shook his head, sending sweat flying.

"Are you okay?" asked Wilson.

"I am now. Let's head back to the control room."

No one in the control room had spoken since Brad and Wilson left. There was nothing to say until they knew whether the two men had succeeded. Shawn looked at his watch. His friends had been gone for nineteen minutes.

Shawn sighed with relief when Brad and Wilson staggered back into the control room. Brad removed his mask and gasped for air, then gave a thumbs up. "Mission accomplished."

"Thank God." Shawn crossed the room. "We'll keep the suits in the breakroom to limit our exposure to radiation. Libby, you're with me. Grab a Geiger counter."

The four men entered the break room. Libby ran the Geiger counter over Brad and Wilson.

"Low levels of radiation."

Shawn nodded. "Take them off."

Brad and Wilson complied. Once out of the radiation suits, they stripped off their blue coveralls and socks, then placed the gear across several lunch tables. There were spare clothes in the building, including underwear, they could change into. However, Shawn knew they had contaminants on their bodies, faces, and hair. Both men should shower thoroughly, but they had neither the time nor resources for this. Brad and Wilson crossed over to Shawn, who read their dosimeters.

"How bad is it?" asked Brad.

"Not bad at all. You received a dose of twenty milliSieverts."

"Thank God." Between fifty and sixty milliSieverts was a lethal dosage.

"What about me?" asked Wilson.

"Only twenty-six milliSieverts."

Wilson chuckled. "Good. I can still have kids."

Brad nudged him. "Yeah, but they might look like something from *The Hills Have Eyes*."

Shawn rolled his eyes and entered the control room, followed by the others.

"What's the pressure level?"

"Seven hundred and sixty-eight and holding," Andy answered.

"Thank God for small miracles," Libby chimed in.

"True." Shawn hated to deflate the mood. "But I have to send another team down to open the valve in the suppression chamber."

CHAPTER TWENTY-ONE

"WHAT THE FUCK did I do to deserve this?" yelled Danielle.

Heavy rain pelted the area from the summer thunderstorm that had moved into the area. Common sense told her to seek shelter before the rain hit, but doing that would delay her even more, and right now time was of the essence.

The rain had begun as a heavy drizzle. At first it felt good, like a lukewarm shower, washing away the sweat and cooling her off. For the first time in days, she felt clean. It slowly increased in intensity until Danielle found herself in the middle of a torrential downpour. The rain soaked her dress until it clung against her body, even her legs. Water pooled on the asphalt and, within minutes, the flats were drenched, her feet squishing every time she took a step. Droplets pelted her face so hard they stung, forcing her to lower her head. Water collected in her hair and ran down her face until she had to wipe it away every few seconds.

Even worse, the storm brought with it more humidity.

The only plus side was that the storm drove everyone else to seek cover, allowing her a brief respite from being constantly on guard for potential danger.

After twenty minutes of drudging through this shit, Danielle came upon an Irving Oil tanker in the center lane. She decided to rest. Crouching, she slid under the tanker, finding refuge from the downpour. Once she had dried off a bit, Danielle inched her way to the left side of the truck to check out her surroundings. The only things in the southbound lanes were a few dozen stalled vehicles and a teenager riding a bicycle in the breakdown lane who appeared more miserable than Danielle.

Glancing north, Danielle saw a clear, sunny sky ahead of the storm clouds. They would get hit with this soon enough. Turning south, she saw that dark clouds dominated the skyline. Dammit, this shit would last awhile. She decided to wait it out a bit longer before continuing. Danielle moved back under the tanker and sat down, her legs crossed in front of her.

After a few minutes, her thoughts wandered back to Kirstie and Shawn.

Danielle worried about her daughter. Kirstie and her friends must be terrified by what went down. She assumed Kirstie must be just as worried about her. At least the girls were together, which helped ease her mind. Regan had a good head on her shoulders and would prevent the group from doing anything foolish. She also worried about Shawn, although not as much. Her brother was more level-headed than her, although Danielle would never admit it to him.

Her thoughts briefly switched to David, hoping him and that bitch were having a much more difficult time than her.

Danielle shifted her thoughts back to Shawn. He would be okay. With luck, he was at the nuclear plant when the power went out and would be safe from—

She suddenly realized that the odds were good that the plant had also lost power because of the solar flare. He went on *ad nauseum* about what happened at that nuclear facility in Japan over a decade ago when it lost power after a massive tidal wave flooded the back-up generators. Without electricity, the reactor cores overheated and the surrounding areas were unlivable because of radiation. What if the same thing happened at Seabrook? She could be walking into a death zone and not even realize it.

Fuck!

Fear now mixed with Danielle's anxiety. She had to find Kirstie and get out of the area as soon as possible.

The downpour had shifted to a steady rain. Now was as good a time as any. Crawling out from under the tanker, Danielle headed north again, quickening her pace despite the pain in her legs and feet.

She had walked a few miles when she spotted a green sign on the side of the highway. Danielle headed toward it and paused.

Salem, NH   12 miles

Manchester   35 miles

Concord   48 miles

"Fuck this shit," she mumbled then kept walking, hoping to cover as many miles as possible before sunset.

CHAPTER TWENTY-TWO

THE GATHERING STARTED awkwardly. Everyone put on a false air of happiness, which proved next to impossible. Those already in attendance chatted idly as the rest sauntered in, talking about anything except the obvious nightmare the community faced. Andrew eventually stepped over and asked the group to gather around the picnic table and lawn chairs. A woman stood beside him with blonde hair down past her shoulders and glasses. Kirstie guessed her to be in her early or mid-forties.

Andrew raised his hands. "If I can have your attention. For those of you who don't know her, this is Kathy."

The woman smiled and waved.

"Kathy is a high school science teacher here in Atkinson. She's going to explain what happened yesterday."

"I'll do my best." Kathy stepped forward. "I'm a biology teacher, not an astrophysicist. In short, Earth was hit with a massive solar flare that fried all electrical systems."

"But aren't we always hit by solar flares?" asked Kirstie.

"We are. The sun constantly admits small amounts of electromagnetic radiation that often disrupt radio waves. But this event was larger than anything our solar system has experienced in recorded history. And we were unfortunate enough to be directly in its path. When the flare washed over the planet, it produced uncontrolled spikes in the electrical currents. Everything connected to the grid burned out, including transformers and power lines. Unfortunately, it knocked out everything on the planet that requires electricity."

"Excuse me." A younger woman holding an infant raised her hand as if in a classroom. "How long before the power comes back on?"

"Best case scenario, five to ten years."

A commotion broke out among the guests. A dozen questions were launched at Kathy at once. Andrew stepped forward and waved his hands for everyone to quiet down.

"One question at a time, please."

A heavyset man with long dark hair and a full beard shouted down the others. "Why the fuck will it take so long?"

"Benjamin," snapped Andrew. "Watch your language. There are kids here."

"Screw that." Benjamin flashed Andrew a glare that could kill then turned back to Kathy. "Well?"

"Ninety percent of the electricity throughout the country is transmitted by large power transformers. There are only a few of them, and they were all disabled by the flare."

"Do you really think it's going to take that long to repair them?" asked an older gentleman.

"They can't be repaired," answered Kathy. "They can only be replaced."

"It shouldn't take that long to get the spares up and running."

"There are no spares." Another commotion broke out, forcing Kathy to talk over everyone. "It takes up to eight months to build one under ideal conditions, and they're produced overseas. Even if they could be built, there is no way to get them here. We have no way of replacing them."

"What about those of us who have solar panels?" The question came from someone in the back. "Were the panels affected?"

"The panels should be fine. It's the connections between them and the appliances that were fried and need to be replaced."

A woman in her thirties looked around. "Does anyone here

know how to do that?"

Kathy shook her head. "Even if we had someone who could repair the connections, every appliance plugged in at the time had its electronics burned out. They'll all have to be replaced."

"How come my toilet won't flush?" asked a young woman. "It's not electric."

"Because you either have a well or you're connected to the town water supply. In either case, a pump is required to get the water from the source to your house, and they're no longer working."

"And my air conditioner?" The question came from an older woman with white hair who sat at the picnic table.

"Anything that requires electronics to operate won't work." Kathy emphasized the word anything. "That includes air conditioners, fans, appliances, cars, trucks, vans, televisions, radios, phones, computers, and furnaces."

"You're saying we're screwed?"

Kathy frowned. "Yes."

A dozen conversations broke out among the group. The white-haired woman gasped. "So, what are we going do?"

"The only thing possible," interrupted Regan. "If we want to survive, we're going to have to learn to fend for ourselves like our ancestors did when they first settled here."

"What the fuck do you know?" shouted Benjamin. "You're only a teenager."

"She may be a teenager," said Andrew. "But she's right."

The crowd calmed down.

"If we want to make it through this, we're going to have to work together. That means pooling our resources, sharing our supplies, and doing what we can to survive."

An auburn-haired woman seated on a lawn chair and rocking a stroller with an infant inside raised her hand. "How long is this going to take? I only have enough food and water in my house to last a few days."

"If we combine all our resources, ration what we have, and share them equally we'll hopefully make it long enough to get back on our feet."

Kathy moved up beside Andrew. "I have seeds at home my students use to grow fruits and vegetables. We can start with that. I also have some manuals on how to filter rain or river water to make it safe to drink. It's a project for my senior class. I'll check my files and see if I have anything else that's useful."

"Good idea." Andrew redirected his attention back to the others. "We can set up a foraging party and go to Plaistow to gather seeds and the necessary supplies at Home Depot."

"Won't they all be looted by now?" asked someone off to the right.

"Hopefully no one else has thought that far ahead, so we might get lucky and find enough to get us through."

"It's five miles to Plaistow," said the auburn-haired mother with the stroller. "That's a long walk there and back."

"Excuse me," interrupted Mikayla. "The Carsons live a mile down the road. They stable horses. Maybe if we let them join the group, they might be willing to let us borrow some of the horses."

"Excellent idea," said Andrew.

"I also figure it would help us get away quickly if we run into trouble."

"Agreed." Andrew paused. "Which brings up another harsh reality we must face. The longer this crisis goes on, the more desperate people will become, and they'll do anything to survive. Besides pooling all our supplies, we need to divide all weapons equally among the group for self-defense."

"Screw that," blurted out a man whom Kirstie recognized as one of the people who had looted Dignam's house. "I ain't giving up my guns."

"Don't you mean Dignam's guns?" Mikayla asked. "You and Joel, as well as some of the others here, are the ones who robbed his house."

"Maybe you were the one who shot him," added Kirstie. "We found his body at the bottom of the basement stairs."

"That wasn't me," he said with a wavering tone as he glanced over at Joel.

"Fuck you, Ralph," snapped Joel.

"That's behind us," said Andrew. "We have to look forward. If some of us are able to do that to one of our own, you can only imagine what outsiders will do to take what we have. We need to share all the weapons equally so we all have a means to defend ourselves, and then we need to set up a neighborhood watch to protect us from outsiders."

"Bullshit," mumbled Joel.

"You don't have to join the group if you don't want to. But if you're not in this from the beginning, you won't be allowed to join later. Once your supplies run out, you're on your own."

"Who the fuck put you in charge?" snapped Ralph.

"We'll take a vote." Andrew scanned those gathered in his backyard. "Who wants Ralph to be in charge?"

Joel, Ralph, and their wives were the only ones who raised their hands.

"Does anyone else want to be in charge?"

No hands went up.

Kirstie jumped in. "Who wants Andrew to be in charge?"

Everyone who had not already voted raised their hands.

"It's settled, then. We'll meet here at eight o'clock tomorrow morning. Bring everything you have of value—food, canned goods, toilet paper, weapons, ammo, anything that's vital to survival. After that, a group of us will head into Plaistow to see what we can scrounge up."

Joel, Ralph, and their wives left abruptly without saying anything. The rest chatted amongst themselves before breaking off one by one and heading home. Andrew and Kathy talked for a few minutes before Kathy said goodbye. Andrew joined the girls.

"Thank you for the support back there."

"My pleasure." Kirstie blushed. "You're the best person for the job. You seem to have everything under control."

"I appreciate that."

"I have a question," said Regan. "When you go into town tomorrow, can Kirstie and I come along?"

"It'll be dangerous. Are you up to it?"

"We walked here from Canobie Lake Park the night of the solar flare," answered Kirstie. "We're used to it."

"That was two days ago. Things will be a lot worse tomorrow."

Regan nodded. "We still want to go."

"Thanks. I'm going down now to check with the Carsons about lending us horses. If they agree, we'll leave at ten o'clock tomorrow after we meet."

The girls said their goodbyes and headed home. Kirstie slowed and pulled Regan aside, allowing Mikayla and Abbey to get ahead of them.

"If I'm going into town tomorrow, I want to be armed. Can you teach me how to use a pistol?"

"Sure." Regan chuckled. "I knew you'd eventually come around."

The rumble of thunder echoed from the south. Both girls turned in that direction. Thick, dark clouds rolled across the horizon, slowly heading in their direction.

"Let's wait until tomorrow morning, though."

Kirstie agreed.

CHAPTER TWENTY-THREE

THE SECOND VALVE that needed to be opened was the pneumonic air-operated one located in the suppression chamber beneath the reactor. A torus, a donut-shaped structure surrounding the reactor and half-filled with water, sat inside the suppression chamber. Any steam that escaped from the reactor's cooling system would be pumped into the suppression chamber where pipes would vent it into the torus. Once there, the steam would cool and convert back into water that would be used to cool the reactor. However, with no power, steam could not be transferred into the torus and converted. As the reactor heated up, the water inside the torus would eventually evaporate and generate even more pressure against the containment vessel, increasing the likelihood of a breach.

What made this trip more dangerous than opening the MO valve was that while the containment vessel had a twenty-foot-thick concrete wall between the team and the reactor, no such protection existed in the suppression chamber.

Being third in line of command, Kevin would lead the team. Libby quickly volunteered to go with him, partially to compensate for the embarrassing incident earlier that day. They donned the Tyvek radiation suits, two of the heavy fire protection suits the firemen had brought, and the boots, then studied the operator's manual to plot a way to the valve. When finished, the two men wrote down the valve number on their gloves and rejoined Shawn.

"The radiation is going to be higher down in the suppression chamber than in the containment vessel, so pay close attention to the Geiger counter. It's set to go off when it hits eighty milliSieverts. When that happens, get out of there quickly."

Kevin disagreed. "If we do that, there'll likely be a vessel breach."

"It's a risk I'm willing to take. If you two get a lethal dose of radiation, there's nothing I can do for you. We have no way to get you to the hospital, assuming it's even operating." Shawn forced a smile and tried to lighten the mood. "Besides, we're short staffed, so I need all the help I can get."

"Thanks," Kevin chuckled.

"Another thing. You only have twenty minutes of air in those tanks, and where you're going will take longer to get to, so don't put on your masks until you reach the doors to the reactor chamber."

"Roger that. We're going to enter the reactor building through the north entrance. It's closer to the valve." Kevin took a deep breath and turned to Libby. "Ready?"

Libby nodded.

"Then let's get this over with."

Shawn watched both men leave the control room, praying they would be successful.

KEVIN AND LIBBY stopped when they reached the northern set of doors to the reactor building, both men building up the courage to go inside.

"What's the reading?" asked Kevin.

"Thirty-five milliSieverts."

Shit. Radiation had begun to spread outside the reactor chamber. Soon the entire facility would be affected.

"I'll lead the way. You keep a close eye on the Geiger counter. Ready?"

"Let's do this."

They put on their hoods and started the air tanks, then opened the first of the doors. It swung aside with a loud, metallic clunk. Kevin stepped inside. Libby followed, closing the door behind him. They followed the same procedure into the suppression chamber.

A white haze filled the area. Kevin could not tell if it was steam or dust, praying for the latter. Steam meant the reactor was overheating and evaporating the water, which signaled an imminent meltdown.

"What's the reading?" Kevin yelled.

Libby checked the Geiger counter. "Seventy-three milliSieverts!"

Kevin led the way along the catwalk until it turned left, then headed to the vale located in the northwest corner. As they passed the maintenance hatch, a buzzing sounded, barely audible through the masks and air flow. Libby paused to lift the Geiger counter.

"The needle hit one hundred! It's at the limit!"

Shit! The radiation down here had already reached dangerous levels, and they were only halfway to the valve. He considered backtracking and approaching from the opposite direction in the hopes the levels on that side would be lower. However, they would run out of air before they completed the mission. Yet if they continued, they would both receive lethal dosages of radiation. However, the alternative could expose the entire community to the same fate. As much as he hated to do it, he made the only reasonable decision.

"Let's go back!"

"We haven't opened the valve yet!"

"We'll die if we try! We'll have to think of another way! Move!"

Libby did not need to be told twice. Both men moved as fast as they could and exited the suppression chamber, securing the doors behind them. They rushed through the darkened building to join the others. After a few minutes, Kevin slowed, exhausted, sweat pouring off his body. He prayed it was from the excessive heat inside the chamber and not the first signs of radiation poisoning.

When they reached the control room, Kevin motioned for Shawn to meet them in the break room. They had already taken off their hoods when Shawn entered. The boss greeted them with a surprised expression.

"That didn't take long."

"We never reached the valve. The Geiger counter hit its limit halfway there, so I made the decision to turn back. Sorry."

"No need to apologize."

"We failed."

"You had no choice. You did the right thing."

Kevin slid out of the fire protection suit. "What's the pressure now?"

"Seven hundred and eighty-three kPa."

"One more thing," added Libby. "We detected moderate levels of radiation outside the chamber."

"How bad?"

"Only thirty-five milliSieverts. But that means the radiation is spreading."

"Fuck," mumbled Shawn.

Both men stripped out of their boots and Tyvek suits. Kevin started to unzip his overalls when he remembered the dosimeters.

"What are the readings?"

Shawn stepped forward and read the dosimeter. His eyes widened.

"How bad is it?" asked Kevin.

"Eight-nine milliSieverts."

"Shit."

"And me?" asked Libby.

Shawn checked the dosimeter and grimaced. "Ninety-five

milliSieverts."

Kevin and Libby stared at each other, realizing they had both received dangerous doses of radiation. Without proper medical facilities, the chances were good those doses would eventually be fatal.

Shawn tried to be comforting. "Strip out of those clothes. I'll bring you new ones. Have something to eat and drink, then go lay down and relax. We'll manage things for now."

"Thanks." Kevin knew neither he nor Libby could relax. It would be hard to knowing death would soon be knocking at the door.

DAY THREE

CHAPTER TWENTY-FOUR

DANIELLE WOKE UP, stretched her arms above her head, and twisted her body from one side to the other and back again. Each move pulled on her tightened muscles, causing the kinks to snap. It hurt each time they did, but the temporary discomfort was worth it when compared to how lose her neck and shoulders felt afterward. She lay back on the car seat, taking a few minutes to rest before hitting the road again. Not since the solar flare had struck had she physically felt this relaxed.

Last night, while looking for a place to sleep, Danielle had stumbled across a 1968 Mustang being transported on a flatbed tow truck north of where I-93 merged with I-495. While she knew little about cars—Shawn always checked the fluids and took the cars for inspections and repairs—she knew enough that a car this old did not rely on electricity to function. Everything worked manually. Climbing onto the flatbed, Danielle had slid into the Mustang's driver's seat, rolled the windows down halfway, locked the doors, and reclined the seat enough so she could not be seen from the highway. Another heavy rain hit a few hours before midnight and lasted... she did not know how long. The rain cooled the temperature and created such a calming, rhythmic pounding on the roof that she fell into a deep sleep and did not wake up for hours.

Lifting her head, Danielle checked the old-fashioned hand clock mounted on the dashboard which still worked. It read 7:55. She had slept for almost ten hours. She needed it. At least now she had enough energy to resume her journey.

Danielle raised the seat and checked the area for any signs of danger. The only people she spotted were a young couple in the far-left lane heading south. They appeared harmless enough, yet she did not want to take any chances. Reclining the seat half-way, she kept an eye on the couple until they passed by the flatbed, thankfully not noticing her. Danielle watched them in the rearview mirror until they were out of sight.

Then she noticed that the Mustang's trunk remained shut. Every other vehicle she had passed the last two days had the doors open and the trunk or hatchback raised, the interiors having been picked clean of anything of value. Somehow, the Mustang had been spared, probably because it sat on the flatbed. With luck, she might find something of use.

Dainelle first checked the back seat and glove compartment but found nothing except the owner's manual. She searched for the trunk release latch and pulled. The trunk clicked open. Opening the door, she slid out and carefully made her way along the edge of the flatbed to the rear of the car, then looked inside.

"Shit," she muttered to herself. Nothing.

Danielle felt around until she found the luggage floor latch and lifted it. Sure enough, there sat the spare tire, jack, wheel nut wrench… and a crowbar.

"Sweet."

Danielle picked up the crowbar. It weighed more than she expected, but not enough to tire her out. Most importantly, it would make a good weapon, which she needed.

She closed the trunk and jumped down onto the asphalt. The landing did little to soothe her sore feet. If only there had been a pair of slippers in the car.

Taking a deep breath, Danielle continued north.

The next few miles were uneventful. The farther north she traveled, the fewer vehicles there were. More importantly, she came across no one wandering the highway.

Right after the exit to Methuen, Danielle came across a Massachusetts State Police cruiser on the shoulder directly behind an old, rusted pick-up truck with a utility bed that reminded her of those used by old-time electric crews. The trooper must have pulled the driver over when the solar flare hit. The doors and trunk of the cruiser sat open. Knowing that rummaging through it would be futile, she checked it out anyways in case something had been left behind but had no luck. Everything of value had been stripped out, even the mounted laptop. God only knew why anyone would bother with that.

Danielle moved forward to the truck. A logo on the door read Thorne's Lawn Service. The bed had been ransacked, the only things left behind being a gas-powered lawn mower, a leave blower, three-foot-long hedge trimmers, and two electronic weed whackers. For some reason, no one had bothered to open the storage compartments on the exterior of the bed. Using the crowbar, she pried open the door on the upper rear compartment.

"Come on," Danielle whispered to herself. "Let there be a gallon of water."

The metal door popped open, revealing five replacement heads for the weed whacker, two plastic containers of motor oil, and spare blades for the lawn mower.

Shit.

Focusing on the compartment beneath it, she pried it open. Empty.

Danielle made her way along the left side of the truck, opening the remaining compartments one by one, and finding nothing but garbage bags, two orange extension cords, a zombie garden gnome (though she had no idea what they would use that for), and a small pair of hedge clippers eighteen inches in length. She contemplated taking the shears as a secondary weapon but would have to hand carry them and decided against it.

Moving over to the right side, Danielle began in the rear and moved forward, again finding nothing of use. Two cabinets remained. She almost gave up but figured she had gone this far and might as well try. When the door sprung open on the top cabinet, it revealed three pairs of heavy work gloves, some dirty hand towels, three tan t-shirts and two tan baseball caps with the company logo on them.

At least I found something, she thought.

Danielle could use the t-shirts to help pad her feet. The hat would shield her from the sun. Taking out one, she slipped it on. It fell across her face. Removing the baseball cap, she adjusted the back strap and placed it back on. This time it fit.

She pried open the last cabinet.

"Thank God."

Inside were a pair of sneakers, two sets of clean socks rolled into balls, a belt, and a twenty-ounce bottle of blue Gatorade. Danielle could barely contain her glee, especially since she had finished off the last bottle of water she had traded sex for. Removing the Gatorade, she unscrewed the top and swigged down half the contents in one gulp, saving the rest for later.

Taking out the sneakers and socks, Danielle opened the door to the passenger side of the truck, climbed into the front seat, removed her flats, and examined her feet. Three large blisters welled up on her left foot with two large and three small blisters on her right. No wonder it hurt to walk. After letting her feet air out for a few minutes, she gently slid on one pair of socks and tried on the sneakers. They were only one size too big, which she could deal with. Slipping back onto the high-way, she bounced on her feet several times. They still hurt due to the blisters, but not as bad as before.

Danielle secured the belt around her waist and returned to the other set of cabinets. Unrolling a garbage bag, she tossed the extra pair of socks, t-shirts, and half-empty bottle of Gatorade inside, then wedged the small hedge shears between the belt and her back.

With everything packed, Danielle headed north, grateful for her find and hoping it meant her luck was changing for the better.

CHAPTER TWENTY-FIVE

K IRSTIE HAD BEEN hoping the weapon training Regan promised would include firing at multiple targets like on a gun range, but that turned out not to be the case.

The two girls had awoken at the crack of dawn, scoffed down a breakfast that consisted of an unheated can of maple-syrup flavored baked beans, then went out into the backyard to train. It was more of a familiarization course. Regan gave Kirstie the .38 caliber revolver then taught her how to hold the revolver, aim it, squeeze the trigger, reload the cylinder, and a few other minor details.

"Do you think you're ready to shoot it?"

"Yes," Kirstie answered excitedly.

"Good." Regan handed her friend four rounds.

"Is this it?'

"We're short on ammo. Maybe after the exchange this morning we'll have more for you to practice with. Besides, I don't expect you to be John Wick. You only need to hit your target. Load."

Kirstie pushed the release button with her left hand and pushed out the cylinder with her right, then loaded the four bullets into the chambers. When finished, she moved the cylinder back into place.

"Now what?"

Regan pointed to a tree ten yards away. A poster of Matthew Lillard from *Five Nights at Freddy's* had been nailed to the trunk. "Fire one shot at your target."

"Appropriate for a villain."

Regan chuckled. "Mikayla let me have it. It's the only thing available that makes a good target. Aim at his chest."

"Why not his head?"

"You're a novice. The chest presents a larger target. Fire one shot when you're ready."

Kirstie lifted the revolver and aimed down the sight, trying to remember everything her friend had told her. She pulled the trigger. The round struck the tree six inches above and two inches to the right of Lillard's head.

"Dammit."

"Relax. You jerked the trigger, and when you did, you raised the barrel. Try it again, only this time take a deep breath and hold it, then squeeze the trigger gently."

Kirstie followed her friend's instructions. The bullet struck the poster between Lillard's head and left shoulder.

"Shit, I missed again."

"But you did much better. You tend to shoot high and to the left. This time, aim a few inches below and to the right of the center of his chest."

Kirstie aimed and fired the last two rounds. One struck Lillard in his left shoulder, the other near his stomach.

Regan patted her on the shoulder. "Good job."

"But I didn't kill him."

"You don't have to kill him, only neutralize him." She handed Kirstie six more rounds. "Reload then let's head over to Andrew's place. It's time for the exchange."

Regan slid her Magnum between her pants and the small of her back. After Kirstie reloaded, she did the same with her .38.

When they reached the backyard, everyone from last night's gathering was present. Over eighty pistols, rifles, shotguns, and semi-automatic weapons, most of them stolen from Dignam's house, lay spread out across the picnic table. A huge stash of food and beverages stood in the center of the cement patio, ready to be distributed evenly among the neighbors. What caught Kirstie's attention were the five horses tethered to the family swing set, casually munching on grass.

"They're beautiful," she said to no one in particular.

"The Carsons lent them to us for ten percent of our supplies," Andrew replied.

Regan did not seem pleased. "That seems like a big cut."

"It's worth it. The more horses we have, the more supplies we can bring back. It also increases our numbers so the odds of us being robbed are much less."

"Where are Abbey and Mikayla?" asked Kirstie.

Andrew pointed to the house across the street. "They're helping Lori round up the supplies from her house."

A man of average height with auburn hair came over holding a clipboard. He had a three-day growth of beard forming around his cheeks and jaw, like the other men. Kirstie assumed shaving had now become a luxury like showers.

Andrew introduced them. "Ladies, this is Keith. He creates video games for a living. Keith, this is Kirstie and Regan, Mikayla's friends."

"Hi." Keith greeted them with no enthusiasm, his attention focused on the clipboard.

"How are we doing for supplies?" asked Andrew.

"Better than I hoped. As of right now, we have enough food and water to last us ten days, even more if we ration it."

"That won't be enough to get us through until the gardens start blooming. And that's assuming we find any seeds to plant."

"True, but it gives us plenty of time to establish ourselves. There are also dozens of houses in the neighborhood that are vacant. We can scavenge through them for the next few days and see what they have. Hopefully, that'll add a week or two to our stockpile."

"Good thinking," Andrew said. "Has everyone from last night reported in?"

"We haven't seen Joel or Ralph yet."

"I doubt we will. Those two assholes will hoard everything

they—"

Keith interrupted him. "Speak of the devils."

They all turned to see Joel and his wife Sarah, and Ralph and his wife Lindsey, coming down the street. Each pushed a wheelbarrow in front of them, one filled with bottled water and canned goods and another with a few weapons. The other two were empty. Kirstie wondered why they brought empty wheelbarrows. She also noticed that the weapons numbered less than those she saw them taking away from Dignam's house. A gut feeling told her something bad was about to go down, a sensation reinforced when Regan broke away and strolled over to the horses.

The couple stopped in front of the picnic table.

"Glad you decided to join us," said Andrew. "Place the guns here and the other supplies with the rest of the stuff—"

Joel reached into the wheelbarrow and lifted out an AK-47 with a drum magazine which he pointed at Andrew. Ralph removed a shotgun and aimed it at Andrew. Sarah removed a pistol from her holster and centered it on Keith.

"We're not joining your group," said Joel. "We're taking what you have for ourselves."

Keith's face turned red. "You fucking bas—"

Ralph swung the shotgun toward him. "Shut your mouth, asshole, or I'll shut it for you."

Lindsey stared at her husband. "What are you doing? You said we were going to team up with them."

"Fuck that shit. These assholes will only last a few weeks if they share it. We'll last several months with their stuff. More than enough to make it to our summer home in Vermont."

Joel motioned toward the horses. "And with those we'll make it there in half the time."

Andrew tried to control his anger. "You'd really fuck us over like this? We're neighbors."

"We live in the same neighborhood. It's every man for himself. You should know that. You were once a Marine."

"We looked out for each other's backs, not stabbed them in it."

"Boo fucking hoo. We're going to take what we need and leave in the morning. You can have what's left. And if anyone tries to stop us, I have no problem gunning you down."

"I'm sure you don't," snarled Keith.

Sarah raised the gun as if ready to fire. "Shut up, asshole."

Lindsey stepped closer to her husband. "We can't do this to them."

"Do as you're told."

"I want no part of this."

"Stay here for all I care."

Lindsey moved away several feet and hung her head in shame.

Joel nodded to Ralph. "Get the horses."

"You can't do that," said Andrew. "They belong to the Carsons."

"They belong to us now." When Ralph hesitated, Joel barked, "Get the damn horses."

Everyone watched as Ralph went over to gather the horses. As he drew near, Regan raised her hands and stepped aside, letting him approach. With his left hand, he grabbed the reins of the closest horse, an all-black Friesian. It neighed and tried to pull away.

"Knock it off!" yelled Ralph.

The horse put up more resistance. Ralph shouldered his shotgun and took the reins in both hands.

Regan reached behind her back, withdrew the Magnum, and fired four rounds into the side of Ralph's abdomen. Chunks of flesh and organs blew out of the exit wounds on the other side. He collapsed face first onto the grass, a puddle of blood forming beneath him.

When Joel and Sarah looked over to see what happened, Andrew and Keith moved forward. Joel saw the movement in the corner of his eye and raised the AK-47, his finger wrapped around the trigger.

"Go ahead. Give me a reason to kill you."

Both men froze.

Fuck this shit, thought Kirstie.

Grabbing the revolver from the small of her back, she fired three rounds into Joel. He spun around and fell backwards against the picnic table, dropping his weapon in the process. Sarah turned to take down Kirstie but not quickly enough. Kirstie fired her last three rounds into the bitch's chest. Sarah collapsed beside her husband's corpse.

Keith raced over and grabbed the AK-47, training it on Lindsey who knelt on the lawn, sobbing.

Kirstie still held the revolver in her hands, dumbfounded by what had happened and how she had reacted. Andrew came over, gently placing his right hand on her shoulder. With his left, he carefully took the .38 and slid it into his pocket.

"Thanks. You saved my life."

"I... I killed them."

"It's okay. They were going to kill us. You did the right thing."

"I know I did." She glanced over and made eye contact with Andrew. "I didn't realize I had it in me."

Andrew took Kirstie in his arms and hugged her. "We're all going to have to rise above ourselves if we hope to survive."

Keith kept the AK-47 aimed at Lindsey. "What are we going to do with her?"

Andrew stepped over and placed a hand on the barrel, pushing it down.

She made eye contact with Andrew, tears flowing down her cheeks. "Please, don't kill me. My kids won't survive on their own. Please."

"Did you know about this?"

"No. I swear. Ralph told me they decided to join you. If I knew what they planned, I would have warned you."

"I believe her," said Kirstie.

"So do I." Andrew helped Lindsey to her feet and placed

his hand under her chin, lifting her head to face him. "But if you show any signs of disloyalty, you and your kids are on your own. Understand?"

"Yes." An anguished smile spread across her face. "Thank you."

"Keith, gather a couple of people and escort Lindsey back home. Round up what they have and whatever you find in Joel's place, then add them to the pile. We'll divvy things up accordingly."

"No problem. What about you?"

"We have to get ready to go into Plaistow and get the supplies we need."

Mikayla and Abbey rushed across the street from Lori's house, pausing when they spotted the three dead bodies. Abbey asked, "What happened?"

"They drew weapons on us and tried to steal the supplies for themselves," Andrew replied.

"And you shot them?"

"Nope. Your friends did."

Abbey's eyes widened. "You mean Kirstie and Regan?"

Andrew grinned. "Yup."

"It doesn't surprise me." Mikayla showed no emotion.

Abbey patted Kirstie on the back. "I didn't know you had it in you, girl."

"Neither did I," Kirstie admitted.

Mikayla tried to comfort her friend. "Don't let it bother you. They were the neighborhood assholes. No one liked them."

"Thanks." Kirstie forced a grin then pointed to Regan. "I had a good teacher."

"You taught her how to shoot?" asked Abbey.

Regan nodded.

"Can you show me?"

Mikayla jumped in. "Me too?"

Kirstie glanced down at the two bodies at her feet. "I think we're all going to need to learn how to defend ourselves."

CHAPTER TWENTY-SIX

S HAWN STARED AT the pressure gauge. The current reading was seven hundred eighty-eight kPa. Despite Wally feeding water into the cooling system for twelve straight hours, the pressure inside the reactor had not decreased.

Brad approached from behind. "Any changes?"

"The pressure is slightly greater."

Brad looked over his friend's shoulder. "At least it's not rising as quickly as before."

"We're only delaying the inevitable."

"Remember, it took almost half a day to start the feed."

Shawn turned around, leaned against the control panel, and rested the palm of his hands on the edge. "Wally contacted me this morning and said they were only pumping half as much water into the cooling system than anticipated."

"Why?"

"The pump on the fire engine is inoperable. They're using a diesel generator to feed water into the system, which doesn't have the same efficiency."

Brad thought for a moment. "They need more time to catch up."

"I hope you're right." Shawn sighed and glanced over his shoulder at the control panel. "I wish we'd been able to open the AO valve to release the pressure in the suppression chamber."

Brad said nothing. Neither man wanted to face the fact that the failed attempt to open that valve had exposed Kevin and Libby to dangerous dosages of radiation for nothing.

"What were the readings when you sent Andy outside last night after the venting?"

"They were minimal," replied Shawn. "I only wish I knew the radiation level downwind from us."

"What good would it do? We have no way of warning the surrounding areas. And even if we did, without power they have no way of getting to a safe location."

"I know." Shawn sighed a second time. "I hate not being in control of—"

A ticking interrupted their conversation. A tense silence fell across the control room as all eyes focused on the source of the noise—the Geiger counter sitting on a stool placed by the door. Gathering his courage, Shawn approached and focused on the counter.

"How bad is it?" asked Brad.

"It's slightly over one milliSieverts an hour."

"That's not too bad," said Libby.

"It depends on how long we're stuck here," added Wilson.

Shawn handed Brad the radio. "Check with Wally. Tell him the radiation levels have finally reached the control room. Ask him what the readings are outside and warn him to keep checking every hour."

As Brad moved across the control room to make the call, Shawn went over to the white board, wiped it clean, and took the cap off the black pen. Across the top, he wrote the words CONTAINMENT VESSEL, SUPPRESSION CHAMBER, CONTROL ROOM, OUTSIDE, and the names of those on duty. Under CONTAINMENT VESSEL, he wrote down the reading recorded there when the team closed the MO valve and, under Brad's and Wilson's names, the dosimeter levels they registered when they closed the valve. He then did the same under SUPPRESSION CHAMBER and Kevin's and Libby's dosimeter readings. He checked his watch, wrote down the time on the far left of the whiteboard, and underneath CONTROL ROOM, jotted down one milliSieverts.

Brad joined him.

"Wally says the outside reading is .8 milliSieverts."

Shawn added the reading to the whiteboard.

"What do we do now?" asked Wilson.

Shawn turned to face his team. "We wait and see what happens next."

CHAPTER TWENTY-SEVEN

DANIELLE HAD NO clue of her location, which was sad. She had driven this route twice a day, five days a week, for years and only now realized how little attention she paid to her surroundings. She had been walking for two days and would have thought she made better progress. The only thing she knew for certain was that she had recently left Massachusetts, a few hours ago having passed a sign on the side of the highway welcoming her to New Hampshire. By the time she reached home, she would have the leg muscles of an Olympic athlete.

Or would need a wheelchair.

The traffic was even lighter this far north of Boston, which Danielle appreciated. The more vehicles on the highway meant the more places for danger to lurk. She assumed no one wandered the highway because they had all moved into the nearby cities where the chances of survival were better, and over the past two days had seen few people. If things were that bad in the cities and towns, more people would have moved back to the highway. A part of her wondered if doing the same would be a good idea. There might be emergency services there distributing food and water, or a place where she could discard her sweat-soaked dress and switch it out for more appropriate clothes.

Every time Danielle considered getting off at the next exit, she remembered the warning the two teenagers who gave her water offered about avoiding Manchester. Maybe no one returned because the outlying towns had become war zones which swallowed them up. She decided to stay on I-93 and continue with what worked.

Danielle walked for another hour when she heard women screaming combined with raucous laughter. Common sense told her to cross over to the southbound lanes and disappear into the woods beyond. Curiosity got the better of her. Two hundred feet ahead sat a stalled tractor trailer, blocking the view of what went down in front of it. Danielle made her way to the rear of the trailer and peered around the corner.

What she saw almost made her wet herself from fear.

Six thugs were taking advantage of a family upon which they had stumbled. A better word would have been tormenting. One man with a long, unkempt beard and wearing a biker's leather vest had his arms wrapped around a young girl no more than fourteen. Two others had the father on his knees and held him in place by the arms, forcing him to watch the other three gang members rape his wife who lay naked on the asphalt, her torn off clothes scattered around her. Each of them took a different orifice and violated it, laughing and catcalling. The daughter sobbed. The father screamed for them to stop, only to be punched several times in the face by one of the men holding him. As each of the rapists finished, he pulled up his pants and relieved one of the others holding down the rest of the family, who then stepped over to join the gang rape.

When the last thug finished, a disgustingly fat guy with a beer belly sticking out from under his t-shirt punched the mother several times in the face, knocking her unconscious. He walked over to the teenager and began to tear off her clothes. Both the father and the daughter screamed for them to stop, the latter struggling to break free and kicking at her attackers. which only excited them more.

Danielle wanted to help the family but could do nothing. If she did not get out of there now, she would be—

A strong hand covered her mouth. Caught off guard, Danielle dropped her bag and the crowbar. The attacker pulled her into him. the bulge in his pants indicating his excitement about assaulting her. The acrid smell of cigarette smoke poured from between his lips.

"Do you like what you see, bitch?"

Danielle shook her head.

"Too bad, because you're next."

The attacker reached around with his free hand and tore open the front of Danielle's dress, exposing her bra. His grime-covered hand grabbed one of her breasts and squeezed so hard Danielle moaned in pain.

"You're going to be doing a lot more of that in a minute."

He spun around and slammed Danielle's upper body on the hood of a car ten feet behind the truck, causing her face to strike the metal. She felt blood flow from her nose. He twisted her left arm in one hand to hold her in place and, with his right, removed the hedge clippers and tossed them on the hood. Reaching down, he yanked the torn dress up around her thighs.

"No panties? What a good little cunt. The guys are going to have fun with you, but I'm taking you first. No more sloppy seconds for me."

She heard him unbuckle his belt and unzip his fly, followed by the sound of them dropping to the asphalt. He moved closer, the tip of his cock pressed against her anus. The attacker leaned over, placing his head by her ear and whispering, "Get ready, bitch. This is going to hurt like—"

Danielle jerked her head back, slamming it into the ass-hole's face. The sound of his nose breaking accompanied his cry of pain. She continued the assault three more times until the back of her head shattered his front teeth. He released her and stumbled back three feet. Danielle spun around. Blood flowed from his nose and mouth. *Good, now the motherfucker knows how I feel.* The attacker spit. The fragments of five fractured teeth sat in the middle of the pool of blood. He stared at them then glanced up at Danielle, his eyes burning with fury.

"You God damn fucking cunt. You'll pay—"

Danielle had already reached behind her and grabbed the hedge clippers, opening the blades. The rapist's dick quickly went flaccid but still made a good target. Placing the angle of the two blades around the base, she rapidly snapped them shut. He groaned in agony and dropped to his knees, both hands covering the wound. Blood poured through his fingers. Staring at the limp organ laying on the ground, he cried several times then looked up at Danielle. His expression changed from pain to fury, and he opened his mouth to call for his friends.

He never got the chance.

Danielle placed the clippers on either side of his neck and slammed shut the blades, then yanked them toward her. They sliced through his skin and muscles, severing the arteries in the process. The attacker's attempted call for help devolved in a pathetic gurgle as blood flowed down his throat. Her anger far from satiated, Daniele kicked him in the face hard enough to break more teeth, though at this point she doubted he noticed. He fell over onto the highway and bled out.

Racing back to the truck, Danielle grabbed her belongings and peered around the corner. The others had finished with the teenager, who lay on the ground in a fetal position, sobbing. The mother still lay unconscious. The father screamed obscenities at the attackers, who responded with laughter. The fat one stepped over in front of the father, pulled a pistol out of his pocket, and shot the father in the face. Startled by their friend's response, the two holding him in place jumped aside and released the father, their clothes splattered in blood. An argument broke out between them and the fat guy.

Danielle did not want to wait around and be next. She ran south, keeping the tractor trailer between herself and the gang, then bounded over the guardrail. Crouching so as not to be seen, she maneuvered between the cars and ran into the woods bordering the southbound lane.

CHAPTER TWENTY-EIGHT

DESPITE THE PEP talk from Regan and the fact that Joel, Ralph, and Sarah got what they deserved, it took Kirstie a while to get over the emotional trauma of taking a human life, even if the people killed were narcissistic assholes who gladly would have done the same to them. She and Regan sat at the kitchen table in Lori's house, the two teenagers talking while the grandmother made them a cup of cold herbal tea. Regan distracted Kirstie by focusing the conversation on positive topics such as how lucky they were to have made it this far and how good their chances were of surviving. Lori helped by lacing Kirstie's tea with two shots of whiskey. After the first sip, Kirstie wanted to ask for an alcohol-free cup but thought better of it. She enjoyed the taste, and the whiskey helped take the edge off.

When ten o'clock rolled around, the two girls made their way over to Andrew's house. Five horses stood in the driveway munching on grass, each wearing a saddle. Two people hovered by the horses. Kirstie recognized one from the barbecue last night but did not remember her name. She was a young woman the same height as Kirstie, in her early twenties, with red hair tied in a bun and a stern expression on her face. The other was a man in his mid-thirties, attractive and slightly overweight, with blonde hair. Andrew sat on the front steps of his house engaged in a dispute with Kathy.

"I need to go into town with you. I'm the only one who knows what to get."

Andrew studied a piece of paper in his hands. "Isn't everything we need on this list?"

"Yes, but there might be other things we could use that you might miss."

"I can't risk it. You're too valuable to the group."

Kathy scrunched her brow. "How am I valuable if I stay here?"

"Because you're the only one who knows how to put together the things we're getting."

"I have a bunch of books that'll tell you how to do that," replied Kathy, frustration evident in her tone.

"Books are for amateurs. You're the expert."

Kathy laughed disparagingly. "Why are you going? You're in charge. Who's going to take over if something happens to you?"

"There are a dozen qualified people who can take over if I'm gone. Besides, I need to get a layout of the situation around us so we can be prepared...." Andrew left the thought unfinished.

Kathy finished the thought. "So we can be prepared if others try to take what we have."

"Exactly."

Kirstie stepped up and interrupted. "Give me the list. I can make sure we get what you need."

"Are you sure?" asked Andrew.

"I had a year of chemistry in high school. I should be able to find everything."

Andrew glanced over at Kathy who finally gave in, realizing she could not win this battle. She took the list from Andrew and handed it to Kirstie, who read it over.

vegetable seeds (corn, carrots, wheat, spinach, peas,
     asparagus, green beans, lettuce, tomatoes)
fertilizer
3 55-gallon plastic drums
2' of 1" 40 PVC pipe

10' of ¾" 40 PVC pipe

1 threaded faucet

5 ¾" PVC slip ons

6 ¾" PVC 90-degree elbows

1 ¾" PVC tee fitting

1 ¾" reducer bushing

2 1" PVC 45-degree slip on elbows

unscented bleach (as much as possible)

5-gallon drums and lids (as many as possible)

screens (as many as possible)

charcoal, sand, gravel (as much as possible)

Kirstie folded the paper and slid it into her pants pocket. "I got this."

"Thanks." Kathy started to walk away then stopped. "One more thing not on the list. Get as many of those large, orange Home Depot pails as you can find."

"What are the pails for?"

"We'll have to use those instead of toilets since there's no plumbing."

Gross, thought Kirstie. "I got you covered."

"Thanks." Kathy forced a smile and headed back to her house.

Kirstie turned to Andrew. "How are we going to carry all of this?"

"The Carsons gave us two harnesses," Andrew replied. "Hopefully, we'll find carts so the horses can haul the stuff back. Let me introduce you to the rest of the team." Andrew led the girls over to the horses. "Guys, this is Kirstie and Regan. They're going with us. This is Meg and Jordan."

Meg waved and offered a curt, "Hello."

Jordan smiled and shook their hands. "Pleasure to meet you. Welcome to the Scavengers."

"Scavengers?" asked Regan.

Meg grinned. "It's the name he gave to our group."

"Makes us sound cool."

Andrew clapped his hands together and pointed to five shotguns and five pistols laying on a blanket. "Grab a weapon and mount up. We have a long day ahead of us."

Kirstie took a 40-caliber Glock and a shotgun and climbed onto her horse. When they were ready, Andrew led the team east along Providence Hill Road toward Plaistow, followed by Kirstie, Regan, and Meg. Jordan brought up the rear.

THE TRIP TOOK under two hours. Andrew picked a winding route along the back roads of Atkinson that led them past the golf course, Atkinson Academy, and the town hall. The neighborhoods reminded Kirstie of her hometown in Dunbarton—upper middle class and quiet. Only now the peaceful nature had been replaced by fear and apprehension. The few people outside warily watched the five armed intruders make their way along the streets. At one ranch-style house, two men stepped onto the front porch, one carrying an AR-15 and the other an AK-47. Andrew waved to let them know his group meant no harm. The two men waved back but stayed on the porch until they passed.

Eventually, they emerged onto Plaistow Street on the north end of town half a mile from Home Depot. Andrew paused and examined the street in both directions.

Kirstie maneuvered her horse alongside him. "What are you doing?"

"Making sure there are no armed gangs around. I don't want to get into a situation we can't manage."

That did nothing to ease her anxiety.

Andrew turned right onto Plaistow Street. The entrance to Home Depot stood a few hundred feet beyond the traffic lights. Andrew led them up the entrance until they came to the store which stood off to their right. The glass doors had been shattered but the place did not appear to have been ransacked, a sharp contrast to the Walmart on the other side of the parking lot that had goods scattered in front of it. They stopped by the entrance.

Meg rode her horse between Andrew and Kirstie. "I'm surprised this place hasn't been cleaned out yet."

"It's only been three days since we lost power. The looters are looking to stockpile food and water. They haven't thought to gather other supplies yet."

Jordan motioned toward the broken glass doors. "Someone's thinking ahead."

Andrew nodded. "Let's hope they're no longer here."

He made his way to the entrance and led his horse inside.

"Shouldn't we leave them out here?" asked Kirstie.

"Horses are valuable now and I don't want anyone trying to steal them," said Andrew. "And I don't want others to know we're here. It might invite trouble."

The rest of the group followed and, once inside, dismounted.

"Regan, you stay here with the horses. Let us know if anyone shows up." Andrew turned to Kirstie. "What are we looking for?"

She removed the list from her pocket and read off the contents. When finished, Andrew nodded.

"Kirstie and I will gather the stuff from the gardening center. Jordan, Meg, you look for the other stuff. Stay together and fire a warning shot if there's any sign of danger."

Each of them grabbed a shopping cart and headed off.

Since the gardening center was in a greenhouse, Kirstie and Andrew had plenty of light to see by. Whoever had raided the store had not been interested in these supplies, leaving plenty of seeds and fertilizer. Kirstie grabbed a stack of orange pails by the door and filled them with all the fruit and vegetable seed packets she could find while Andrew packed his cart with bags of fertilizer. Once full, he took it back to the entrance and returned with an empty one.

When all the seed packets had been loaded into the pails, Kirstie searched for items to assist in gardening like work gloves, garden tool-and-tote sets, gardening weasels and hoes, and wooden stakes for supporting plants. It took over an hour, but she managed to fill four pails with everything they needed to produce a self-sufficient garden. As she loaded the last pail into her cart, Andrew came up pushing his own cart filled with fertilizer.

"Are you almost done?"

"I think I have everything we need."

"Good. I want to get back while it's still light."

They made their way to the entrance. Several carts sat by the horses. Seven were filled with five-gallon water bottles for coolers.

"Who found these?" asked Kirstie.

"Meg did," answered Regan. "We get a double bonus on these."

"What do you mean?"

"We have plenty of water to drink, and we can use the empty containers to gather rain."

Meg arrived at that moment with another cart filled with two more water bottles. "That's the last of them."

"Good." Andrew looked around. "Where's Jordan?"

Meg shrugged. "He got excited a few minutes ago and ran off."

"Jordan!"

"Coming," he yelled from the center of the store. A few minutes later he appeared pushing a cart filled with rolls of toilet paper. "Look what I found."

Meg shook her head. "They weren't on the list."

"You'll appreciate these when the toilet paper we have runs out."

Andrew chuckled. "Let's pack these up and get out of

here."

They found a flatbed trailer in the parking lot sitting amongst the pick-up trucks for rent. Using chains and rope from inside the store, the group attached the trailer to the harnesses on Regan's and Meg's horses, brought it over to the entrance, and began loading.

Halfway through, Andrew mounted his horse. "Jordan, you're in charge here. I want to check out something at Walmart."

Jordan studied the store and then glanced over at Andrew. "Are you sure? I doubt there's any food left."

"I'm not looking for supplies. If I'm not back in fifteen minutes, head back to Atkinson. I'll catch up with you later."

Kirstie mounted her horse. "I'm going with you."

"No, you're not. It could be dangerous."

"All the more reason I'm going. If there's trouble, you'll need back up."

Andrew hesitated.

"The days of chivalry are gone. I'm either part of the team or I'm a burden." Kirstie nudged her horse's flanks. "Come on."

The two crossed the parking lot, keeping a wary eye on both the store and their surroundings. Kirstie did not see anyone around, at least not near the doors. It made her feel more at ease until Andrew slung the shotgun off his shoulder and laid it across the saddle, his right hand resting near the trigger. She followed his lead.

The area in front of Walmart looked as if a riot had taken place. Shards of glass from the shattered doors and windows. Abandoned items, mostly clothes that had been dropped as the looters fled the area. A turned over cart that had been carrying a sixty-five-inch HDTV. Various frozen foods that had long since melted. A torn apart package of toilet paper ruined thanks to last night's rain. And right in front of the entrance, a small pool of blood with a dozen broken teeth mixed in it.

Andrew reached the sliding doors, leaned forward, and led his horse inside, checking over his shoulder to make certain Kirstie followed. When she entered, he led them past the registers and turned left.

"Shouldn't we dismount and leave the horses here?"

Andrew shook his head. "I want to make a fast getaway if needed."

The inside of Walmart was an even worse mess than the parking lot. The entire store had been ransacked, with those items not looted scattered across the floor. Magazines, greetings cards, cleaning supplies, and so many other products littered the aisles. Anything edible, including the candy and junk food snacks up front, had been stolen. Now that they had left the register area where daylight poured through the windows, the store plunged into darkness. Kirstie's anxiety returned, and she listened carefully for any signs of intruders.

Once past the Subway shop, which had also been looted, Andrew paused and muttered a single word.

"Fuck."

Kirstie moved up alongside him.

Ahead of them stood the pharmacy. From what little light came from a nearby skylight, Kirstie could see the area had been as badly ransacked as the food section. The shelves had been cleared of every over-the-counter product from aspirin to cold and flu meds to supplements. Someone had pried open the gates to the pharmacy and cleared the shelves of all prescription medications.

"The looters were thorough," noted Kirstie.

"I hoped nobody had thought to raid this area yet. We could have used this stuff, especially Kathy."

"Kathy?"

"She's diabetic and needs daily insulin injections.'

"I didn't know. Why didn't she include it on her list?"

"That's the way she is. She puts the needs of the group before herself." He sighed in frustration. "We better get back before the others leave without us."

Turning their horses around, the two made their way back to Home Depot. The rest of the team had finished loading the cart and were waiting for Andrew and Kirstie. They mounted their horses as the pair approached.

"This is the most dangerous part," warned Andrew. "With all these supplies, we'll be a prime target. Hopefully, no one is desperate enough yet to try and rob us but be on the lookout just in case. Keep your eyes open and stay frosty. If we do run into trouble, protect Meg and Regan and cover their retreat. And don't hesitate to take the first shot. Our group and the supplies have top priority, no one else. Any questions?"

There were none.

"Let's move out."

Andrew led the way out of the parking lot and back onto Plaistow Road. Meg and Regan followed, their horse pulling the cart. Kirstie and Jordan brought up the rear.

CHAPTER TWENTY-NINE

"WE HAVE A problem!" yelled Brad.

Shawn woke up from his much-needed nap. "What is it?"

"The reactor pressure is climbing again."

Fuck, thought Shawn. There could only be one reason for that.

"Can you hook the car battery up to the reactor's water level monitor?"

"It'll take a minute."

"Do it."

As Brad frantically worked to switch the connections, Shawn stepped over to the Geiger counter. It read 7.2 milliSieverts per hour, just above the safe dosage level. The longer his team stayed here, the greater their chances of suffering radiation poisoning. Common sense told him to evacuate, but there was no other location on site to control the reactor. If they stayed, they were signing their death warrants. If they evacuated, no one would be left to contain the reactor, which meant an inevitable meltdown and tens of thousands of locals, if not hundreds of thousands, would die from radiation poisoning.

"That's not good," mumbled Wilson.

Shawn turned to face the control panel. Brad and Wilson stared at the monitor, both men concerned. He went over and checked.

The reactor's water level indicator read far below normal, which meant a large portion of the core was exposed with no way of cooling it down. Images of what had happened to the reactor core at Chernobyl flashed through his mind.

"What are we going to do?" asked Andy.

"We have to get more water into the reactor ASAP."

Without taking his eye off the gauge, Shawn removed the radio from his belt and pressed the TALK button.

"Wally, can you read me?"

No response.

"Wally, are you there?"

"*I'm here. I'm busy right now. The God damn injection line isn't working.*"

"What?"

"*I said, the God damn injection line isn't working.*"

"Let me call you back." Shawn turned to Brad. "Hook the battery up to the pressure gauge for the suppression chamber."

Brad seemed confused. "Why the suppression chamber?"

"Just do it."

Brad shrugged and proceeded to remove the panel to the electrical circuit for the suppression chamber gauge. Shawn paced the floor, not wanting to rush his friend, though he had a gut feeling he knew what the results would be. After several minutes, Brad stood and wiped his hands on his coveralls.

"Done."

Shawn did not want to look at the gauge. "What's the reading?"

Brad stepped over to the wall and muttered, "Shit."

"What's the reading?"

"Six hundred and eighty-nine KPA."

Andy glanced between the two men. "What does that mean?"

"It means the lack of water is increasing the heat and pressure in both the containment vessel and suppression chamber. A meltdown or an explosion is inevitable if we don't reverse the situation soon." Shawn stepped away from the others and rekeyed the radio. "Wally, are you there?"

"*What's up?*"

"You can't feed water into the suppression chamber because the kPa is six hundred and eight-nine."

"*God damn it. How did that happen?*"

"The reactor core is exposed and generating excessive heat and pressure."

"*Then we're screwed.*"

"No, we're not. I'm sending a team down to the suppression chamber to release the pressure. Once they do that, hopefully you'll be able to start pumping water back into the injection line. We still have a chance of getting this situation under control."

"*A God damn slim one.*"

"Yeah, but it's better than none at all. I'll let you know when that's accomplished. In the meantime, check the spent fuel rod pool. If the water gets too low there, the rods will be exposed and emit dangerous amounts of radiation."

"*Roger that.*"

"One other thing." Shawn paused. "Since the core is exposed, keep a close watch on the radiation levels outside."

"*Great. Any more good news?*"

"We're not dead yet." Shawn's joke fell flat.

"*Give it time. Let me know the moment we can start pumping again.*"

"I will. Good luck."

Shawn slid the radio back onto his belt. When he turned to his team, they all stared at him, fear and concern in their eyes.

Brad spoke for them all. "I hate to ask, but how do you plan to relieve the pressure inside the suppression chamber?"

"Wilson and I are going down to open that valve."

A stunned silence fell over the control room.

Wilson finally summoned the courage to speak. "You realize that's a death sentence."

"There's no choice if we hope to prevent a meltdown. That's why I'm going with you. I can't ask any of you to go in my place."

Libby stepped forward. "You're needed here. Let me go."

"No. You and Andy are the youngest members of the team, which means you'll both be more effected by the radiation than any of us. In fact...." Shawn removed one of the radios from the console and handed it to Libby. "I want you and Andy to evacuate to a safer location."

"Screw that," said Andy.

"Besides," added Libby. "There's no safe place around here."

"Go to the guard shack and wait until you hear from me."

Andy shook his head. "We're part of the team."

"I need you as backup in case something happens to the rest of us." When the two men tried to disagree, Shawn shut them down. "This has nothing to do with your performance. The situation here is spiraling out of control. I want the two of you to evacuate to the guard shack and wait. If any of us succumb to radiation poisoning, I'll call you back to take over. There's no need to expose all of us. You can relieve us when we get this situation under control."

"And what if you don't get the situation under control?" asked Libby.

"Then the three of us as good as dead. In that case, you two have a chance of surviving."

Libby shook his head. "No way. We wouldn't be able to live with ourselves if we retreated to a safe place while you three put your lives on the line."

"What if I order you to wait at the guard shack?"

"You may be the boss," Andy chuckled. "But you can't make us leave."

"We're staying," added Libby.

"Thank you." Shawn turned to Wilson. "Let's suit up."

WALLY SLID THE radio into his back pocket and headed over to

Katherine and Carlson, who oversaw the pumping of the water into the injection line.

"Any luck?"

"None." Katherine wiped the sweat from her brow. "Do you know what's wrong?"

"Shawn called from the control room. The pressure inside the suppression chamber has spiked, so trying to pump water into the system is useless. They're going to vent the chamber. In the meantime, he wants us to shift our attention to the spent fuel pond and make certain it has enough water so the rods don't become exposed."

"Makes sense," said Carlson.

"One more thing. The reactor core is exposed, so the radiation levels out here might be increasing. What's the reading on the Geiger counter?"

Carlson glanced down at the device located against the exterior wall.

"It's reading 1.4 milliSieverts per hour."

"God damn it." Wally contemplated his next move. "You two get Eric and take a break inside the cab. Tell Josh and Rogers to suit up, then have them switch out the hose from the injection line to the rod pool. We'll work in one-hour shifts to limit our exposure to radiation. Get moving."

CHAPTER THIRTY

DANIELLE DID NOT stop when she reached the woods. In fact, she quickened her pace, not wanting the gang to catch her if they came looking for whoever had killed their friend. Every few minutes, she changed course. By now, she had no clue where she was. Hopefully, neither did they.

Pausing to catch her breath, Danielle leaned against a tree. It took a few minutes for her breathing and pulse to return to normal. All the while, she listened for any signs of being chased. She heard yelling, but it came from the highway. No rustling came from the woods behind her, so the odds were good they did not care enough about their friend to hunt her down. Thank God for small miracles. Still, she refused to take any chances. After a minute, Danielle took off again, not running as fast as before, but still changing direction every hundred yards.

Ten minutes into her escape, Danielle heard a noise off to the right. She froze and listened but could not detect anything.

Damn it, Danielle chastised herself. *Stop overreacting and focus on—*

A rustling came from her right. She spun around. It sounded again, closer but moving slowly. One of the gang members must be trying to sneak up on her. Now that he had been discovered, he would attack. Danielle could run but knew she would not make it far before being caught, especially if he called the others for help. Then she would meet the same fate as the two women on the highway. Better to die fighting.

Danielle raised the crowbar like a baseball bat, ready to

defend herself.

The rustling drew closer. It came from behind the tall bushes only a few feet away. The leaves gently shook. What the fuck was he waiting…?

The bushes parted. Danielle lunged and swung the crowbar. Her foot slid on the damp soil and she stumbled, missing her target by more than a foot. Fuck, she had blown her one chance of winning. Danielle yelped as her left knee slammed into a rock but ignored the pain, glancing up to see how her attacker planned to respond.

A frightened racoon spun around, darted back into the forest, and quickly disappeared among the trees.

Danielle chuckled. Thank God Shawn and Kirstie had not witnessed this. They would never let her live down this embarrassment. She had a long way to go if she ever hoped to be an apocalypse warrior.

Once her heartbeat returned to normal, Danielle climbed to her feet, groaning and trying to ignore the throbbing in her knee. At least it distracted from her aching feet. Limping lightly, she continued through the woods.

A few minutes later, Danielle exited into a clearing. In front of her stretched scores of large homes with acres of backyard space and a lake on the other side. She had stumbled across an upper-middle-class neighborhood. Sitting down and resting against a tree, she relaxed for a moment to check out the area, not wanting to leave the frying pan only to burn in the fire.

Half an hour passed, and no one appeared in or around any of the houses. Maybe they were holding up to prevent assholes like the gang members from preying on them. However, it could just as easily be that the owners were at work when the solar flare hit, like she had been. Still, better to be safe than sorry. She decided to wait it out a bit longer.

When the sun began to set, Danielle descended the hill and headed for the nearest residence, a two-story, colonial revival-style house with a three-car garage. Approaching through the backyard, she cautiously climbed the stairs to the deck and knocked on the French doors, hoping the owners did not answer with a blast from a shotgun. She got no response, so she knocked again, this time harder. Still nothing.

Danielle tried opening the door, but it was locked. Not surprising. She considered using the crowbar to break the glass but did not feel right about breaking into someone else's home. Fuck it. She needed a safe place to rest.

Using the edge of the crowbar, she wedged it between the door and the jamb and twisted it until, eventually, the lock snapped. Sliding the door aside, she stepped in.

"If anyone's here, I'm not a threat. I'm only looking for a place to stay for the night."

Silence.

Danielle slid shut the door and entered, heading into the kitchen. She crossed over to the refrigerator and opened it. The odor of decayed food wafted out, turning her stomach. She rummaged through the contents until she found five bottles of lukewarm spring water. Taking two, she drank them down one at a time, not stopping until halfway through the second. The other three she placed in her trash bag.

Danielle then checked out the cabinets, almost squealing with joy. They were well stocked. Canned goods, cereal, an opened loaf of whole grain bread, and peanut butter. She scooped up the bread and peanut butter, rummaged through the drawers until she found a knife, then took her bounty into the living room. An eighty-five-inch TV screen was mounted on the wall opposite the fireplace with a U-shaped sofa set in front of it. Kirstie and Shawn would never leave this room if they lived here.

Danielle's heart sank a bit over not knowing whether her daughter and brother were safe.

Sitting on the sofa, she made herself a peanut butter sandwich, her stomach growling in anticipation of the first meal she had eaten in days. Finishing the first one in no time, she made a second and wolfed it down.

By now, the sun had dropped to the tree line across the lake. It would be dark soon. Throwing the bread, peanut butter, and knife into the bag, she headed upstairs.

The master bedroom was spacious, with a king-size bed against one wall and a long bureau with a large-screen TV opposite. Placing her stuff on the floor by one of the nightstands, Danielle entered the bathroom, stepped in front of the sink, and turned on the faucet. Water poured out. Not certain how long her luck would last, she rapidly cleaned the crud off her face and hands and threw a few handfuls of water onto her hair. The flow stopped after less than a minute, but the quick wash had been refreshing.

At least for her face. The rest of Danielle still felt grungy after being on the road for three days in the rain, heat, and humidity. She stripped out of the tattered red dress and tossed it on the floor by the toilet, happy to finally be rid of it. The sneakers, socks, and bra she placed on the counter by the sink. Pulling a facecloth off the rack near the shower, she stepped inside and slid shut the door, then turned on the faucet. A stream of cold water blasted her in the face and immediately tapered off. Danielle soaked her body and the facecloth as much as possible before the flow stopped, then spent the next few minutes cleaning herself. When finished, she dried off with a towel.

Danielle swirled her tongue around her mouth. The little water she had did nothing to cleanse the dirt that had built up these past few days. A pair of toothbrushes, dental floss, and a bottle of Scope sat on a glass tray to the left of the sink. For a moment, she debated whether to use them. God only knew what diseases the owners' might have, but quickly erased all such nonsense from her thoughts. Being the end of the world, what did it matter? She rinsed her mouth out with Scope, used one of the toothbrushes on the counter to clean her teeth, flossed, then rinsed her mouth out with Scope again.

Staring at her reflection in the mirror, Danielle wished her appearance matched her cleanliness. The gang member had not broken her nose, but bruises covered it. She then noticed black and blue marks on her forehead where it had banged against the hood. Danielle touched them and winced. They were sore, and would worsen over the next few days, but nothing that would not eventually heal. Other than that, she seemed fine, though she would not be able to start an Only Fans account any time soon.

Danielle carried the toothbrush, floss, and Scope back to the bedroom and tossed them in her bag.

Next, she checked out the walk-in closet. It contained more cloths than every closet in her house combined. The mistress of the house must have been petite because all her clothes were two sizes too small. Thankfully, the husband was her size and only slightly taller. She picked out a pair of worn jeans that fit comfortably, though she needed to roll up the bottom of the legs, a tan t-shirt with no logo on it, and a pair of hiking sneakers that surprisingly fit. Danielle felt human for the first time in days.

A black book bag sat on the top shelf. Pulling it down, she brought it into the bedroom and emptied the contents of her trash bag into it. This would make traveling a lot easier.

Before going to bed, Danielle went back to the bathroom. The sun had dropped below the horizon, minimizing the light. She rummaged through the drawers until she found a pair of tweezers and some band aids, then took a roll of toilet paper and returned to the bed. In the dimming light, Danielle used the tweezers to clip small holes in each of the blisters and drained the water onto pieces of toilet paper. Tonight, she would sleep barefoot to let them heal and bandage them in the morning.

Laying down on the bed, she placed the crowbar and shears beside her. With a sigh, she leaned back into the pillows and relaxed.

Danielle sensed her confidence returning. She had made it halfway home and now had decent walking clothes, three bottles of water, and food. Chances looked good for making it home safely so long as she stayed off I-93 and took the back roads. She might make it through this nightmare after all.

In the light from the aurora, Danielle lapsed into a deep sleep.

CHAPTER THIRTY-ONE

T HE SCAVENGERS RETURNED from Home Depot late in the afternoon.

Kirstie felt a sense of relief when she spotted Lori's house a few blocks ahead. Though everything had gone according to plan, she had been on edge the entire trip, expecting something to go south. With luck, this experience would give her enough self-confidence so the next time out she could concentrate more on the task at hand. Kirstie only hoped she could maintain her cool when inevitably one of these runs went FUBAR.

Several neighbors came out to wave. One family applauded. As they approached Keith's house, he exited and crossed the lawn, meeting them in the street. Andrew stopped his horse, followed by the rest of the team.

"How did it go?"

"Perfect," replied Andrew. "We didn't run into any trouble."

"No one tried to steal your supplies on the way back?"

Andrew shook his head.

Meg smiled. "There was that one woman."

Keith grew concerned. "What happened?"

"A woman came up to us wanting to know if we had any water to spare for her four kids."

"What did she say when you told her you had none?"

Meg grinned and nodded to Jordan. "He gave her his bottles of water."

Keith turned to Jordan. "Really?"

Jordan smiled. "What else could I do? The poor woman

was desperate and terrified. Her husband never returned home. She was so grateful she offered me her husband's Colt. 45 in exchange."

"Did you take it?"

Jordan shook his head. "I told her she needed to keep it on her at all times and not talk to anyone. That there were dangerous people out here. The others handed over whatever water they had left."

"You must be thirsty."

"We are," said Regan.

"Head on over to Kathy's house. She's been checking the road for you every fifteen minutes. I'll get some water and bring it to you."

Keith rushed off to get the bottled water.

As they approached Kathy's house, she bounded down the front steps and ran over to the team.

"I've been worried sick. Is everything okay?"

"No problems," said Andrew.

Kathy's expression eased. "Were you able to get everything?"

"Everything except the bleach. Sorry."

"No problems. I have some at the high school. We can get it tomorrow."

"Another supply run?" asked Meg.

Andrew glanced over at her. "You don't want to do any more of these?"

"On the contrary, I enjoyed it. It beats hanging around here." Meg leaned forward and scratched the horse's neck. "Besides, it's been years since I've ridden a horse."

While Andrew, Kathy, and Meg chatted, Abbey and Mikayla ran up to their friends.

"Are you all right?" asked Mikayla.

"We're fine," answered Kirstie.

"Did you get to kill anyone?" asked Abbey.

All three girls stared at their friend.

Abbey became embarrassed. "Just asking."

Kathy interrupted them. "I owe you all an apology. I forgot to add one thing to the list. Wire fencing to prevent wildlife from eating what we grow. I had some at my house, but there's not enough to protect what we plan to grow. Sorry."

"Do you need us to go back?" Andrew asked apprehensively.

"We'll get by."

"Excuse me," said Mikayla. "If you want, we can plant the vegetables in my grandmother's garden. Her backyard is fenced off, and she has several flower beds out back we can tear up and use for growing food."

"Will she mind?" asked Kathy.

"I doubt it."

"Good." Kathy grinned. "You can put the cart in my garage tonight so nothing happens to it. We'll start planting tomorrow."

Andrew nodded.

"Sorry for asking," began Jordan. "What about that family we ran into?"

"What about them?" asked Andrew.

Kathy's expression changed to one of concern. "What family?"

"A mother with four children asked us for water. Her husband never came home and she has no way of keeping the kids alive. They'll be dead in a week. Should we ask her to join us."

"We can't take in everyone who needs help." Andrew spoke the words sternly. "If we do, we won't survive."

"I'm not asking to take in everyone, only this family. They'll never survive on their own."

"Just this one time," Meg pleaded.

"The kids can help tend the garden," added Kirstie. "That way they'll earn their keep."

Andrew looked to Kathy for guidance. She smiled.

"If we use the kids in the garden, that will free up adults for guard duty."

Andrew conceded defeat. "Shouldn't we ask the others first?"

"I will, but I doubt there will be an issue."

"If they agree, we'll stop by tomorrow and ask the family if they want to join us. Their house is on the way to the high school. Right now, let's get the cart stored away. You girls go back to Lori and let her know what's going on, then pull the flowers so we can plant tomorrow. I'm going to tell the Carsons that we'll need their horses for another day and will return them tomorrow. Jordan, you're with me."

CHAPTER THIRTY-TWO

S HAWN AND WILSON donned the Tyvek radiation suits, the heavy fire protection suits, and the boots. Neither man spoke because they knew what they were getting themselves into. When Kevin and Libby had attempted this earlier, they abandoned the effort when the radiation level inside the suppression chamber reached one hundred milliSieverts. That was twenty-four hours ago. Considering the pressure inside the containment vessel and suppression chamber had increased since then, Shawn assumed the radiation levels had also spiked, which did not bode well.

As they were getting ready to leave, Brad moved closer to Shawn and whispered, "Let me do this."

"No."

"You're needed here. I'm expend—"

Shawn cut him off. "You've already gone down once. Doing it a second time with those levels of radiation would be a death sentence."

"It could be lethal for you, too."

"But I haven't been exposed as much as you have." Shawn turned to Wilson, effectively ending the argument. "Ready?"

"No, but let's get this over with."

Both men left the break room and headed down to the northern set of doors leading into the suppression chamber.

"What's the reading?" asked Shawn.

"Sixty-one milliSieverts."

Shit. The radiation level outside the chamber had almost doubled.

"I'll lead. You keep a close eye on the Geiger counter. Okay?"

Wilson nodded.

Both men put on their hoods and started the air tanks, then opened the first set of doors. Shawn stepped inside, with Wilson following and closing it behind him. They followed the same procedure through the interior door.

Steam filled the chamber, which confirmed the reactor was overheating and evaporating what little water remained. If they failed to open the valve, the pressure would increase and Wally's team would not be able to pump water into the cooling system, which meant a meltdown or reactor breach—or both—was imminent.

"What's the reading?" Shawn yelled to be heard through the hood and air tank.

Wilson checked the Geiger counter. "Eighty-three milliSieverts!"

Shawn peered over the side of the catwalk. Between the lack of light and the steam, he could not see the bottom of the chamber. He stopped and clutched the railing.

Wilson bumped into him. "What's wrong?"

"I'm afraid of heights!"

"Do you want to wait here while I open the valve?"

Shawn shook his head, though Wilson did not see it under the hood. "I got this!"

Taking a deep breath, he led the way along the catwalk then turned south, heading for the corner housing the locked valve. When they reached the maintenance hatch, where Kevin had turned back earlier because of the spike in radiation, Shawn turned to Wilson.

"What's the reading now?" he yelled to be heard through the protective hoods.

"The needle's at one hundred!"

"Let's haul ass!"

The two men continued, having to walk slowly so they did

not miss the walkway leading to the AO valve on the turos. Shawn found it because he ran his hand along the guardrail, banging it against the metal when it turned inward. A moment later, they reached the outer wall of the turos. The valve sat four feet above the catwalk. Shawn checked its identifier.

"Valve 25A!"

Wilson checked his glove to verify. "Valve 25A!"

"What's the pressure reading?"

Wilson stepped over to the monitor and checked. "It's at eight hundred and twelve."

Shawn prayed the chamber did not rupture while they were inside. If it did, neither of them would make it out alive.

Grabbing the latch-lever, Shawn jerked his hands away, startled by the heat of the metal even through his radiation suit. He tried again, ignoring the discomfort as he attempted to pull the lever into manual mode. It was stuck in place due to lack of use. Shawn tired himself out after a few seconds.

Wilson tapped him on the shoulder. "Let me!"

Shawn leaned against the guardrail to catch his breath but backed off when he realized the metal was as hot as the lever. Even worse, the high temperature made him lightheaded. If he passed out now, he would be as good as dead, though it would be a slow, agonizing death.

Wilson took over and pulled the lever, but it still refused to budge. It took a minute for him to finally switch it into manual mode. Shawn noticed his friend's shoulders slump from exhaustion.

"I'll take over!"

Wilson moved aside and let Shawn in. The mechanisms to the valve were also stiff from lack of use but, after thirty seconds of pulling, slowly gave way. Once it did, he rotated it as far to the right as possible.

"Valve 25A, open!" yelled Shawn.

"Roger! Valve 25A, open!" confirmed Wilson.

"Let's get the fuck out of here!"

Both men spun around and rushed back to the exit, with Wilson in the lead. Since they knew where they were going, they made good time.

They reached the maintenance door when Wilson suddenly stopped. Shawn ran into his friend, almost knocking him over.

"What's wrong?"

"I can't breathe!"

Shawn checked the gauge on Wilson's air tank, shocked to find it empty. They must have been down here for more than twenty minutes. Then he realized that Kevin and Libby had used the tanks earlier, so he and Wilson had entered the chamber with depleted oxygen levels.

Fuck!

He moved in front of Wilson. "You've run out of oxygen! Take a deep breath, pull off your hood, and run for the exit!"

Wilson stared at him in terror, but only for a second. He bolted along the catwalk, removing his hood in the process.

They were fifty feet from the exit when Shawn's tank also ran out of oxygen. He inhaled deeply, yanked off his hood, and pushed past Wilson as he raced to the interior door. The first attempt to open it failed. The heat had caused the metal to expand.

Shawn placed all his weight on the lever and pushed. His lungs strained against the burden, desperate for air. Shawn closed his eyes and pushed even harder. The lever finally gave way, but the sudden movement caused him to exhale. He pulled open the interior door, trying not to breathe. Glancing to his side, he noticed Wilson standing beside him. He pointed for his friend to go first. Wilson rushed through, but in his haste tripped over the lower jamb and fell to the floor, blocking the exit. The man tried to stand, his movements hampered by the suits.

Shawn's lungs ached from the lack of oxygen. He considered rushing past Wilson and pulling him away from the door, but that would require energy he did not have. When he began to feel lightheaded, Shawn closed his eyes and prayed.

Opening his mouth, he took a deep breath of the irradiated air inside the suppression chamber.

Wilson rolled across the floor, allowing Shawn to jump out and slam shut the door behind him. Once secured, he opened the exterior door. They exited quickly. Shawn closed the exterior door, leaned against the outer wall of the chamber, and slid to the floor, too hot and exhausted to move.

"Sorry about that," Wilson said while gasping for air.

"Not your fault." Shawn paused to catch his breath.

"Did you breathe in any of that air?"

Shawn nodded. "What about you?"

"Twice."

"Shit."

"I know." Wilson stood and held out a hand to Shawn, helping him up.

Both men slowly made their way back to the break room, barely able to walk between the temperature and the exertion. Once inside, Shawn dropped into one of the chairs and rested, watching Wilson strip out of his radiation suits.

Brad raced in from the control room. "What the hell happened down there? You've been gone more than thirty minutes."

Shawn ignored the question. "What's the pressure inside the suppression chamber?"

"Eight hundred and thirteen kPa."

"Fuck." The two of them had exposed themselves to dangerous dosages of radiation all for nothing.

"Will you tell me what happened?"

Shawn relayed the events of the past half hour as he slowly stripped out of his suits and clothes. Libby, Andy, and Kevin had joined Brad, all three staring aghast as Shawn related the story, especially about breathing in the irradiated air. When he finished, none of them spoke.

Wilson broke the silence with a mumbled, "Shit."

"What is it?" asked Brad.

Wilson held up his dosimeter. "I received a dosage of one hundred and twenty-four milliSieverts."

"Jesus Christ," mumbled Libby as he took a step away from the two men.

Brad turned to Shawn. "What about you?"

"I'm afraid to look."

Brad removed the dosimeter from Shawn's coveralls, checked it, and stared blankly at his friend.

That did not bode well. "How much?"

"One hundred and forty-one milliSieverts."

Shawn remained silent. What could he say? Without access to proper medical care, that reading was a death sentence, especially if he stayed at Seabrook much longer. But what choice did he have? He sat back in the chair, the top of his coveralls hanging down around his waist.

Brad moved closer. "Let me help you out of those clothes?"

"It's not like it'll do any good." Shawn thought for a moment. "Contact Wally and advise him of the situation. Let him know we opened the valve but the pressure hasn't changed. Tell him to take his crew back to the fire station where they'll be safer. We'll let them know when... if the pressure drops."

"Are you sure?"

Shawn nodded.

As the others headed back to the control room, Shawn and Wilson finished undressing and put on clean underwear and coveralls, neither of them wanting to dwell on the fate that awaited them.

"WALLY, THIS IS Brad. Are you there?"

Eric picked up the radio from the dashboard.

"Hang on a minute. I'll get him."

Eric blared the horn. Once he got the attention of those

outside, he opened the driver's door and waved for them to come over. They rushed over to the pumper and removed their hoods.

"What's up?" asked Wally.

Eric handed him the radio. "Brad wants to talk to you."

The chief took the radio. "This is Wally."

"We opened the valve in the suppression chamber but it did no good. The kPa is six hundred eighty-nine. And the heat around the toros is climbing rapidly. We're in the early stages of a meltdown but, with the pressure so high, you won't be able to feed water into the cooling system. Shawn wants you to fall back to the fire station where it's safe. When we get the situation under control here, you can come back and start pumping water into the cooling system."

"Roger that. Keep me posted. And good luck."

Wally handed the phone back to Eric.

"Are we heading back to the station?" asked Carlson.

"I'll be God damned if I'm running, though if any of you want to go back, you have my permission. No one will think any less of you."

None of the team took him up on the offer.

Wally broke into an uncharacteristic smile. "Thank you."

"What now?" asked Katherine.

"We'll figure out a way around this." Wally turned to Carlson. "Is there any way we can vent the chamber from out here?"

"I'm not sure." Carlson considered the opportunities. "It's possible we could do it if we opened the valve to the injection line and disconnected the hose. The chamber might bleed out through there. But...."

"What?"

"If we're successful, irradiated air is going to flow out to where we are."

"God damn it." Wally spun around and studied the injection line. The pumper sat in front of the opening, which meant if they did relieve the pressure, they would be directly in the line of contamination.

He turned back to his team. "Everyone go inside the reactor building and wait in the control room. You'll be safe there until I get this pressure bullshit under control. Once I do, come out and join me."

"You're not joining us?" asked Eric.

"Someone has to open the injection line and keep an eye on the pressure."

Katherine shook her head. "With all due respect, we're staying out here with you. We can take twenty-minute shifts, which will lessen our exposure."

"Besides," added Josh. "Once the pressure is down, we need to get the hoses hooked up and pump water into the system quickly. You can't do this on your own."

"What if I order you to go inside?"

"We'll refuse." Katherine grinned. "What are you going to do? Fire us?"

Wally had never felt so proud of his team in all the years he had been on the job and showed it in his usual gruff manner.

"You're the biggest bunch of God damn assholes I've ever worked with, and I'm grateful for you."

Katherine chuckled. "Coming from you, that's a compliment."

Carlson tapped Wally on the shoulder. "Come on. You'll need help opening the injection line."

DAY FOUR

CHAPTER THIRTY-THREE

A LOUD NOISE roused Danielle from her sleep. She stared at the ceiling, confused, wondering for a moment where she was. Then it dawned on her—she had spent the night in the house she had broken into yesterday. But what caused—

A sound reverberated from downstairs. Shit, someone was breaking in. Being upstairs, she had no way to escape.

Danielle slipped on her socks and sneakers as the pounding continued, rapidly tying the laces.

On the fifth try, the front door burst open. She heard footsteps entering the foyer. They stopped, and someone called out, "We know you're in here. Show yourself."

Danielle froze, desperately figuring out what her next move would be. She reached for the crowbar to defend herself when the voice called out again.

"This is your last chance to show yourself. If we have to come and find you, it won't end well."

That was the second time he used the word "we." There must be at least two of them. Her chances of fighting off two assailants were not good. If they came looking for her, her chances of taking them both down were slim. If there were more than two, she had no chance of overpowering them. Danielle placed the crowbar back on the bed.

"I'm upstairs in the master bedroom."

"How many are there of you?"

"Only me."

"Come downstairs with your hands behind your head. If you try anything funny, we'll shoot."

"I'm on my way."

Danielle placed her hands behind her head and left the bedroom. Visions of what she had witnessed yesterday on the highway flashed through her mind.

Descending the stairs into the living room, she noticed three people standing in a semi-circle at the bottom. One man aimed a 9mm Glock at her, the second a shotgun. A woman stood off to the right brandishing a baseball bat. Danielle felt a little more relaxed when she realized the man holding the pistol wore a New Hampshire State Police uniform.

When she reached the floor, the state trooper ordered, "Turn around and keep your hands behind your head."

Danielle obeyed. The trooper stepped closer, the pistol still in his right hand, and began to frisk her, apologizing when he felt between her cleavage for any concealed weapon. When finished, he backed off several feet.

"Turn around."

Danielle obeyed.

"Is there anyone else with you?"

"No."

"Are you telling the truth?"

She nodded.

The trooper motioned to the man with the shotgun. "Daniel, go upstairs and check. If you find anyone, shoot them."

As Daniel ascended the stairs, the woman blurted out, "What are you doing in the Siegfrieds' house?"

"I'm not here to steal anything."

"Really. Those are Harry's clothes you're wearing."

"Please, hear me out. I was in Boston when the solar flare hit. I've been on the road for three days. I only broke in here to get a change of clothes, some food, and a good night's sleep."

"It checks out," said Daniel coming down the stairs. He had slung the shotgun over his shoulder and carried her soiled, tattered dress, bra, flats, book bag, and the crowbar and shears, which he placed on the floor.

"No one else up there?"

Daniel shook his head.

"What's in the bag?"

Daniel lifted the bag, opened it, and went through the contents. "A couple of water bottles, bread, peanut butter, Scope, a toothbrush, dental floss, and bandages."

"Those are not yours," said the woman.

"Kellie, quiet." The trooper holstered his pistol and waved for Danielle to sit on the sofa.

Danielle did as told. The trooper sat on the sofa opposite her. Kellie stood behind him. Daniel stood to the side. He had unslung the shotgun and kept the barrel pointed at the ground, though ready to use it in a second's notice if necessary.

"I'm Rick. What's your name?"

"Danielle."

"What are you doing here?"

"I'm trying to make my way back to Dunbarton to check on my daughter."

"Was she home at the time of the incident?"

"No. She was at Canobie Lake Park with her friends."

"That's not far from here," said Daniel. "Did you check there for her?"

"No. She has a good head on her shoulders, so I assume she tried to go home."

Rick grimaced. "I understand how you feel. My daughter is attending college in Washington, D.C."

"I'm sorry."

"So am I."

An awkward silence descended over the room.

"What's it like out there?" Rick asked.

"It's a fucking nightmare. No power. Looters everywhere. I got off the highway when I ran into a gang that raped a mother and daughter while making the father watch, then murdered them."

"How many were there?"

"Seven, but one of them attacked me so I killed him."

"That's confirmed by the blood on her dress and shears," added Daniel.

"Where did this happen?" asked Rick.

"On I-93 on the other side of the woods."

"Did they follow you?" shouted Kellie.

"If they did, she'd be dead by now." Rick turned his attention back to Danielle. "Anything else?"

"No."

"What's it like in Boston?" asked Daniel.

"Things there are even worse. People are trapped in subways and high rises. None of the hospitals are operating. And there are thousands of people wandering around aimlessly."

"Dear God," mumbled Kellie.

"I know." Rick leaned back in his seat. "And that was three days ago. Now that the shock has worn off, Boston must be a warzone."

Another awkward silence.

Danielle spoke next. "When will the police and the National Guard step in and put things right?"

"We lost power to our cars and communications. If we're lucky, it'll be months before we get organized. Until then, we're on our own." Rick paused, then stood and pointed to the bag and weapons. "Grab your gear and head on out."

Kellie became indignant. "You're not going to let her walk out of here with the stuff she stole!"

"Why not?"

"It's not hers!"

"I doubt we'll ever see the Siegfrieds again, or anyone else who wasn't here when the flare hit. She needs that stuff if she ever hopes to see her daughter again. So, be quiet."

Kellie turned, stormed into the kitchen, and began rummaging through the cabinets for supplies.

Rick shook his head and turned to Danielle. "Follow the lake north. It ends near Route 111. From there, you can follow the back roads home. And be careful. With every day that passes, the bad guys are going to get tougher and form gangs, and the good people will either die of starvation or fall victim to them. It would be safer for you to stay here—"

"I can't. I have to find my daughter."

"I understand." Rick offered his hand. "Good luck."

Danielle shook it. "Thanks."

Daniel came over and hugged her. "I'll say a prayer for you, hon."

"I'm going to need it."

Danielle grabbed her stuff and left the house before they changed their minds. Once outside, she headed toward the lake and made her way to Route 111.

CHAPTER THIRTY-FOUR

"YOU GOT THIS?" asked Kirstie. She stood by the garden bed. Mikayla and Abbey pulled the last of the grandmother's flowers from their soil and dropped them into a single pile.

Mikayla nodded and wiped her brow with the back of her hand. The heat and humidity today were unbearable, and it was only nine in the morning.

"I always help my grandmother with her flower garden. Besides, Theodora is coming over in an hour. She had her own vegetable garden and offered to help us out. She's also going to show us how to use the flowers we tore out to make a compost heap."

"You'll be busy today."

"Yeah." Mikayla frowned.

"What's wrong?"

"I can deal without my cell phone or laptop." Mikayla stood and stretched her neck, the strained muscles popping audibly. "But the lack of air conditioning is killing me."

"I hear you."

It had been four days since anyone in the neighborhood had a shower or enough running water to wash their face and hands. Sweat and grime covered them all and, thanks to the summer heat, half of the neighborhood reeked of body odor. Kirstie hated the grungy feeling. In another week, she would trade her virginity for a long, hot shower.

Regan opened the back door. "Are you almost ready?"

"I need to grab my weapons."

Abbey chuckled. "I bet that's something you never thought you'd say."

"Tell me about it." Kirstie wished her friends luck and went back into the house to grab her pistol, shotgun, and two bottles of water. When she joined Regan in the driveway, Meg and Jordan were already mounted on their horses while Andrew argued again with Kathy.

"No," Andrew sternly told her. "You're not going with us. We need you here."

"I already gave Becca and Justin instructions on how to set up the water filtration systems and storage tanks."

"That's not the point. We're screwed if something happens to you."

"What if something happens to you?" protested Kathy.

"We went over this yesterday. I'm expendable. You're not. You're the only one who knows how to set up our survival equipment."

Kathy placed her hands on her hips defiantly. "I'm also the only one with keys to the school."

"Give them to me. I know how to open a door."

She ignored the snarky comment. "There are items in my classroom we might be able to use."

"Then make me a list."

"We don't have time for that. Besides, I won't know what we can use until I get to check my classroom."

Andrew hesitated. "We don't have an extra horse for you."

"She can have mine."

Meg dismounted and handed her shotgun and pistol to Kathy, who took them before Andrew could intervene.

"Face it," said Jordan with a grin. "You're not going to win this one."

"I give up," Andrew sighed. "You can come along. But I'm staying close to you the whole time."

"Deal."

Kathy climbed onto Megan's horse.

"What will you do?" Andrew asked Meg.

"I'll help Becca and Justin."

Kirstie and Regan mounted their horses.

Jordan moved his horse over to Andrew. "What about the mother and her kids?"

"I talked with the others last night. Everyone concurred so long as the five of them pull their weight and are not a burden to the group. We'll stop by on our way to the school and, if they accept our offer, we'll pick them up on the way home."

"Thanks."

"It's cool," Andrew replied, then nudged his horse to begin the trip to Timberlane Regional High School.

THE TRIP PROVED more unbearable than yesterday's excursion, both humans and horses sweltering in the heat.

After an hour, they came across another horse farm. Andrew checked with the owners to see if it would be okay to let the horses drink from the water troughs. No one was home, so Andrew led the team out back. As the horses refreshed themselves with water and munched on a bale of hay, Kirstie and Regan checked the stable. Eight horses had been corralled inside. Two were dead from lack of water and heat exhaustion, flies and maggots already infesting the bodies. The other six were not far behind. The girls freed them, and each horse raced outside to find food and water. Andrew decided to stop on the way back and, if the residents still had not returned, commandeer the remaining six horses. They would be of use around the compound. Besides, feeding them and putting them to work seemed preferable to leaving them to die.

Less than half an hour later, the team reached the house where the mother had begged them for water yesterday.

Jordan placed his hand over his mouth. "Dear God."

Four bodies lay on the lawn—the mother and three children, all elementary school age. Each of them had been shot in the back of the head with a shotgun. Thankfully, the bodies lay face down in the grass, concealing the exit wounds.

"What happened?" asked Kirstie.

Andrew grimaced. "It looks like the mother asked the wrong people for help."

A noise came from inside the home.

Andrew moved his horse in front of Kathy, unslung his shotgun, and aimed it at the residence. The rest of the team did the same.

"I know you're in there. Come out with your hands up."

The front door opened slowly. The group raised their weapons, prepared to fire back if attacked.

Instead, a teenage girl with blonde hair centered herself in the doorway, her hands above her head, her body shivering from fear.

"Please don't shoot. There's nothing left. The other group took everything we had."

Kathy maneuvered her horse around Andrew. "Haellie?"

The teenager's eyes widened. "Mrs. V? Is it really you?"

"Yes."

Kathy dismounted and ran toward the teenager. Haellie bounded off the porch and rushed into Kathy's arms, hugging her tightly and sobbing.

"You know her?" asked Andrew.

"Haellie is one of my students." Kathy broke her grip and wiped the tears off the teenager's cheeks. "What happened?"

"A group of men came by while the kids were playing out front. When they approached the house, mom came out to see if they had any food or water to spare. The leader lined them up, made them get on their knees, and asked my mother questions. After she gave them the information they wanted, the leader shot them in the back of the head. Then the group ransacked the place. Whatever they didn't take they destroyed."

"How did you survive?"

"When they stormed the house, I hid in the attic. I was afraid they would kill me as well, and...."

Haellie broke down. Kathy held her close, trying to comfort her.

"When did this happen?" asked Andrew.

"Last night, a few hours after a group of travelers gave her water."

"That was us," said Jordan.

Haellie looked at him, her eyes glazed. "Thank you."

"How many were there?" asked Andrew.

"Six. All men in their twenties and thirties."

"Were they on horseback?"

Kathy glared at him. "Stop asking her questions."

"We need to know in case we run into them."

"It's okay." Haellie wiped the snot from her nose. "They were walking. They headed in that direction."

She pointed to the road ahead of them.

"It's okay. We'll take you back to our compound where you'll be safe."

Haellie glanced over at the bodies of her mother and siblings. "I... I can't leave them like this."

"Is there anyone still in the house?" The question came from Andrew.

Haellie shook her head.

"Wait here."

Andrew dismounted and entered. A few minutes later, he returned with a blanket and three sheets which he placed over the bodies.

"Come with us," offered Kathy.

Jordan held out his hand. "You can ride with me."

Haellie balked. "I'd... I'd rather ride with Mrs. V, if that's okay."

"Of course, it is."

Kathy climbed back on her horse then pulled Haellie up in

front of her, holding the reins with one hand and hugging the teenager with the other. Andrew led the group back onto the road and continued toward the high school, only this time with the shotgun resting across his lap. Kathy followed. Jordan brought up their rear, also keeping his shotgun at the ready.

Kirstie stayed back, staring at the four bodies, blood already soaking the sheets and blanket.

Regan moved up alongside her. "Are you okay?"

A long pause ensued before Kirstie finally turned to her friend. "What the hell is happening to the world?"

"It's only going to get worse." Regan tapped Kirstie's shoulder. "Come on. We need to stay together."

The two girls nudged their horses and fell in behind the others.

CHAPTER THIRTY-FIVE

S HAWN SAT AT his desk, trying to clear his head. His team had been active for close to seventy-two hours and were exhausted. Adrenalin had been keeping them going most of that time, but that had started to wear off. He wished he could add coffee to the mixture, an impossibility without electricity. Each of them had tried taking a nap, but only Wilson fell asleep due to the high level of radiation he had received. Between the heat and humidity that permeated the control room and the concerns over the increased radiation throughout the facility, none of them could relax. The physical exhaustion did not bother him as much as the mental strain. He needed to keep a clear head if he hoped to avoid a major fuck-up.

Standing, Shawn entered the control room and stepped over to the Geiger counter resting on a table by the door. It registered 14.5 milliSieverts, double from a few hours ago. He headed over to the control panel. Brad stood by the pressure monitor to the containment vessel.

"What's the reading?"

"Eight hundred and twenty-one."

Shawn's eyes widened. "Are you serious?"

Brad stepped aside. "See for yourself."

Sure enough, the needle hovered at the eight hundred-and-twenty-one mark. Despite the efforts to open the valve in the suppression chamber, they had failed. He and Wilson had more than likely forfeited their lives for nothing.

"Is the reading accurate?" he asked.

"It has been up until now. Every time one of us went down

there, I compared the readings the team took with those up here, and every time they matched."

"Is there anything we haven't tried yet?"

Brad shook his head. "Wally called to say they're trying to bleed off some of the pressure through the injection line. Apparently, it didn't work."

"I give him an A for effort." Shawn closed his eyes and massaged his temples. "I could use a cup of coffee right about now."

"Screw that," chuckled Brad, trying to lighten the mood. "I could use a few shots of whiskey."

"When this is over, I plan on swilling down a few bottles."

Libby strolled up to join the conversation. "If you're that desperate for coffee, there's half a pot in the break room left over from last shift."

"That was four days ago," said Shawn light-heartedly. "It's stone cold and probably tastes like shit."

Brad grinned. "I could bring it down to the reactor and heat it up for you."

"Andy made the pot," added Libby. "The radiation might improve the taste."

From the other side of the control panel, Andy smiled and extended the middle finger of his right hand.

Shawn laughed. "If the cars worked, I'd send one of you into Seabrook for a Dunkins run."

"I wish." Brad's humor drained. "Sadly, it'll be awhile before—"

The control room shook, accompanied by a muffled explosion. The walls vibrated violently. Tiles and dust fell from the ceiling, the latter creating a haze in the room. Those around the control panel dropped to the floor and covered their heads. Shawn crouched and looked around the control room, hoping the area did not sustain substantial damage. After a few seconds, the noise and rumbling died off, leaving the control room quiet.

"What the fuck was that?" Libby coughed.

Shawn stood and waved his hand in front of his face to clear the dust. "An explosion occurred somewhere, more than likely in the reactor."

Brad stared at the pressure gauge and mumbled a single word. "Fuck."

"What?"

"The pressure inside the containment vessel dropped to below two hundred." Brad met Shawn's gaze, fear in his eyes. "It's been breached."

Picking up the radio, Shawn pressed the TALK button. "Wally, are you there?'

No one answered.

"Wally, are you there?"

No response.

"Can anyone hear me?" he yelled into the microphone.

Still nothing.

Shawn pocketed the radio and headed to the door.

"Where are you going?" asked Brad.

"To check on Wally and his team."

WALLY STOPPED BY the injection line to check on the Geiger counter. It read 3.35 milliSieverts. Each reading showed an increase in radiation. The God damn reactor was overheating and already in the early stages of a meltdown. He would check with the control room when he returned to the pumper to see if the pressure inside the containment vessel had dropped. He prayed that it had. If they did not inject water into the system ASAP, they would have another Chernobyl or Fukushima on—

An explosion rocked the area outside the reactor. Wally leaned against the exterior wall and covered his head with both arms. At first, he thought he heard rain hitting the ground around him. However, when a small piece of concrete slammed into his back, he realized it was debris from the reactor building. He heard something heavy crash against metal, followed by a muffled scream. The falling debris continued for several seconds before stopping. When Wally looked up, a haze of dust covered the entire area, dropping the visibility to zero.

Reaching down, Wally picked up the Geiger counter and wiped the dust from the faceplate of his hood. Thank God it had not been damaged. He checked the meter. It read 21.8 milliSieverts and climbing. The God damn reactor must have exploded.

Wally made his way toward the pumper, unable to see it through the haze, though he heard moaning nearby. After ten feet, it emerged from the cloud. Four of his team huddled outside the cab, each of them dazed and covered in dust. Then he noticed a huge chunk of concrete had crashed into the right side of the cab. He quickened his pace.

"Is everyone okay?"

Carlson glanced over at the chief. "Thank God you're alright."

"What about you?"

"Eric has a gash on his head and a broken right arm." Carlson nodded his head toward the pumper. "Katherine didn't make it."

Wally stared inside the cab. The chunk of concrete had collapsed the roof on the right side of the cab. Katherine's crushed body lay sprawled in the seat, blood flowing down her body and pooling on the floor. He closed his eyes and said a silent prayer for her.

"Do you know what exploded?" asked Carlson.

"No. Where's the radio?"

"On the dashboard."

Wally climbed up, avoiding looking at Katherine, and grabbed the radio. That's when he heard Shawn yelling through the speaker.

"*Can anyone hear me?*"

Wally pressed the TALK button. "I'm here."

"*Jesus Christ, I was worried. Is everyone okay?*"

"Katherine died in the explosion. Eric sustained injuries, but nothing life-threatening. Do you know what exploded?"

"*We think it was the containment vessel. The pressure dropped to below two hundred right after the blast.*"

Wally assessed the situation. If the breach occurred in the containment vessel rather than the reactor, the drop in pressure meant they could begin pumping water back in the cooling system and hopefully prevent a meltdown. But with the spike in the radiation level, doing so meant a death sentence for his team. Not that it mattered. The area for miles around would be dangerously irradiated. They could run, but that would merely delay the inevitable. If they stayed behind and attempted to cool the reactor, they could, with luck, prevent a meltdown and limit the threat to the surrounding communities.

"Where are you now?" asked Wally.

"*I'm almost at the exit to the building.*"

"Don't come out here. The radiation level is at 21.8 milliSieverts."

"*Fuck.*"

"I know. Listen, with the pressure down, we're going to try and inject water into the cooling system. I need you to stay inside and let me know if we're successful. Can you do that?"

"*Yes, but....*"

Neither man wanted to talk about the fate that awaited the fire unit.

Shawn broke the silence. "*Do you want me to bring down our Tyvek suits for you?*"

"It's not going to prevent the inevitable, and they'll only hamper our efforts. If you'll excuse me, I need to start feeding the system. Keep me posted on what's going on."

"*Roger that.*" A pause. "*Good luck.*"

"Thanks. We're going to need it."

Wally broke the radio connection and climbed out of the cab.

"Did the reactor explode?" asked Eric.

Wally shook his head. "Shawn thinks the pressure inside the containment vessel caused the explosion because the pressure inside the vessel has dropped to below two hundred. Let's hook the hose back up to the injection line and try to get that God damn reactor under control."

None of his team protested despite knowing their fate.

"Josh, hook up the hose to the injection line. Carlson, make sure the generator is still functioning and that we have enough diesel fuel to keep it going. Eric, check the hoses between here and the tributary. If any of them are ruptured, let me know and we'll get replacements from inside the building. Any questions?"

None.

"Move out."

SHAWN STARED AT the radio. He admired Wally for his heroism. Both men knew the fire unit would be dead in a few days from radiation poisoning. But, if they were successful, the team would limit the contamination to the immediate neighborhoods, saving close to a million lives. The only thing Shawn's team could do was make sure they helped out Wally's people any way they could.

He headed back to the control room.

When he entered, Brad ran over to him. "What's the situation outside?"

"Most of them survived the blast."

"Most?"

Shawn ignored the question. "Wally is going to try and inject water into the cooling system. Hopefully, the only damage was to the containment vessel. I want you to switch the battery to the temperature gauge on the reactor so we can monitor their progress."

"I can do that." Brad nodded. "Anything else?"

"Pray they're successful."

CHAPTER THIRTY-SIX

DANIELLE REACHED THE end of the lake and crossed through the trees, pausing when she spotted Route 111. Fear gripped her. What if the gang of rapists she had encountered yesterday remained in the area? The chances were good they had long since left the area, but better to be safe than sorry. Brandishing the crowbar, she cautiously made her way to the end of the trees, pausing behind a tree every few seconds to build up her courage, then moved forward. Only when certain no one was around did she venture past the tree line.

All four lanes were filled with rush hour traffic, vehicles long since abandoned by their drivers. Danielle positioned herself by a pole supporting a road sign and scanned the road for several minutes, not spotting any movement. Not surprising. Summoning her courage, she crossed the road to the westbound lanes and headed toward Dunbarton.

Danielle realized she had no clue about her location or how to get home using back roads. Sure, she knew Dunbarton and the surrounding towns by heart but had rarely traveled outside the area except to do errands or go to the mall, which she now needed to avoid at all costs. This was new territory for her. If she fucked up, she could easily stumble across a major city, or worse, get lost and add several more days before she made it back to Kirstie.

If Kirstie had made it home.

Up ahead, six lines of vehicles stretched east and west along the road at a traffic signal that no longer worked. One of them, a Walmart truck, had been ransacked for anything of value. On

one corner sat a Dunkin coffee shop, with a gas sta-
tion/convenience store opposite it. She moved over to the trees
on the side of the road and studied the area for any signs of
trouble. After several minutes, once confident no one was
around, she made her way along the road.

Danielle paused at the end of the tree line and studied the
convenience store. It had been looted. A body lay on the
cement in front of the store, a pool of dried blood beneath it.
She intended to cross the road and continue when a crazy idea
suddenly struck her. Taking a deep breath to steady her nerves,
she crossed the parking lot.

The body had already begun to rot. Flies and wasps hovered around it, and maggots infested the body, especially the
large exit wound on its back.

Danielle stepped inside the store. As she predicted, everything edible or drinkable had been stolen. Debris littered the
floor, making it difficult to move without stepping on something. She made her way to the registers where a second body
lay on the floor, a heavy-set guy with long, scraggily hair and
three gunshots to his chest. Insects overran the corps, and
maggots formed pools in the exit wounds. It sat in a pool of
congealed blood, dried chunks of flesh and organs covering the
coffee station behind it. Propping herself on the counter and
leaning forward, she checked behind it, hoping the weapon
used to kill him was still there. The clerk lay against the
cigarette rack, most of her head blown off. Gore covered the
rack and floor, and dried blood puddled on the floor. She could
not see any guns. Someone must have stolen them along with
every pack of cigarettes and cheap cigars available. For some
people, beer and smokes were a priority during the apocalypse.

Danielle moved down to the end of the counter and almost
squealed with joy. The map stand had been knocked over, with
dozens of maps spread out and trampled. She rummaged
through the pile until she found what she needed—a map of
New Hampshire. Picking it up, she spread it out by the lottery

stand.

Route 111 would lead her into Nashua, one of the largest cities in New Hampshire. Manchester sat twenty miles to the north, and between them sat the large, sprawling town of Merrimack. Making her way through these cities was not an option. Luckily, a stretch of highway four miles in length ran between Merrimack and Manchester and passed through the suburbs. Danielle had a good chance of crossing there without being in too much danger. After that, she faced only lightly populated back roads leading to Dunbarton. She estimated it was approximately forty miles between here and home, a two-day trip. The most difficult part of the journey would be finding a way across the Merrimack River which flowed through the three cities. The only bridges across were in the cities, and going into them would be too dangerous. She would have to find some other way across.

Judging by the map, she should reach the stretch of road between Merrimack and Manchester before nightfall. That gave her plenty of time to find some way across, hopefully a small boat or canoe. Shit, at this point, she would be willing to cross in a pool float. Once she figured that out, Danielle would rest, cross late in the evening when hopefully no one would be around, and by tomorrow morning would be on her way home.

With luck, she had put the worst behind her.

Danielle studied the roads she needed to take, then folded the map, slid it in her bookbag, and continued on her way.

CHAPTER THIRTY-SEVEN

THE SCAVENGERS REACHED Timberlane Regional High School a little over an hour after leaving Haellie's house. For Kirstie, it seemed like an eternity now that she knew a gang of murderers were nearby.

As they veered off Greenough Street into the parking lot, Kirstie was surprised at the size of the school. It consisted of three interconnected buildings—Timberlane Regional High School to the left, the Timberlane Performing Arts Center in the middle, and Timberlane Regional Middle School to the right. No cars were in the parking lot, which did not surprise her. Being summer, not even the most dedicated teachers wanted to be here unless they had to. She scanned the front of the buildings but saw no indication anyone had broken in.

So far, so good.

Andrew led his horse up to the main entrance of the high school, dismounted, and pulled on the doors.

Locked.

"At least we know the place hasn't been looted."

"Yet," said Jordan.

"Isn't that we're about to do?" joked Regan.

Andrew grinned. "When we do it, it's called survival."

Kathy helped Haellie down then climbed off herself. She handed the reins to the teenager, unlocked the double glass doors, and stepped inside. Andrew and Haellie led the horses into the corridor, with the others dismounting and following.

Andrew faced the team.

"Jordan, you guard the horses."

"Is there any place larger I can take them?"

Kathy pointed to the left. "The gym is down there. It has plenty of room. Take a right when you get to the end of the corridor. The gym is a few doors down on your left."

"Thanks."

"Kathy, how long will it take you to gather everything you need?" asked Andrew.

"Half an hour, maybe less if Haellie helps me."

The teenager nodded.

"Where's the lab?"

"Down the end of the hall. Room 126."

Kirstie spoke next. "Regan and I are going to check out the cafeteria in case something was left behind we could use."

"Good idea," said Andrew. "If you find anything, pile it up by the doors. We can come back for it later if we have to."

"Where is the cafeteria?"

"Follow Jordan." Kathy pointed down the corridor. "It's right before the gym."

"I'm going to check the nurse's office," said Andrew. "Where is it?"

Kathy pointed behind him. "Right there."

"That was easy."

"There are a few bottles of insulin in the fridge in case I needed them in an emergency as well as several syringes. Please bring them."

"Roger that."

Kathy smiled. "Thank you."

"Head out and be careful. We'll meet in the gym in thirty minutes. Fire a warning shot if you run into trouble."

JORDAN HAD TROUBLE leading the horses down the corridor because of the narrow space. They were agitated and resisted going, but he eventually eased their anxiety and gently ushered them to the gym. Once inside, their attitude changed. On seeing the open space, they entered and spread out, unsuccessfully looking for a place to graze.

Jordan crossed the court and took a seat in the lower row of bleachers. After a minute, his horse sauntered over and stood by him.

"What's up, boy?"

The horse nudged his arm with its nose.

"You want affection." Jordan stood and petted its neck.

The horse rubbed its head against him.

Jordan smiled. He could easily do this for the next thirty minutes.

IT TOOK KIRSTIE and Regan longer than expected to find the cafeteria because they were stuck behind the horses. Once there, they pushed open the doors and stepped inside.

The tables were neatly arranged in two rows of twelve, the chairs folded and stacked on top. The cleaning crew had come in earlier and buffed the floor until the tiles gleamed. Kirstie could not remember the last time she saw a school cafeteria this spotless.

"I doubt they kept any food over the summer," said Regan. "What do you hope to find here?"

"That." Kirstie pointed to three vending machines lined up side-by-side on the wall to the right. One contained various soft drinks and juices; the second Gatorade, Red Bull, or Monster power drinks; and the third dozens of bottled water.

"Damn, girl, you're really getting the hang of this apocalypse stuff."

Kirstie grinned as she crossed over to the machines. All the rows had recently been stocked.

"Those should keep us hydrated for at least a week."

"How are we going to carry all of these?"

"We can't. But if we pack them up, we can come back tomorrow with the cart and retrieve them. Let's check out the kitchen. Maybe there are more stacked in there we can use."

The two headed for the kitchen.

ANDREW TRIED THE door to the nurse's office. It was locked. Fuck it. Using the stock of his shotgun, he smashed out the glass pane, unlocked it from the inside, and entered.

A locked cabinet containing medicines hung on the wall between two hospital-style beds. He went over, shattered the glass, and packed the bottles into the empty book bag he had brought with him. Most were over-the-counter meds such as Tylenol, Ibuprofen, and antacids. Others were orange in color with labels bearing the names of various students and the dosage. Judging by the medicine names, he assumed they were prescription anti-depressants and anti-anxiety pills. Since he had room in his book bag, Andrew took them. They might come in handy as the situation grew worse.

Stepping over to the minifridge on the opposite counter, Andrew opened the door. The interior remained relatively cool, so anything inside hopefully had not gone bad. He rummaged around until he found five bottles of insulin bearing Kathy's name. He added them to the others.

Next, he rummaged through the drawers and wooden cabinets. Not only did he find an opened package containing eleven syringes, he also came across a variety of bandages and gauzes, disinfectant wipes, alcohol pads, rubber gloves, and hand sanitizer.

Damn, he had hit the jackpot.

Andrew stuffed everything that would fit into the book bag.

KATHY STEPPED INTO the classroom and paused, taking in her desk, the lab tables, the posters on the walls, and everything else that made this her space. It felt comfortable being in familiar surroundings.

"Is everything okay, Mrs. V?"

"God only knows when these classrooms will be used again."

"I never thought I'd say this, but I'd be willing to go back to school early if it meant things would return to normal."

Kathy motioned toward the window shades. "Raise them so we can get some sunlight in here."

As Haellie complied, Kathy made her way to the back of the classroom where she kept the chemicals in a metal cabinet. Unlocking the doors, she removed a bookbag and laid it on the closest lab table, then went through the contents until she found the bleach they needed to complete the water filtration project and placed the twin bottles beside the bookbag.

"Anything I can do to help?"

She glanced over her shoulder at Haellie. "Load those two bottles in the bag. I'll pass along some more stuff. Most of them will be glass, so be careful."

Kathy searched for anything they might need, quickly deciding to take them all since she had no idea if any of the chemicals might come in handy later. She removed the bottles one by one and handed them to Haellie, who carefully placed them in the bookbag.

"How are we doing for space?"

"We still have about a third left."

"Good."

Spinning one bottle around, Kathy read the label: Hydrofluoric Acid. Might as well bring back that one. She pulled a hand towel off the top shelf.

"Haellie."

"Yes?"

Kathy handed the hand towel to the teenager. "Wrap this

around this bottle before putting it in the bookbag. And be careful."

"What is it?"

"Hydrofluoric Acid. If you get that on your hands, it'll eat through your skin."

"Thanks for the warning."

Haellie spread out the towel on the lab table and placed the bottle in the center. Before she had a chance to wrap it, a voice came from the front of the classroom.

"Well, look what we have here."

Kathy spun around, an expression of horror on her face. Haellie glanced over her shoulder and gasped.

Two men stood inside the classroom, blocking the door. The taller of the two, who wore a Red Sox baseball cap and had a lit cigarette dangling out of his mouth, cradled a hunting rifle in his arms. The other, a few inches shorter and a good thirty pounds heavier, gripped a .357 Magnum.

Kathy tried to keep her fear under control. "What do you want?"

"We originally came here looking for supplies, but it seems we found ourselves some nice pussy to fuck."

CHAPTER THIRTY-EIGHT

K IRSTIE AND REGAN were ten feet from the kitchen when two men emerged from inside, one a teenage Latino and the other an older guy with close-cropped hair, each carrying two twenty-four-bottle packages of water. Both groups stopped, surprised by the presence of the others. For a split second, they stared at each other.

The two men suddenly dropped the bottled water. The older guy reached for the AR-15 semiautomatic rifle slung over his shoulder while the Latino pulled a revolver from its holster. Both girls brought their shotguns to bear. All four aimed at each other at the same time but no one fired.

"We don't want any trouble," said Regan.

The older guy nodded. "Then lower your guns and there won't be any."

Kirstie shook her head, "No fucking way."

"Then we have ourselves a Mexican standoff," said the older guy.

The Latino extended his arm closer to Regan's face, the Magnum barrel inches from her. "And there's no fucking way I'm gonna lose that standoff."

Both sides stared down each other.

JORDAN RUBBED HIS forehead against the horse's nose when he heard the gym doors open. He moved away from the bleachers to see which team had returned when an unfamiliar voice said,

"What the fuck? These weren't here half an hour ago."

Jordan froze but had already exposed himself.

Two men stood in the open doorway. One was younger, of medium height and build, and wore glasses. The other was a heavyset guy with dark, scraggly hair. The latter spotted Jordan. His eyes widened and he raised a rifle.

"Show yourself, asshole."

Jordan stepped out a few feet, enough to show himself but still be close enough to duck behind the horse if necessary.

"Freeze or I'll shoot."

"Don't fire," said the younger guy with glasses. "You might hit one of the horses. We can use them."

Jordan shifted his gaze to the right. His shotgun rested on the bleacher fifteen away.

THE TALL GUY holding the rifle stepped over to Kathy and placed the barrel inches from her face. She winced from the stench of cigarette smoke on his breath.

"Don't try anything stupid, bitch. I'd hate to ruin that pretty mouth before I have a chance to fuck it."

The fat guy crossed over to Haellie, who leaned back against the lab table, paralyzed with fear. He holstered the Magnum and stared at the teenager's breasts.

"Look at the size of those tits. This is going to be fun."

"Fuck her and then we'll switch out. We'll save the MILF for last."

The fat guy tore open Haellie's blouse and grabbed her breasts, squeezing hard. The teenager gasped. Kathy could not bear to watch one of her students being raped and was about to offer herself up to the assholes.

In a split second, Haellie's expression switched from fear to fury. Clasping the bottle of acid in her left hand, she smashed it into her attacker's face, shattering the glass. He screamed in agony, his cry covering the sizzling of his flesh as the acid began to burn it away. Raising his hands to cover his face, the fat guy stumbled to the side.

"You fucking cunt!"

The tall guy swung the hunting rifle toward Haellie. Kathy lunged, placed her hands on the barrel, and pushed it toward the ceiling as he pulled the trigger.

ANDREW HEARD THE blood-curdling scream followed seconds later by a gunshot. Things had gone south fast.

His Marine training kicked in. Taking the bookbag of meds and his shotgun off the table, he raced out into the corridor.

THE COMMOTION CAUGHT the two men in front of Kirstie and Regan off guard. The older guy lowered his weapon for a moment.

It was all Kirstie needed.

She pulled the shotgun's trigger. The older guy's head exploded, splashing the Latino with blood, brain matter, and pieces of shattered skull. The lifeless body dropped to the floor.

Despite being covered in gore, the Latino surged forward. In one quick move, he knocked the pistol from Regan's hand, wrapped his arm around her neck, and pulled her close to him, using her as a shield. Regan clasped his arm, struggling to break free, stopping only when he placed the Magnum's barrel against her temple.

"Drop your gun or the bitch dies."

THE SCREAM AND weapon fire could be heard all the way to

the gym.

Jordan used the opportunity to make a move toward his shotgun.

A shotgun blast echoed off the walls and blood splashed across Jordan's face. At first, he thought he had been hit. When the horse he had been petting collapsed, he realized the round had struck it instead.

The gunfire scared the remaining horses. They bolted for safety, which happened to be the gym doors where the two attackers stood.

Jordan used the opportunity to grab his shotgun and ran to the center of the gym. The guy with the glasses ducked into the corridor to avoid being crushed while the scraggly-haired attacker moved along the gym wall, making himself the perfect target.

Raising the shotgun, Jordan pumped off three rounds. The first two missed, blasting chunks out of the wall and scaring the horses even more. The third struck the scraggly-haired guy in the left leg, ripping it to shreds. He cried out and slid down the blood-covered wall, dropping his weapon in the process. Jordan raced forward and kicked the shotgun out of the wounded man's reach.

The scraggly-haired guy covered his face with his arms and pleaded, "Don't kill me."

Jordan ignored him. Keeping the barrel trained on his target, he made his way to the door to find the other attacker.

CARBONE HEARD THE horses close behind him. He threw himself against the wall and closed his eyes, praying he would not be crushed in the stampede.

The horses raced by him. One of the saddles clipped his back, sending a jolt of pain through his body. Thankfully, nothing crippling.

Once the horses passed, he considered going back for Brian until he heard three gunshots and his friend scream in pain. Fuck him.

Carbone chased after the horses and headed for the exit.

"WHAT THE—"

Four of their horses turned the corner and raced down the corridor, heading straight for Andrew. He hugged the wall as they ran past. Andrew decided he would chase them later. They would need time to calm down. First, he needed to check on his team. Hopefully, none of them had been killed.

As he ran down the hall, a guy wearing eyeglasses raced into the T-section of the corridor, stopping when he spotted Andrew. Andrew raised his weapon into the high-ready position.

"Freeze!"

The guy bolted. Andrew fired off a round which missed, the pellets imbedding into the wall. Andrew ran after him. He reached the end of the corridor to see the intruder push his way through the side door. By the time Andrew reached the exit, the guy had crossed the street and headed for the house across the way. He wanted to chase after him, hunt down and kill the bastard, but common sense told him to make sure his people were safe.

Andrew headed back inside the school.

AS KATHY STRUGGLED with the tall guy to wrest away the rifle, Haellie rushed forward, body slamming him and shoving him into Kathy's desk. Kathy stumbled to the side, letting go of the hunting rifle. As the tall guy fell, she wrenched the weapon out of his hand and stepped back a few feet.

The tall guy leaned against the front of the desk and raised his hands. "Don't shoot."

Haellie ignored him. "This is for my little sister."

Haellie lowered the rifle and fired, blasting off his left foot.

He screamed and clutched his leg. "What the fuck! I'm trying to surrender!"

"This is for my sister."

She shifted the rifle to the side and fired again. The bullet struck the lower right left leg, gouging out the flesh. The tall guy screamed again, kicking his legs in agony. Blood spurt from the second wound, meaning Haellie had hit an artery.

"This is for my brothers."

The first shot hit the attacker in the right hand, blowing off three fingers. The second hit his left wrist, severing the hand. Pain and loss of blood overcame the tall guy, who lay there whining.

Haellie stepped closer and aimed at his face.

"And this, motherfucker, is for my mother."

"Pl... please. No more." Tears flowed down his cheeks.

She pulled the trigger. The attacker's head disintegrated.

Haellie dropped the rifle, fell to her knees, and sobbed. Kathy knelt beside her student and held her close.

"It's okay. Let it out."

Haellie sniffed back the snot pouring from her nose. "These... these were the bastards who murdered my family."

"They got what they deserved."

Only then did Kathy notice the burns on Haellie's left hand from where she had struck the fat guy with the bottle of acid.

"Let me look at that."

Haellie shook her head. "There were six of them, so there are four more around. We need to find the others."

The idea of more attackers being in the building terrified Kathy. She glanced over at the fat guy who sat against the wall, moaning and covering his face. They did not have to worry about him. Letting go of Haellie, she picked up the book bag with their supplies, gathered their weapons and those of their attackers, then led the teenager out into the hall to find the others.

KIRSTIE STEPPED UP to the Latino and shoved the shotgun into his face.

"Let her go."

He dropped the pistol and slowly moved his arm from around Regan's neck. Her friend pushed away, picked up the pistol, and aimed it at the Latino.

Both girls noticed he had pissed his pants.

"I… I did as you asked. Will you let me go now?"

"No."

His eyes widened as Kirstie pulled the trigger. Gore and blood splattered the wall behind him. The blast threw the headless body back three feet into the kitchen. Kirstie kept the weapon trained on his corpse.

Regan placed a hand on her friend's shoulder and squeezed gently. "It'll be okay."

"No, nothing will ever be the same again." Kirstie lowered the shotgun and patted Regan's hand. "This is our life from now on."

Regan gathered up the weapons from the floor. "Come on. Let's find the others."

KIRSTIE AND REGAN found the rest of the team in the corridor near the main entrance. Andrew bandaged Haellie's hand while Jordan and Kathy kept guard. Jordan looked relieved when he spotted them.

"Thank God you're all right."

"What happened here?" asked Kirstie.

"Two guys attacked us in the lab," said Kathy. "Haellie hit one with a bottle of acid and burned her hand in the process."

"What happened to the other one?"

"I killed him," the teenager replied coldly. "They were the assholes who killed my family."

"Two others attacked Jordan." Andrew did not look up from tending to Haellie's wounds. "He wounded one. The other escaped. That leaves two more."

"We ran into them in the cafeteria."

Andrew glanced up. "What happened?"

"I killed them."

An awkward silence fell over the group.

"What now?" asked Jordan.

"We gather what we came for and get out of here before the one who escaped comes back with reinforcements." Andrew finished bandaging Haellie.

Kathy motioned toward the book bag. "We have everything we need."

"There's a large supply of water and other drinks in the cafeteria," said Kirstie.

"We can't take them with us. We can come back later for them."

"Where are the horses?" asked Regan.

Jordan pointed down the corridor. "The gunfire spooked them. They ran and gathered down there. I'm giving them time to calm down."

Andrew removed his pistol. "You five gather the horses and meet me out front in ten minutes."

Kirstie looked confused. "What are you going to do?"

"I want to interrogate the survivor."

WHEN ANDREW WALKED into the gym, the scraggily-haired guy had tried crawling to his weapon but gave up because of the pain. Jordan had blown off the lower half of the guy's left leg. Blood gushed from the wound. He would not make it much longer without medical care. The bastard could die for all Andrew cared.

The scraggily haired guy looked up when Andrew approached. "Help me, man. That asshole fucked up my leg."

"You deserve it. You shot first."

"Self-defense, man. Help a guy out."

Andrew crouched beside him. "Maybe. First, I want to ask you a few questions."

"Fuck you."

"That's not very cooperative if you want my help. How many of you are there?"

"Six. What happened to my friends?"

"My people took care of them. You're the only one left. Were they the only ones with you?"

"On the raiding party, yeah."

"That means there are others."

The scraggily haired guy went silent.

"How many in total?"

"Fuck you."

Andrew slapped the wounded leg with the stock of his shotgun. The scraggly-haired guy winced. "That fucking hurt."

"I'll ask again. How many are there in total?"

"Fuck you."

Andrew placed the barrel into the wound and pressed. The scraggly-haired guy screamed.

"I can keep this up all day."

"Okay, okay. There's about fifty of us."

"See. That was easy. Where are you located?"

"I... I can't tell you."

"Wrong answer." Andrew placed the barrel back into the wound and twirled it around.

The guy screamed again, grabbing his thigh to stop the pain. "I can't tell you. Stratman will kill me."

"I'll kill you if you don't talk." Andrew moved the shotgun

toward the wound.

"Wait! We're held up in the VFW Hall in Kingston. We're just trying to survive. We don't mean any harm."

"Then why did you kill that mother and her three kids yesterday?"

"You... you know about that?"

Andrew smiled and stood. He went into the gym to check on Jordan's horse. It was dead. Good. It saved him from having to put the poor animal out of its misery. As he left, the scraggly-haired guy called to him.

"Wait. At least kill me so I don't have to bleed out."

"Nope."

"Come on, man. Have some mercy."

"Like you showed that family yesterday? Not a chance."

Andrew walked out, shutting the gym doors behind him to drown out the swearing of the scraggly-haired guy. When he exited the building, the others were waiting by the horses.

"Did you get anything out of him?" asked Jordan.

"Yes. Nothing good."

"Shit," mumbled Kirstie.

"We'll talk about it later." Andrew mounted his horse. "Right now, I want to pick up those horses abandoned at the stable and get back to the compound."

Kathy stepped over to him. "I want to make one quick stop on the way back."

"It's getting late."

"It's on the way, and it'll only take a minute. But it's important."

"Okay. But let's get moving. And keep your guns at the ready in case we get ambushed."

Kathy mounted her horse then helped Haellie into the saddle behind her, a task made more difficult with her burnt hand. Regan let Jordan have her horse and rode with Kirstie. When ready, Andrew led the way out of the parking lot and back home.

FROM ACROSS THE street, Carbone watched the group move west down Greenough Street.

God only knew what Stratman would do to him if we went back and reported that the others in his party had been lost, but it would not be pleasant. However, if he went back with information about another group who not only survived but were flourishing, a group they could raid to bolster their own supplies, Stratman might go easy on him.

Might.

Carbone waited until the horses were out of sight then set off after them, keeping to the tree line so he would not be spotted.

CHAPTER THIRTY-NINE

S HAWN STOOD IN front of the urinal, the end of the flashlight wedged between his chest and chin while he pissed. He had considered holding it in one hand and doing his business with the other but thought better about it. With his luck, he would wind up peeing all over himself. He did not want to add urine-drenched coveralls to the four days of sweat and dirt he already had to deal with.

Once finished, Shawn slid himself back into his pants and began zipping up when a wave of nausea struck him. He dropped to his knees and vomited into the urine-filled toilet, emptying his stomach three times before dry heaving, another sign of radiation poisoning. He already experienced mild exhaustion and disorientation, which would get worse with time. Right now, he pushed through his discomfort and tried to maintain a strong front for his team, afraid that if he physically broke down it would have a negative impact on the others. Well, maybe Libby and Andy. Brad was well trained, had a good head on his shoulders, and could easily take over command. Shawn did not want to place the burden of a meltdown on him until necessary.

The last reading half an hour ago inside the control room reached 21.3 milliSieverts. That would progressively get worse unless Wally's team could inject water into the reactor and cool it down. At least Shawn's team only had to contend with the radiation seeping through the containment vessel and the walls of the facility. The fire unit outside was exposed to high-level radiation from the reactor due to the breach in the containment vessel. Though no one would dare say it out loud, every realized, including Wally, that his team would not survive this.

Zipping up, Shawn exited the restroom and made his way to the medical unit. Wilson rested on one of the cots. He slept soundly, which at least momentarily spared his suffering. Shawn quietly made his way over and studied his friend.

Everyone had received levels of radiation well beyond normal standards. As of right now, Brad, Libby, and Andy would have to endure a long recovery period and then, ten or twenty years in the future, face terminal cancer. Assuming they could stop the meltdown and decrease the radiation levels.

He and Wilson faced a much worse situation. The doses they had received would more than likely kill them in the next few days. He could not understand why Wilson suffered so much and not himself. Maybe because he was older and had built up more immunity by working at Seabrook for so many years. Whatever the reason, the reprieve would only be temporary. Soon he would be joining Wilson on one of the other cots.

Shawn placed the back of his hand against Wilson's forehead. As expected, his friend ran a fever.

Wilson opened his eyes. Shawn forced a smile.

"How do you feel?"

"Like shit." Wilson coughed. "This is worse than when I had COVID."

"At least you're not contagious."

Wilson chuckled, then suddenly leaned to the other side and vomited onto the floor, blood mixing with the puke. Not a good sign. Wilson continued heaving but nothing came out. Spitting out the last remnants of vomit, he tried to lay down again and became disoriented. He started to fall out of bed but Shawn grabbed his shoulder and pushed him onto the mattress.

"Thanks." Wilson coughed. "How are things going?"

"Good," Shawn lied. "Wally's team is pumping water into the cooling system. We should have the situation under control in a few hours."

"Sorry I'm not there to help."

"Don't worry about it. There's nothing we can do until Wally gets things under control. You rest up. When the others get tired, I'll call you to fill in for them."

"Apologize for me. I hate taking it easy while they're busting their asses."

"They understand."

"Thanks. I don't want to be—" Wilson leaned to the side and vomited again, then gasped for breath. He settled down after a minute and fell back onto the cot, his body shivering. "Sorry about that."

"No problem."

Shawn went over to the cabinets on the opposite wall and searched through them until he found a pair of blankets. One he draped over Wilson and the other he used to wipe up the pool of vomit. He then took the waste barrel from the corner, tossed the blanket inside, and placed it beside Wilson.

"That ought to make things easier for you."

"I appreciate it." Wilson closed his eyes. "If you don't mind, I'm going to take a nap."

"Sure thing. Get your rest. Brad will check on you later. Let me know if you need anything."

Shawn waited until Wilson dozed off, which only took a few seconds. He admired his friend's bravery under the circumstances. Shawn doubted he could endure the same. The worst part was he had no way of sparing his friend from the misery he endured other than taking Wilson's life, something Shawn could not bring himself to do. Hopefully, the end would come quickly for Wilson.

Shawn quietly left the medical unit, headed back to the control room, and walked up to Brad. His friend glanced over his shoulder as he approached.

"How's Wilson?"

Shawn frowned. "Not good. He has all the symptoms of

radiation poisoning."

"Do you think he'll live?"

"I doubt it."

Brad shook his head. "He'd be better off dying now."

Shawn agreed but did not vocalize it, changing the subject. "What's the temperature inside the reactor?"

"Seven hundred and twenty-six."

"Fuck."

"Yeah, but the good news it's been holding at that level for the past four hours."

"Could the pressure inside the containment vessel be rising again?"

Brad shook his head. "I thought about that and switched the battery to the pressure gauge. It's down to one hundred thirty-nine."

"Thank God for small miracles."

"On the downside, the battery is running low on power. Without a way to recharge it, we'll be lucky to get two more days out of it."

"By then, we'll either have the situation under control or it'll no longer matter." Shawn prayed the first option would happen. "I'll take over for you now."

"There's still a little over an hour to go before shift change. Go take a nap. You need to rest after your jaunt down to the suppression chamber. I'll call you when it's time."

"Thanks." Shawn patted his friend on the shoulder and headed for one of the offices down the corridor.

He could not get out of his mind what Brad had said about Wilson being better off dying rather than suffering through the next few months without medical care. Though at first it sounded callous, Brad was correct. While in management training, Shawn had read extensively about the effects of radiation poisoning on the human body. Wilson would suffer a long and painful death. Even if by some miracle he survived, without proper medical care his future would be one of intense pain.

Shawn made two fateful decisions. Despite it going against everything in his nature, when Wilson's condition became worse, he would find a way to peacefully end his friend's life.

And, when his time came, he would ask Brad to do the same for him.

CHAPTER FORTY

F OR THE FIRST time in days, Danielle felt at ease.

At ease was not the correct phrase, but she did not feel
on edge like she had been while traveling north along I-93. She
had spent the last hour walking through a residential neighborhood, which meant fewer stalled vehicles and fewer people.
The only ones she had encountered were a young couple
moving a wheelbarrow of supplies, the man pushing the cart
while the woman carried a shotgun. She kept a wary eye on
Danielle but posed no immediate threat. Danielle nodded as
she passed them. The woman maintained a stern expression
but nodded back.

The only other person she came across had been a middle-
aged man who exited his house as she passed, standing on his
front porch clasping an AK-47 semiautomatic rifle, a warning
not to mess with him. Danielle lowered her head and continued
walking.

Fortunately, trees lined the road, which shielded her from
the sun. Since the heat and humidity were less than the past
few days, it made the journey almost pleasant.

Almost.

Danielle turned a bend in the road, surprised to see a
makeshift roadblock fifty feet ahead of her. The locals had
pushed two pick-up trucks across the road. Six men and a
woman meandered around the vehicles, each armed. They
spotted Danielle a second later. No one aimed their weapons at
her, but she noticed six of them moved behind the beds of the
pick-ups in case there was trouble. Danielle still held the tire

iron. She kept both hands by her side, trying to appear as non-threatening as possible.

An older man with a crewcut and a slight paunch approached. He had a firearm holstered by his side, his hand resting on the grip.

"May I help you?"

Danielle stopped ten feet in front of him. "I'm passing through."

"Is anyone else with you?"

"No."

"Where are you going?"

"Dunbarton. I live there. I'm trying to get home to see my daughter."

The man's expression softened. "How old is she?"

"Sixteen. She's been alone since the solar flare."

"I can relate. My daughter is on deployment in Okinawa. I haven't heard from her in days." He looked over his shoulder. "Coach, will you escort this young lady to the next roadblock?"

"Thank you, but you don't have to do that."

"I do if you want to pass through here." He took on an apologetic tone. "No offense."

"I understand."

A young African-American came around the rear of one of the pick-ups and shouldered his AR-15. "If you'll follow me, please."

As Danielle passed by the older man, he said, "Good luck."

"Thank you."

Danielle fell in beside Coach and they continued through the neighborhood.

"Why do they call you Coach?"

"I'm the athletics director for a school in Manchester. At least until all this shit went down. Where are you coming from?"

"Boston."

"You've traveled all this way from Boston?"

Danielle nodded.

"What's it like out there?"

"Horrible. Rape gangs and looters have taken over I-93. I almost got attacked by one of them. And from what I've heard, gangs and rioters have taken over Manchester."

"We heard that, too." Coach shook his head. "And it's only going to get worse."

"Is that why you set up the roadblocks?"

"Yeah, but so far, we haven't run into any of them. Two days ago, a bunch of punks broke into one of the houses to rob it. Unfortunately for them, the owner was home."

"What happened?"

"The owner killed one of them. The other two are being held under guard in one of the basements. That's why we set up the roadblock. The sad thing is, if any of those gangs come looking to loot the area, we're screwed."

Danielle's stomach turned at the thought of Kirstie and her friends running into one of them.

A few minutes later, they reached the roadblock at the other end of the neighborhood. Like the previous one, it consisted of two pick-ups blocking the road protected by seven armed men and women. They eyed the pair suspiciously until Coach waved, letting them know things were okay.

When they reached the roadblock, Coach stopped. "You're on your own from here. But you realize you're going to have to pass through Manchester or Nashua to get home."

"I do, but I have that worked out."

"How are you set for supplies."

"Not good. Every place I passed had been looted."

"Damn." Coach turned to one of the men. "Ryan, get me two bottles of water."

"Those are our supplies."

"This woman is trying to get to Dunbarton to check on her daughter."

Ryan frowned but pulled two water bottles out of a cooler,

brought them over, and handed them to Danielle.

"Thank you so much."

Ryan flashed her a disapproving glare and walked away.

Danielle turned to Coach as she slid the bottles into her book bag. "I appreciate this."

"No problem. We have to look out for each other. I hope you make it home safely and find your daughter."

"So do I."

Danielle shook Coach's hand, passed through the roadblock, and continued north.

CHAPTER FORTY-ONE

THE SCAVENGERS WERE halfway home, a trip during which they were all on edge after what had happened at the high school.

Kirstie studied the group. Everyone was tense but holding themselves together, ready for any encounters. Everyone except Haellie. Kathy did not go into details about what had taken place at the school, but it must have been bad. Haellie pressed her torn blouse tightly against her chest with her burned hand and held on to the saddle with the other. The poor teenager looked as if she might have a nervous breakdown at any second. Not that Kirstie could blame her. Considering the shit show they now found themselves in, you either folded or became hardened. Kirstie had chosen the latter. Thank God she did or she would be dead by now.

Yet it bothered Kirstie that taking the lives of the two assholes in the cafeteria did not faze her. When this was over... if this was ever over... she would never be the same again.

At Atkinson Academy, Andrews veered the horses left onto the side street when Kathy rode up.

"I need to go to the library."

"It's getting late, and we still have to gather those horses that were abandoned."

"The library is a hundred yards down the road. Besides, I'll only be a few minutes."

"Is it that important?"

"We'll have a better chance of surviving."

Andrew contemplated for a moment then conceded, leading the Scavengers straight ahead.

The Atkinson Library was a relatively small building, although a good size for such a small town. Two sedans were parked at the far end of the lot, more than likely belonging to employees stranded when the solar flare hit. It seemed as if no one had been here since the incident.

Kathy stopped her horse near the front entrance and dismounted.

Haellie clasped her hand. "Don't leave me."

"I'll be back in a few minutes." Kathy squeezed the teenager's hand. "Andrew will take good care of you."

As if on cue, he pulled his horse alongside Haellie and stopped.

Kathy looked at Kirstie. "Will you join me?"

"Sure."

Kirstie slid off her horse, careful not to knock off Regan. She held the shotgun in a low-ready position and nodded. Kathy led the way inside.

The library had large windows that allowed plenty of sunlight into the building.

"Is anyone here?" called out Kathy.

When she got no answer, Kathy made her way to the card catalogue file in front of the main desk and began searching through the files. Kirstie strolled through the library, checking behind the main desk for anyone who might be hiding, then walked by the aisles between the bookshelves in case anyone waited to ambush them.

"Here we are." Kathy ripped out a card and headed for the shelves. She paused beside Kirstie. "Do me a favor. I'm part of a bird watching club that meets here on the weekend. We have binoculars stored in a box at the librarian's station. Could you get them?"

"You plan on bird watching?"

"No, but the binoculars will come in handy when guarding the compound."

"Okay. Yell if you run into any trouble."

Kirstie crossed over to the main desk and checked behind it. It took only a few seconds to find the cardboard box containing the five sets of binoculars and two books on bird watching. By the time she removed the binoculars, Kathy had returned holding a book.

"Are you set?" Kathy asked.

"Got them."

"Let's get out of here."

When they joined the others, Andrew asked, "Did you get what you wanted?"

"Yes." Kathy handed him the book.

Andrew read the cover. "*A Prepper's Guide To Surviving the Apocalypse.?*"

"It'll tell us everything we need to know to build projects that'll keep us alive." She smirked. "Was it worth the detour?"

"Yes," he conceded with a smile, then switched back to Marine mode. "Let's move out."

CHAPTER FORTY-TWO

THICK CLOUDS COVERED the area, blocking the sun and lowering the temperature by ten degrees. Wally wished it would rain, not only to cool off him and his team, but also to cleanse the radiation from the air. The sky had been overcast since late morning and still no precipitation. Wally doubted they would get any. Not that it made much of a God damn difference. Being near the coast, the humidity remained unbearable, causing their clothes to stick to their skin as if they were in a sauna. And the constant high doses of radiation were catching up to them.

Sam had been the first to collapse two hours ago. Wally and Josh had attempted to help him into the driver's seat of the pumper, but the minute they opened the door the stench of rotting flesh from Katherine wafted out, making Josh puke. Wally shut the door and, instead, propped Sam up against one of the rear wheels. He had laid there since, only moving twice to vomit blood.

The rest of them, including Wally, were slowly becoming exhausted and disoriented. Wally gave each of them a task to keep their minds and bodies occupied. Since Eric nursed an injured head and arm, Wally posted him by the injection line to make sure a steady flow of water passed through the hoses into the cooling system and to monitor the Geiger counter. He sent Carlson out to check the hose leading to the tributary to make certain it functioned properly, mostly a time-consuming task. Josh checked the cars in the parking lot to find any jerry cans they could and mark which vehicles ran on diesel fuel in case the supply from the pumper ran out. Once those chores were completed, Wally would have to come up with some other tasks to keep them busy.

Wally made his way over to Eric, who crouched by the exterior wall, leaning against it for support.

"How are things here?"

Eric glanced up. "Fifty-fifty. We're having no trouble feeding water into the cooling system but, despite our efforts, the radiation levels are still rising."

"What are they now?"

Eric leaned over to check the Geiger counter. "Thirty-one point eight milliSieverts."

"God damn."

"That's an understatement."

Wally removed the radio from his pocket and pressed the TALK button. "Shawn, are you there?"

A voice on the other end responded. "*This is Shawn.*"

"We've been feeding water into the cooling system for twelve hours now but the radiation level out here is still climbing. Any idea what's up?"

"*We have the same problem in here. What's your latest reading?*"

"Thirty-one point eighteen milliSieverts."

"*Fuck.*"

"No shit. Any idea what's wrong?"

"*The pressure inside the containment vessel is still dropping. It's below one hundred kPa now. And the heat inside the reactor is holding steady at seven hundred and seven degrees, which is a good sign. My best guess is the water you're pumping into the system has not yet replaced what was already lost. Are you having issues with feeding in water?*"

"No. But the diesel generator we're using only operates at two-thirds the capacity of the one on the pumper."

A momentary pause elapsed before Shawn came back online. "*The reactor had entered the early stages of meltdown mode for quite a while. It's going to take time to replenish the cooling system. So long as we're pumping in water faster than it evaporates, we'll eventually refill the cooling system and give the decay heat a chance to burn off."*

"And if that doesn't happen?"

"Then welcome to Chernobyl II."

"God damn," said Wally, not realizing he had pressed the TALK button.

"All we can do is our best. Keep up the work you're doing and let me know if there's any changes. I'll do the same on our end. Do you need me to send out anyone to help you?"

Wally could certainly use the help. He had one person dead, one seriously wounded, and four others, including himself, lethally affected by radiation poisoning. But to request assistance would be issuing a death sentence to Shawn's team. He would keep his team working until they either got the situation under control or enough of them were down due to radiation that they needed help.

"We're fine, thanks. Let me know if there's any changes to the readings."

"I will. Good luck."

Wally slid the radio back in his pocket and sighed.

"Everything okay?" asked Eric.

"The pressure inside the containment vessel is dropping but the temperature inside the reactor is holding steady. With luck, we're about to hit the tipping point."

"Good." Eric coughed. "I hope we're around long enough to see it."

CHAPTER FORTY-THREE

I T TOOK LONGER than anticipated for Danielle to make her way to the Merrimack River, mostly because she stopped several times to consult the map. A few miles east of Nashua, she picked up Route 128 and headed north for several miles, circling around Londonderry and the commercial areas, before turning west onto one of the residential roads leading to the river. Now she truly relied on the map and, though it took a while, she eventually reached her destination.

The skylines of Nashua and Manchester lay to the south and north, respectively. On the opposite bank, a few commercial buildings were spread out among the trees. If she had read the map correctly and, so far, she had done a good job of it, beyond the industrial area were sparsely populated neighborhoods and back roads leading all the way home.

Luck was on her side today.

As Danielle sat in the shade by the tree line scanning the riverbank for a place to cross, she spotted three rowboats and a canoe resting at scattered intervals on the east side. She assumed they belonged to locals who used them to get away from the cities. Thankfully for her, no one had stolen them. That would make her crossing that much easier.

Danielle opened her book bag and searched through it until she found one of the bottles of spring water Coach had given her. Twisting off the cap, she drank a third of the contents, tightened the cap back on, and slid it into the book bag. She would save the rest for later. God only knew when, or if, she would find any more.

Danielle leaned back against a tree and relaxed. The sun would be going down in a few hours. She would cross the river early in the morning. Hopefully by then, most of the locals would be settled in for the night, decreasing her chances of running into trouble. That would also give her several hours to clear the area and be well on her way home.

For the first time since this nightmare began, Daneille had a chance to sit back and take in what had happened. Only now did she realize how peaceful it seemed here. All she could hear were birds chirping and the Merrimack River flowing by. The world suffered through an apocalypse, and two of the state's largest cities were nearby, yet they remained silent. No sounds of traffic. No sirens. No airplanes. Not even screaming or gunshots. That surprised her the most. She had assumed that by now the world would be one huge warzone.

The more Danielle thought about it, the more sense it made. Once the initial shock of the disaster wore off, people did what they needed to in order to survive. She had done the same and was not proud of it. By now, everything necessary to live through this nightmare had most likely been looted, and everyone still alive held up somewhere waiting out the chaos. It explained why she had not seen a single living person for the past few hours. She wondered how many others like her were still on the road desperately trying to get home.

Judging by what she could see of Manchester, the situation must have been bad. The top floors of the city's Brady Sullivan Building had been gutted by fire. Dozens of plumes of smoke rose from both cities where conflagrations were burning themselves out. Her mind flashed back to the chaos she and Brian witnessed that first night when escaping Boston. And Boston was relatively small. She did not want to imagine the hell holes major cities like New York City and Los Angeles had become. She closed her eyes and thanked God for the good luck. So far.

A rustling from behind Danielle snapped her out of her

reverence. She jumped up, grabbed the crowbar, and spun around in a fighting stance.

Two children emerged from the woods—a girl no more than eleven clutching the hand of a small boy around six or seven. Both looked unharmed, though neither had washed in days. Greasy hair clung to their heads. The boy had food stains on his shirt.

The girl hugged the boy and turned to the side, protecting him.

"Please don't hurt us."

"I won't." Danielle lowered the crowbar but kept a firm grip on it in case there were adults nearby using the kids as bait. "What do you want?"

"We… I saw you passing through our neighborhood and hoped you would help us. You seemed like a nice person."

"I am. You just startled me."

"Sorry. We'll leave you alone."

"That's okay." Danielle motioned toward the tree. "Have a seat."

"Are you sure?"

"Yes."

The two kids sat down. The little boy seemed terrified. So did the girl, but she had enough common sense to put herself between him and Danielle.

"What are your names?"

"I'm Elisabeth, but everyone calls me Liz. This is my brother, Kyle."

"I'm Danielle. Where are your parents?"

"Our dad is in the military. He's deployed in Iraq. My mother is a nurse at Elliott Hospital in Manchester. She was on duty the day this started and never came home."

That explained their fear and anxiety. "You've been alone all this time?"

"Not all of it. We had a babysitter."

"What happened to her?"

"The bitch left us on the second day." Kyle spat out the words, his tone filled with contempt.

Liz gently slapped him on the head. "Watch your language."

Danielle suppressed a grin as she remembered how many times Shawn had done that to her. "What happened to her?"

"She left us to go home," said Liz. "She wanted to be with her family."

Kyle snarled. "She took most of the bottled water with her."

"We've been living off of canned vegetables and baked beans the past few days."

Danielle was horrified. "That bitch."

Kyle smiled and glanced over at Liz. "See. I told you so."

"When did you last have a drink?" asked Danielle.

"Yesterday."

"Hang on." Danielle stepped over to her book bag, removed the last bottle of water, removed the cap, and handed it to Liz. "You and your brother drink this."

"Are you sure?"

"Yes. Please, take it."

Liz took the bottle and handed it to Kyle, who drank half of the contents in one gulp. He handed the bottle to his sister. She looked over at Danielle.

"Do you mind?"

"Go ahead."

Liz finished the bottle in seconds and handed the empty container back to Danielle.

"Thank you."

As Danielle placed it in her book bag, the girl reached into hers, removed a can of baked beans, and offered it to Danielle.

"I can't take that from you."

"Yes, you can. We have a few more in here. Besides, you look hungry."

Danielle could not argue with that. She had not eaten in a

while. As she popped open the can, Liz pulled a spoon from her book bag and handed it to her.

"You'll need this."

Danielle wolfed down half the can of beans and then offered it to the kids.

Liz shook her head. "We're sick of that stuff."

"I want to go to McDonalds," said Kyle.

"I told you, they're all closed for now," said Liz.

Kyle frowned. "I'd kill for a McFlurry."

"We all would." Danielle thought for a moment. "Did you ask your neighbors for help?"

"Most of them were at work and never made it home. I asked some of the people I knew if we could stay with them until mom got back, but they all turned us away. They said they didn't have enough food and water to feed us."

"They're assholes," mumbled Kyle.

Danielle chuckled, saving the boy from another head slap. "You tried everyone?"

"Everyone but Mr. Higgins."

"He's a predicant," added Kyle.

"Pedophile," Liz corrected him, then turned to Danielle. "He rounded up all the abandoned kids and said they could stay with him."

The expression on Liz's face indicated she knew what those children must be going through.

An awkward silence passed between them.

Liz stood. "We won't bother you anymore."

"You're not bothering me."

Danielle's mind raced. She could not abandon these two. They would be dead in a week, or worse, would stay with the pedophile but would have to do unspeakable things to survive. Yet taking them with her would only slow her down. Even worse, it would make her a target for every sicko out there and would impede her ability to fight or escape. The torment tore her mind apart, but eventually her better half prevailed.

"You're welcome to come with me. I'm heading home to check on my daughter."

"Really?" Excitement tinged Liz's tone. "You wouldn't mind?"

"I can't leave you alone. Let's go back to your house and leave a note for your mother so she knows you're safe."

"We already did," blurted Kyle.

The surprised expression on Danielle's face must have been evident because Liz became embarrassed.

"Before we followed you, I left a note for my mother saying we went with a nice lady and would call her as soon as we could, and not to worry."

"You expected me to take care of you?"

"You seemed nice when I saw you walking through our neighborhood." Liz forced a smile. "I was right."

Danielle grinned. "You were. Get some rest. We're going to cross the river tonight when no one can see us."

"Yay," squealed Kyle. "I haven't ridden in a boat since last summer."

"It's across the river. Then we have a long walk ahead of us. Are you up to it?"

"Yes." Liz ran over and hugged Danielle. "Thank you."

Danielle fought back tears.

What type of nightmare had the world devolved into?

CHAPTER FORTY-FOUR

THE SCAVENGERS MADE it home shortly before sundown.

They had stopped at the stable on the way home and rescued the six horses found earlier, bringing them back to the compound. Kirstie and Regan had checked out the stalls and found enough saddles and saddle bags for them. Andrew would bring the four horses back to the Connors later that night plus one from the stable to make up for Jordan's horse killed at the high school. Jordan agreed to ride with him leading an extra horse so Andrew did not have to walk back.

Keith stood guard duty along Providence Hill Road and sent a runner ahead to let the others know the team had returned safely. A crowd had gathered to greet them by the time the Scavengers reached the compound.

Becca tended to Haellie's burns. The hand would definitely be scarred and have limited mobility, but so long as it did not become infected, the teenager should be okay.

Andrew explained to those present what had gone down at the high school, which generated fear and concern among the others. He tried to console them, saying they would be okay for tonight but tomorrow they needed to discuss better ways to protect themselves.

Kirstie and Regan helped unload what supplies they had into Kathy's garage and cleaned off the cart. Andrew had decided to make one more run tomorrow back to Timberlane to retrieve the water and other drinks the girls had found in the cafeteria. He agreed it would be risky, but that much water would keep the compound going long enough to set up the water infiltration and storage systems. Then they would stop by the stables and pick up hay to keep the horses fed. Although this time, they would be well armed in case they ran into trouble. After that, they would hunker down and set up a defense system around the compound.

Justin, an engineer at BAE in Manchester, had a large, enclosed backyard and agreed to keep the horses there until they could set up better accommodations for them.

As Kirstie and Regan led the horses to Justin's house and got them settled, Abbey and Mikayla joined them.

"We heard you got into a gunfight at the school," Abbey said excitedly.

"We did," Kirstie replied stoically.

"What happened?"

When Kirstie did not answer, Regan jumped in. "Six guys were in the school looting it. Jordan killed one. Haellie killed two more, and—"

"Wait," interrupted Mikayla. "Who's Haellie?"

"A teenager we picked up on the way. The same guys who attacked us murdered her family. Anyway, she killed two of them, and Kirstie killed two more. One escaped."

Abbey tapped Kirstie on the shoulder. "You're a real bad ass, girl."

Kirstie spun around to face Abbey, her face red with rage. "I'm not a bad ass!"

The two girls backed off. "Sorry."

"You should be. Do you think I enjoy taking lives? If I hadn't, Regan would be dead right now."

"And I appreciate that." Regan gently touched Kirstie's arm, hoping to calm her.

It did not.

"I did what I had to survive. Sooner or later, we're all going to have to kill someone. Do you think you'll be able to? Could you take a life to save yourself, or to protect one of us?" "I... I don't know," Abbey stammered. "Maybe?"

"You better figure that out now. We're living in a new world, a kill or be killed world, and I intend to come out of this alive."

Kirstie stormed out of the yard, slamming the gate behind her, and ran down the street. She needed to be alone for a few minutes and calm down.

She was furious, but not at Abbey. Her rage came from what she had become.

Stopping at a bend in the road, she sat down on the hood of a stalled car and cried. Kirstie despised herself. She had never been like this before. Fuck, she used to be one of those people who slammed on the brakes of her car to avoid running over a squirrel. The most violent things she had ever done involved playing *Call of Duty* or *Fortnite* or reading horror novels. Now she had become a killer. Sure, she could tell herself *ad nauseum* that every incident was in self-defense, but that did not change the fact that she had already taken down three people. And they were not even one week into the fucking apocalypse. She had always despised those Westerns where the hero kept notches on the grip of his pistol for every person killed. Shit, at this rate, she would have the grip on her shotgun filled within a month.

Kirstie stared into the woods, her mind still in turmoil.

How much more shit would she have to go through before this nightmare ended?

CARBONE CROUCHED BEHIND a bush a few houses down from where the others had gathered to greet those assholes who had murdered his friends.

He was exhausted from the battle at the high school and then following the riders back here. Those motherfuckers had horses while he had to walk all the way. Walk, my ass. For the past several hours, he had waited for the riders to turn a bend in the road, then ran forward to keep track of them. By now, he could easily curl up here and sleep for several hours, but not only would that be stupid, it would make him vulnerable to detection.

Carbone would fall back a few miles, find an empty house to hold up for the night, then return in the morning to the VFW Hall and tell Stratman what he had found. The bastards had a nice set up here, something Stratman would be interested in taking for his own people.

CHAPTER FORTY-FIVE

S HAWN SAT BY the cot in the medical unit, watching over Wilson in case he woke up and needed anything. It seemed more like a death watch.

Wilson's fever kept rising, though without a thermometer Shawn had no way of knowing by how much. His hair had started to fall out in small clumps and erythema, red splotches as a result of capillary congestion caused by the radiation, covered his hands and face. The foul stench of shit filled the room. Shawn first noticed it when he entered the room. Rolling Wilson onto his side, both his friend's pants and mattress were soiled. Blood mixed in with the feces. It was only a matter of time now.

The radiation levels had already started to affect the rest of the team. Libby and Brad had begun vomiting earlier in the day, and the entire team had developed fevers. The only thing that had prevented them from collapsing in exhaustion, including himself, was the adrenalin from trying to secure the reactor. However, that task now fell to Wally and his team. The control room could only monitor the readings and pray that things—

Andy burst into the room, startling Shawn who had started to doze off.

"You got to see this."

At first, Shawn thought something else had gone wrong until he noticed the excited expression on the kid's face. He jumped to his feet and ran for the door.

"What's up?"

"The temperature inside the reactor is dropping."

The two raced into the control room. Brad studied the gauge, the index and middle fingers of his right hand crossed. Libby and Andy hugged, patting each other on the back. Shawn ran up to Brad who turned toward him, a smile on his face.

"Did Andy tell you?"

Shawn nodded. "How far has it dropped?"

"Quite a bit. It's currently at seven hundred and one. Wait!" Brad sounded excited as if he had seen the last ball of the Mega Millions and won the jackpot. "It dropped to six hundred and ninety-nine."

"Thank God." Shawn allowed himself a few seconds of happiness before the shift supervisor in him took over. "What's the radiation level?"

Libby checked the Geiger counter by the door. "It's at 13.3 milliSieverts."

"With luck, that will start declining soon." Shawn paused. "Has anyone told Wally yet?"

Brad shook his head. "I wanted to make sure it wasn't a fluctuation."

"Do you think that's a possibility?"

Brad shrugged.

Both men watched as the temperature dropped another degree. Brad glanced over at Shawn and grinned.

"I think we got it under control."

"I'll let Wally know." Shawn stepped over to the control panel and removed the radio from the console. "Wally, can you read me?"

"*WALLY, CAN YOU read me?*"

Wally heard the call but did not register it at first, focusing all his energy on emptying a jerry can of diesel fuel into the generator. He finished the transfer and secured the cap back onto the generator's fuel tank. On the fourth call, he removed the radio from his pocket and responded.

"This is Wally. What's up?"

"*The temperature inside the reactor is dropping. It's gone down eight degrees in the last twenty minutes.*" Somebody yelled out something in the background. "*Make that nine degrees. You guys did it. We're getting the reactor under control.*"

"Finally." Wally did not have the same level of enthusiasm in his voice that Shawn did.

"*What's the radiation level out there?*"

"Hang on."

Wally summoned what energy he could and staggered over to the Geiger counter by the exterior wall. Eric leaned against it, not having moved in over half an hour. When Wally crouched beside him, Eric opened his eyes halfway.

"What's up?"

"Shawn said the reactor is cooling off."

"We were successful?" Eric barely got out the words.

"We were. Shawn wants a radiation reading."

Eric leaned to one side to read the gauge but immediately started to fall over. Wally pushed him back against the wall.

"It's okay. I'll do it."

"*Thanks.*"

Wally checked the gauge and called Shawn. "It's 39.8 milliSieverts."

A momentary pause passed before Shawn responded. "*With luck, that should start dropping soon.*"

"It better."

"*I'll keep you posted. And Wally, you and your team did a great job. You saved thousands of lives today.*"

"Thanks."

Wally pocketed the radio and leaned against the wall, desperately needing a break. He tried to be excited about finally getting the reactor under control, which was difficult considering the price of their success. Katherine had died in the explosion that breached the reactor wall. Carlson had succumbed to radiation poisoning a little over an hour ago. When Wally had gone over to check on him, Sam had passed away quietly in his sleep. He did not inform the others and left the body leaning against the pumper. Considering Eric's condition, he would be joining his friend soon.

The only ones capable of functioning were himself and Josh. If you could call their condition functional. All three of them had been pissing and vomiting blood since early that morning. They took turns every hour refilling the generator with fuel, but even that fifteen minutes of work exhausted them. They would be lucky to make it through the next thirty-six hours.

The three of them would continue feeding water into the cooling system until they were no longer able to function and, with luck, get the reactor under control.

DAY FIVE

CHAPTER FORTY-SIX

"MISS DANIELLE. IT'S time to get up."

The voice was as gentle as the nudge on her shoulder. Danielle opened her eyes. Slowly, she recognized her surroundings. Liz and Kyle sitting beside her. The trees near the edge of the river. The dark skylines of Nashua and Manchester standing in stark contrast to the aurora. Pushing herself into a sitting position, Danielle stretched and twisted her neck, trying not to groan like an old lady when her muscles cracked.

"Are you okay?" asked Liz.

"Just tired." It then dawned on Danielle night had fallen. "What time is it?"

"It's a little after midnight." The young girl pointed to her Hello Kitty watch. "You've been asleep for six hours."

"Sorry. I didn't mean to sleep so long."

"You needed it. I only woke you because you said you wanted to cross the river before sunrise."

"Thank you." Danielle stood and arched her back, resulting in more snapping muscles. "Did you see anyone while I slept?"

Liz shook her head.

Kyle pointed toward Manchester. "But someone set up camp over there."

Danielle followed Kyle's finger. South of the city, the glow of a campfire could be seen above the treetops. She reasoned that someone trying to get home would stay near the riverbank and not let their presence be known. Whoever set up camp on

the highway was either asking for trouble or meant an organized group, more than likely manning a roadblock into
Manchester. In either case, she needed to avoid them.

Crouching in front of the children, Danielle whispered,
"We're going to cross the river now. I need you both to stay
close to me and not make any noise. There are a lot of bad
people out there, and we have to avoid them. Are there any
questions?"

The kids shook their heads.

She hugged them. "Let's go."

The three made their way to the riverbank. Danielle ignored the canoe and headed for the nearest rowboat.
Thankfully, a pair of oars sat on the bottom. She helped the
kids inside and had them sit up front. Pushing the boat into the
river, Danielle jumped in, mounted the oars in the crutches,
and rowed toward the opposite shore. The current proved
stronger than she expected, taking her toward Nashua, so she
rowed upstream while crossing.

Something banged into the side of the boat, pushing against
the oar and resting against the starboard side. Liz gasped and
covered her brother's eyes. A body lay face down in the water.
Danielle reached over, grabbed its belt, and pulled the corpse
around the stern. Only then did she notice scores of bodies
floating down the river. Her stomach turned. Someone must be
disposing of the corpses from the city.

"Keep your eyes closed until we reach the other side," she
quietly warned the kids, who willingly obeyed.

It took a few minutes and several more encounters with the
corpses before they finally reached the other side. Jumping out,
Danielle pulled the boat onto the shore, helped the kids climb
out, and then dashed inland.

She led the kids through an open field until they reached a
small copse of trees along Route 3 where she paused to check
their surroundings. Across the street sat a private residence
and, beside it, a bowling alley. She rushed Liz and Kyle across

the open space, then stayed close to the row of trees separating the house from the bowling alley, her eyes switching between where they were going and the house to make certain no one watched them. At the end of the backyard, she maneuvered the kids into the woods behind the house.

When they emerged on the other side, Everett Turnpike lay ahead of them. As with I-93, dozens of abandoned vehicles sat along both lanes. Danielle carefully surveyed the area. The only people she spotted were a group of men sitting around the campfire they had spotted earlier, laughing loudly and drinking. Thankfully, they were two miles away and would not notice her as long as she and the kids remained silent.

Danielle crouched in front of the kids again. "Those are probably bad people, and we don't want them to notice us, so stay low and close to me. And remember, don't make any noise."

Liz gave her a thumbs up. Kyle mimicked pulling a zipper across his lips.

Crossing to the nearest vehicle, a FedEx van with the rear doors open and torn-apart packages strewn around the highway, she paused, checked the area for people, and then rushed the kids over to the guardrail. An SUV sat in the center lane. She saw no one. Helping the kids over took less than a minute. After one final check for danger, the three raced across the highway, using the SUV as cover, and rushed into the woods beyond the turnpike.

Danielle paused, listening for any indication someone might be lurking nearby or following them. After several seconds with no sounds, she ushered the kids through the woods. After walking for half an hour, they emerged into a clearing extending through the forest that allowed access to the electric power lines running through the countryside. Danielle stopped and turned to the kids.

"We should be safe now. We'll follow these power lines until we reach a road. Once I know where we are, we'll go

from there. Stay with me and don't make a sound, and if you
see anything unusual, let me know. We should reach my house
by this time tomorrow. Ready?"

Kyle nodded.

"We trust you, Miss Danielle."

Danielle smiled. She hoped someone nice was helping out
her daughter.

She led the way along the clearing.

CHAPTER FORTY-SEVEN

K IRSTIE FELT AT ease when she spotted the compound ahead of them.

Compound. Andrew had been calling the neighborhood that for days and the rest of the group had taken up the mantra. It seemed ominous, like they were on a military installation in a war zone. Which, technically, they were. Unlike the compounds she had seen in movies, this one could not easily be defended.

This morning, the Scavengers made their last supply run back to Timberlane Regional High School to retrieve the water and other drinks she and Regan had discovered yesterday. Andrew led the team, which included her, Regan, Jordan, and Meg. Only this time, each brought along two shotguns and a second pistol in case they ran into trouble which, fortunately, they did not. They filled half of the cart with water and power drinks and returned to the stables, filling the rest of the cart with a trough for water and as many bales of hay as they could fit. Andrew mentioned as they left how these supplies should keep the group viable for almost a month.

The only disturbing part of the trip came when they passed Haellie's house. During the night, animals had pulled off the sheets covering the bodies on the front lawn and started eating the corpses, something none of them would mention to the others. Sadly, Kirstie knew they would all be seeing much worse in the next few weeks.

Several members of the group came out to greet them and help unload the drinks into Kathy's garage. The riders then rode on to Justin's house. They parked the cart with hay in his garage along with the saddles, then settled the horses in his backyard.

Justin came out to help.

"I always wanted a horse but never thought I'd own a stable," he joked as he dropped a bale in the center of the yard and cut the ropes holding it together.

"We appreciate you taking on the responsibility," said Andrew. "For the next few months, the horses are our only means of transportation."

"I wish it would rain soon," said Jordan. "They're going to use up a lot of our water if it doesn't."

Andrew agreed. "Justin, if you don't mind, I'm going to have the team set up one of the water filtration systems and a container in your yard for the horses."

"No problem."

"Thanks." Andrew turned to his team. "Tonight, I'm going to hold a meeting on rationing our supplies and defending the compound. I want to be ready in case anyone tries to take what we have."

A fearful expression crossed Meg's face. "Do you think that's a possibility?"

"It's a certainty. There are a lot of groups out there like the assholes we ran into yesterday. We need to be ready for it."

An uneasiness settled over the group.

"We'll work out the details tonight," said Andrew. "Right now, you need to get some rest. I've pushed you hard the last few days."

"Andrew's Raiders?" joked Justin.

"I prefer the word rangers." Andrew grinned. "Raiders makes us sound like the bad guys. Right now, I want you all to relax. Tonight is going to be important to our survival."

CHAPTER FORTY-EIGHT

"**W**HAT DO YOU think?" asked Brad.

Shawn did not answer right away, instead trying to comprehend the events of the last twenty-four hours. What a day ago had been an imminent massive disaster took a one-hundred-eighty-degree turn overnight. Not that it bothered Shawn. A sense of relief washed over him though he could not believe their luck.

The temperature inside the reactor began to drop yesterday and continued throughout the night. From a high of eight hundred and twenty-one, which indicated the core had begun melting down, the readings had dropped to five hundred and ninety-one degrees. Still far from ideal, but much better than they had anticipated. Shawn attributed that to the remnants of the decay heat which, along with the breakdown of the cooling system, had helped contribute to the incident. Thanks to Wally's team, they had been able to feed water into the system and stabilize the situation. Once the decay heat died out, the situation would return to normal.

Normal? Nothing that happened over the last five days could be defined as normal. The best description would be a clusterfuck on steroids.

Seabrook had sustained irreparable damage. Protocol required that the reactor be shut down and the facility dismantled, a process that would take years. In the current situation, that would not happen. While they had contained the meltdown and prevented further damage to the core, they had no means to reverse the damage already done and had no way to assess its extent without physically checking the core and the containment vessel. Normally, they would use drones and probes equipped with cameras to enter these areas and report back what they had observed. Thanks to the solar flare, that would be impossible. The only alternative would be to send down a team to physically observe the damage. Considering the dangerously high doses his team had already received, such a move would be a death sentence.

And futile. They had no means to fix what had already occurred.

Shawn and Brad agreed that the breach occurred inside either the containment vessel or, more likely, the suppression chamber. They had no way to confirm if the explosion had damaged the core but assumed if it had, the damage was minimal. Had the core been breached, the radiation levels would be much higher than they currently were and most of them would be dead by now. The explosion had released highly irradiated air from the chamber which contaminated the area. Like with Chernobyl and Fukushima, the only safety precaution that could be taken would be to evacuate the surrounding area to limit the number of civilians who would be subject to radiation poisoning. Under the circumstances, that would be impossible.

Shawn avoided thinking of how many people in the surrounding community would die because of what had transpired here the last few days.

When Shawn did not answer, Brad asked again, "What do you think?"

"I think our job here is done."

"Are you sure?"

"What else can we do? We got the reactor under control. There's nothing we can do about the radiation."

"What now?"

The rest of the team had joined the conversation. Libby asked nervously, "Does this mean we can go home?"

"I don't see why not."

"What about the radiation outside the facility?" asked Andy. "Won't it be dangerous out there?"

"No more so than staying here." Shawn made eye contact with each of his team members. "Our work here is done. I want to head home and check on my sister and niece. I'm sure most of you have loved ones you want to be with. Anyone who feels more comfortable staying here is welcome to do so. But I'm leaving. Who's with me?"

The rest of the team raised their hands.

"Good. Gather up all the supplies we have left. We'll divide them equally and head out in a few hours. Any questions?"

"What about Wilson?" asked Brad.

Shit. In his excitement to leave, Shawn had forgotten about him. Wilson would not be able to travel in his condition.

"I'll go check on him. Brad, contact Wally and tell him we're heading out soon, and they should do the same."

"Roger that."

Shawn made his way to the medical unit. The reek of diarrhea and vomit almost overwhelmed him, forcing him to swallow down the bile rising in the back of his throat. Wilson lay on the cot, not moving. The red blotches had spread, covering his hands and most of his face, The only signs of life were the belabored rising and falling of his chest as he struggled to breathe.

Shawn walked over and gently shook Wilson's arm. "Are you awake?"

"It's not like I can sleep the way I feel." Wilson's attempt at humor fell flat. "What's up?"

"We have the situation under control. The temperature inside the reactor is dropping. We've stopped the meltdown."

"Sorry I wasn't there to help."

"There's no need to apologize. You went above and beyond opening that valve in the suppression chamber."

"Thanks. Don't forget, we both did that."

Shawn tried not to think about that. He would soon suffer the same fate as his friend. He changed the subject.

"I've given orders for the team to prepare to evacuate the reactor."

Wilson chuckled, which turned into a coughing fit. He leaned over the side of the cot and vomited into the barrel, then laid back down.

"I doubt I'll be leaving here."

"I know." Shawn placed a hand on Wilson's shoulder. "I'll stay with you if you want."

"Screw that. Get out of here while you have a chance."

"I can't leave you alone."

"Yes, you can." When Shawn tried to argue, Wilson cut him off. "We both know I'm not going to get better. Staying with me will only lessen your chances of getting home. I'll be fine."

"But...." Shawn had no idea what to say.

Wilson shook his head. "No buts. I'm not going to make it. If you stay, there's nothing you can do for me. Besides, I'm single and don't have a family to worry about. You do. Leave me to die in peace. Check on me one last time before you go."

"Are... are you sure about this?"

Wilson nodded. "Now, if you'll excuse me, this exhausted me. I need to take a nap."

Shawn stayed by his friend until he dosed off, which took only a few seconds, then returned to the control room.

"How is he?" asked Brad.

"Bad. He won't make it much longer."

Brad sighed. "One of us should stay with him."

"I volunteered, but he refused. Hopefully, he'll pass on before we leave. Did you reach Wally?"

"I tried for five minutes but no one answered."

"Fuck." Shawn tried not to imagine the fate that awaited Wally and his team. "We'll check on them when we leave. Let's get ready."

CHAPTER FORTY-NINE

D ANIELLE AND THE kids traveled only a few miles before they reached a two-lane road and headed north. After a quarter of a mile, they came across a crossroad and rested in the woods until dawn when Danielle had enough light to consult the map.

"Where are we?" asked Liz.

"As far as I can tell, we're south of Bedford." She pointed to the road they had followed last night. "This is Wallace Road. It'll take us to Goffstown, and from there it's not far to my house."

The girl raised her eyebrows. "Define 'not far'."

"About twenty miles."

Kyle sighed melodramatically.

Danielle chuckled and rubbed his head. "Come on. You'll be fine."

The three continued walking north. As the morning progressed, the heat and humidity worsened, making the trip less comfortable. Danielle ignored that. With each passing mile, she felt more at ease. The homes became fewer and more isolated, and they walked for several hours without coming across anyone. Even more reassuring, there were no signs of violence or looting. The area seemed as peaceful as if it was early on a Sunday morning.

After walking for several hours, Liz stopped and tugged on Danielle's sleeve.

"Miss Danielle, I hear men talking."

Danielle raised her forefinger across her lips to indicate

silence and then mouthed the words "Thank you." Motioning for the kids to get behind her, she moved off the road to the tree line and cautiously approached the bend, fearing the worse.

A roadblock stood at the intersection of Wallace and New Boston Roads. A sense of hope surged through Danielle. She counted seven National Guard soldiers, a New Hampshire State Trooper, and four local sheriff's deputies. None of them wore armor plating or helmets, and their weapons were either slung over their shoulders or casually laid against a stalled pick-up truck. Twelve horses with saddles were tied to nearby trees. A dozen people sat on the side of the road in the shade, ranging in age from toddlers to men and women in their fifties or sixties. One National Guardsmen crouched by a mother holding a two-year old girl, all of them laughing as he played peek-a-boo with the child.

Danielle felt a tug on her shirt sleeve and turned to see Liz staring at her, eyes tinged with concern. She leaned close to Danielle's ear.

"Are they bad people?"

"No, sweetie. They're the good guys. Come on."

They stepped back into the center of the road and made their way to the roadblock.

When two hundred feet away, one of the Guardsmen spotted them and called out, "Hey, lieutenant. We have three more coming."

A young woman in a camouflage uniform slid out of the driver's seat of the pick-up. She was attractive with a pleasant smile and brunette hair tied into a long ponytail. On spotting Danielle and the kids, she waved, then spoke to two of her men who immediately jogged down the road toward them. As they approached, Danielle noticed that both men looked like they had recently graduated from high school.

The taller of the two greeted them. "Good afternoon, ma'am. I'm Corporal Davis and this is Private Lennox."

She smiled, finding great comfort in their attitude. "I'm Danielle. This is Liz and Kyle."

The two kids waved.

"Are you all okay? Any injuries?"

"No. Just tired and thirsty."

"You're in luck, ma'am. We have food and water left. Please, follow me."

"That sounds wonderful. Thank you."

As they walked back to the roadblock, Davis asked amicably, "How long have you been on the road?"

"I was in Boston when this all started. I've been walking for five days."

"You and your family walked all the way from Boston?" asked Lennox, surprised.

"I did. I met these kids last night. They were abandoned and needed help, so I said they could come with me."

"That's awfully kind of you." Davis glanced down at the kids. "Has she been treating you well?"

Kyle nodded. Liz replied with an adamant, "Yes."

"You're lucky you made it this far. Things are getting bad out there."

"It hasn't been easy."

"Well, you're safe now."

When they reached the roadblock, the lieutenant stepped forward to greet them.

"I'm Lieutenant Trudeau. Welcome to our little corner of the world. Glad to see you're okay."

Danielle smiled. "Thank you. It's nice to finally meet some good people."

"I hear you, ma'am. Follow me, and I'll get you something to drink."

They approached the pick-up. Trudeau reached under the bed cover and pulled out three bottles of spring water and three protein bars which she handed to Danielle and the kids.

"Sorry the water is warm but we have no way to keep it

cool."

"That's fine, lieutenant. It's good to have something to eat and drink."

"Join the others and rest. Oh, and I'll need to take your weapons while you're with us. We can't be too careful."

Danielle hesitated.

"It's okay, ma'am. You're safe with us."

Danielle relented, realizing she would not need them with armed people around her. She would retrieve them once they were on their way.

The three took their water and protein bars and joined the others in the shade. Those already there nodded or waved at the new arrivals.

A few minutes later, Trudeau came over with two more bottles of water and handed them to the kids.

"Thank you," said Danielle.

"You're welcome. I want to make sure they're well hydrated. As you can imagine, medical care is rare at the moment."

"Tell me about it."

"Corporal Davis said you walked all the way here from Boston. What's it like out there?"

Danielle spent the next five minutes relating to the lieutenant what she had gone through. When Danielle finished, Trudeau whistled between her teeth.

"Man, you're damn lucky." She looked over at the kids. "Sorry."

Liz chuckled. "I've heard worse from my parents."

"What's it like around here?" Danielle asked.

"It's getting bad, but we're taking care of it. We've had several encounters with gangs over the last few days and have had to detain them. Two groups opened fire on us. I lost three men in those encounters."

"Sorry to hear that. At least the government is getting things under control."

"We haven't heard from anyone in control since this whole

thing began. What we're doing is a local initiative. The mayors of the five surrounding towns got together and set this up. My guardsmen are all locals who now work for the mayors. Same with the sheriff's deputies. The Statie happened to be on patrol when the solar flare hit and joined up with us. We've established roadblocks along all the main roads and have patrols roaming through the towns to keep things under control."

"What's it like outside this area?"

"I have no idea. All communications are down. And honestly, I don't care. We're stretched thin enough keeping our own area safe."

"Well, you seem to be doing a good job."

"Thanks. Let me know if you need anything."

Kyle had already finished his second bottle of water and laid down on the grass to take a nap. Liz sat beside him, switching between eating her protein bar and nursing along her first bottle of water.

"What now, Miss Danielle?"

"We're in Goffstown. Dunbarton is the next town over. That's where we're heading. With luck, we should be home by nightfall."

"Good. I'm tired."

"I know." Danielle leaned over and hugged her. "You rest up. We'll head out soon."

Twenty minutes passed when a carriage drawn by two horses came down the road. Seven people sat in back, all in civilian clothes. Three National Guardsmen and a Goffstown deputy rode horses on either side of the carriage, their weapons resting on their laps.

Trudeau stepped over to the group. "You're ride is here. Time to get going."

Danielle roused the kids then went over to the lieutenant. "Thank you for the hospitality. If you don't mind, I'll grab my weapons and we'll be on our way."

Trudeau seemed confused. "Sorry, ma'am, but I can't

allow that."

"But I live in Dunbarton."

"This entire region is under martial law. No one is allowed to travel on their own. It's not safe out there."

Panic welled up inside Danielle. "We're almost home."

"I understand, but I can't allow it. You'll have to join the others."

The carriage had stopped and those who had been resting on the grass had begun to climb aboard.

"Where are you taking us?"

"A refugee center has been set up at SNHU Arena in Manchester. All the necessary supplies are being gathered there. The mayors assured us the location is safe. Once the situation has been stabilized, you'll be allowed to go home."

"What if I don't want to go?"

"You have no choice." Trudeau spoke the words as friendly as possible as Davis and Lennox moved up behind her, weapons in their hands. "Please, ma'am. Don't make this difficult."

For a moment, Danielle had no idea what to do. Then Liz tugged on her sleeve.

"We should do as they ask."

Realizing she had no other options, Danielle acquiesced and helped the kids onto the carriage. Trudeau followed and assisted Danielle on board.

"Please, trust me. I wouldn't make you do this unless I had been assured you'd be safer there."

Danielle said nothing. Maybe this was a good thing. With luck, she would find Kirstie at the refugee center.

Once everyone boarded, the carriage turned around and headed north.

CHAPTER FIFTY

KIRSTIE LOOKED AROUND Andrew's backyard. Everyone from the compound attended, seated in a semi-circle, all of them expressing concern.

Regan sat beside her. She leaned over, nudged her friend, and whispered, "Am I the only one getting a bad vibe about this?"

"We all have that vibe."

Andrew stood and centered himself in front of the group.

"By now you all know what happened yesterday at the high school. We're facing a precarious situation. We've gathered all the supplies we could find to survive. Now we have to concentrate on defending what we have."

"Wait a minute," interrupted Keith. "I thought you killed all but one of the gang members. What threat can he pose to us?"

"I interrogated one of the members before he died. He told me there are fifty others held up in the VFW Hall in Kingston, which is not far from here. And that's the one gang we know of. Given the state of the world, I assume there are more out there that pose a potential threat."

"But none of them know we're here."

"The one who escaped knows we exist," said Jordan. "If he makes it back to the others, he'll tell them there's a group somewhere nearby that is stocked up to sit this out."

"Which means they'll come looking for us," added Meg.

"Exactly," agreed Andrew.

"Maybe they can be reasoned with," suggested Theodora.

Haellie snorted. "Good fucking luck with that."

"What do you mean?"

"You don't have to tell them," Kathy whispered.

"They need to know." The teenager took a deep breath. "Two of them found me and Mrs. V alone and tried to rape us. I killed them."

"You killed them?" asked Abbey.

"Yes. It was kill or be killed. These people can't be reasoned with. I watched them murder my mother and siblings. If they find us, they're going to rape the women, murder all of us, and take what we have."

A stunned silence fell over the group as those who had yet to come to the realization of how bad things were suddenly realized the extent of the situation the group faced.

Justin broke the silence. "Let's build a wall around the compound."

"I thought of that," said Andrew. "But it won't work."

"Why not?"

"Andrew and I already discussed this," said Kathy. "The area is too large to put up a wall."

"We would have to scavenge every Home Depot and Lowe's within a fifty-mile radius, which puts too much of a strain on the horses. Even if we did, the best we could do is a plastic or chain link fence which would barely slow down an attack. And without heavy equipment, we have no way of setting up one. Besides, we have to assume the gang will find us sooner rather than later. We need to focus our efforts on something we can build quickly with the supplies we have on hand."

"What are you suggesting?" asked Keith.

"A series of defensive positions throughout the compound."

"How can we do that?" asked Kirstie.

"It's not as difficult as you think if we work together. We'll dig as many foxholes as we can and use the dirt to make firing berms around them. It's going to be a lot of hard work, but the more we have the better our chances of defending ourselves. We'll also set up around-the-clock patrols of the neighborhood as well as checkpoints on all the roads leading in."

"How will we communicate?" asked Keith.

"If you see anyone coming, fire three warning shots. That will be the signal for us to man our positions." Andrew paused. "Another thing. We need to always carry weapons with us in case we're ambushed."

"I hate guns," said Quinn.

"Get over it," snapped Haellie. "I did. Guns are why Mrs. V and I are alive today."

"I'm not disagreeing with you," said Keith. "But do you think we're up to this? We have people who have never fired a gun before. And we have kids and teenagers in the group."

"I've already killed someone in order to survive," said Haellie.

"So have I," said Jordan.

"We have, too." Kirstie pointed to Regan.

Andrew raised his hands to stop the argument. "I know what I'm asking is not easy. But remember what Joel and Ralph tried to do to us, and they were our neighbors. The people out there are even worse than those two. And as time goes on, it's going to become a nightmare. Trust me. I know."

"What do you mean?" asked Theodora.

"Do you really want to know how bad it's going to get?" asked Andrew.

"They need to be told," said Kathy.

"While in the Marines, I was on a task force assigned to study various emergency situations and what the outcome would be. My group studied the effects of a world-wide EMP." Andrew's tone became increasingly intense. "The electricity is out around the globe, which means we no longer have the ability to produce food unless we grow it ourselves. All supply chains are cut off, so what we have in the area are our only means of survival, and every grocery store has already been raided. Everyone is on their own. Most people only had enough food and water to last three days, which is the barest minimum needed to survive. That means by now at least a billion people around the world have perished. By this time next week, that number will be close to three billion. Within a month, it'll reach eight billion."

Mikayla gasped. "That's the entire population of the planet."

"Exactly. In one month, there'll only be a few million people around the world still alive, and they'll be fighting for what little supplies are left. Large cities will be death zones with handfuls of people fighting each other to survive. The only ones who will make it through that first month are farmers, preppers, and those who have taken over food warehouses, and they'll be targets for those who have nothing. It'll be at least six months, maybe a year, before the state and federal governments can restore order and bring things back under control. During that time, no one will be bringing us humanitarian aid. There'll be no Red Cross to help with the sick. Those who survive the first few weeks will be entirely on their own. Which brings up another…."

Andrew stopped.

"What?" asked Kirstie.

Andrew hesitated.

Kathy finally prodded him. "Tell them."

Andrew sighed. "Eight billion people are going to die and remain unburied. As they rot, disease is going to run rampant, especially in cities and large towns like Plaistow. The chances are good that pandemics will begin. Those will be spread by people leaving populated areas and by the rats and insects that, once they run out of food, will spread out searching for food elsewhere. If one of those reaches us, we're screwed."

"We're fortunate the flare hit during the summer because it gives us time to prepare for the winter. Once the cold weather and snow hits, we're going to suffer big time. We must grow as much as possible and can the produce to make it through the winter. There'll be no electricity to heat our homes, so those with fireplaces will have to take in those who don't have one. Anyone who comes down with pneumonia will have to be isolated so it doesn't spread to others. Right now, we're playing the survival game on beginner's mode. We have to get ourselves to expert level by November while defending this compound from outsiders, which is not going to be easy."

Everyone stared at Andrew, shocked by the reality they now faced.

Meg finally broke the silence by mumbling, "Dear God."

"I'm a man of faith," said Andrew. "But at this stage of the game, God will only help those who help themselves. The next eight months are crucial to our survival, and that's only if we can stave off any attacks from those who want to take what we have."

"What's the good news," joked Justin, trying to break the sullen mood.

Andrew grinned. "The good news is if we survive until spring, and the chances of that are not good, then we might make it through this nightmare."

"What now?" asked Kirstie, not sure if she wanted to hear the answer.

Removing several sheets of paper from his back pocket, Andrew handed them to the group.

"Kathy and I have worked out a roster for everyone. She's in charge of getting us supplied for winter and I'm in charge of defending the compound. Everyone will work two eight-hour shifts, one helping set up our survival network and one patrolling the compound. The other eight hours are for rest."

Kathy jumped in. "Look over the roster and let us know if we overlooked anything. If anyone wants a change, we'll see if we can accommodate you."

"Also," added Andrew, "everyone travels in pairs while on the compound so we're not ambushed."

"What about our pets?" asked Quinn.

"We hadn't thought about that," said Kathy.

Andrew considered his answer. "You'll have to feed them out of your rations. We'll set aside some extra food and water for your dogs so long as you bring them along on patrols. They'll be useful in detecting anyone who comes near. Any other questions?"

They had hundreds of questions, but no one dared ask them.

"Okay. First shift begins at four o'clock, which is in an hour. I suggest everyone have an early dinner. Those of you not on the first shift, get some sleep. The next few weeks are going to be hard on all of us."

Kirstie and the girls waited until the roster made its way to them and checked it out. Abbey and Mikayla were assigned first shift with Andrew and several others to start building defensive positions. Kirstie and Regan had that shift free, then took over guard duty at midnight.

Regan nudged her friend. "Night patrol. We finally made bad-ass status."

"You think that's a good thing?" Kirstie did not hide the irritation in her voice.

"Lighten up. We're in a much better position than most people out there."

Most people out there included Kirstie's mom and uncle. Given what Andrew had told them, she wondered how they were faring.

CHAPTER FIFTY-ONE

A S IF TO reaffirm their decision to leave, the car battery lost power an hour before the team departed. The last temperature reading inside the core was one hundred and twelve degrees.

Half an hour before departing, the team changed out their old coveralls for a new set. The new clothes made them look better than they had in the past five days. Too bad none of them felt that way. Their bodies stunk from sweat and grime. Each of them had a five-day growth of beard and their hair, oily and unkempt, stuck to their heads. He could deal with that. What would make the trip unbearable was that each of them suffered from different degrees of radiation poisoning. Each of them had begun vomiting in the last twelve hours though, thankfully, no one had suffered yet from diarrhea. And all of them were fatigued. The only things keeping them going now were adrenalin and the excitement of getting home to be with their loved ones.

Assuming they lived long enough to make it that far.

Supplies were limited. Each team member had two bottles of water and half a dozen snacks. Considering how sick they were, that would not last long. All but one of the flashlights had run out of power within the last few hours. Shawn hoped the remaining one would last long enough for them to get out of the building.

They had decided to leave behind the dosimeters and Geiger counters. No sense of keeping track of the inevitable.

Once their book bags were filled, Shawn stood in the center

of his team.

"Is everyone ready?"

He received three half-hearted replies.

"Let's head out. But I want to check on Wilson first."

Shawn led the way, leaving the control room for the last time.

At the medical unit, Shawn entered to check on his friend while the others stayed in the dark corridor.

Wilson lay on the cot, breathing heavily but steady. Shawn went over to check on him. He had decided to ask Wilson one more time if he wanted him to stay. He gently shook his friend's shoulder.

"Wilson, it's Shawn. We're leaving."

No response.

Shawn shook him a little harder. "Wake up."

Wilson did not. Only the belabored breathing indicated he was still alive. Wilson must have slipped into a coma. At least his friend would not know they had left him alone and, with luck, would die peacefully in his sleep. It was the best he could hope for Wilson, though Shawn would have to live for the rest of his life knowing he had abandoned his friend to die alone so he could make it home to see Danielle and Kirstie. He prayed God would forgive him, then wondered if there God existed and, if he did, why he would submit the world to such a nightmare.

As Shawn exited the medical unit, Brad asked, "How is he?"

"He's in a coma."

"Good," replied Andy, then looked at the other team members. "You know what I mean."

"Let's go."

A few minutes later, they exited the building. As if one cue, the flashlight went dark.

"That's ominous," chuckled Libby.

"We don't need it any longer." Brad pointed up.

The aurora flowed across the night sky, providing enough illumination to see by.

"Wait here," said Shawn. "I want to check on Wally's team."

"We'll go with you," said Brad as he fell in behind Shawn.

They found Wally and his team spread around the area. One leaned against the wall near the injection line, with three against the pumper. Wally lay by the generator, which no longer ran. A jerry can lay by Wally, its contents spilled on the asphalt. He must have been trying to refill the tank when he collapsed.

Shawn went over to check on the team, feeling for a pulse. All of them were dead. He said a silent prayer for them and rejoined the others.

"Are they...?" Brad could not bring himself to finish the question.

Shawn nodded.

"Damn." Libby glanced over at the fire team then back to Shawn. "They gave their lives to save everyone and nobody will ever know the sacrifice they made."

"We do," answered Shawn. "We're alive because of them."

"Yeah," sighed Andy. "But for how long?"

The others stared at him disapprovingly.

"Sorry."

"Forget about it," said Shawn as he walked down to the main gate.

The rest of the team fell in behind him.

When they reached the gate, the two guards were missing. Shawn peaked inside the shed, expecting to see them dead, only to find it empty.

"No one's here."

"The bastards deserted us?" blurted Libby.

"I don't blame them," said Brad.

"They were supposed to protect us."

"From what?" Shawn glanced over at Libby. "It's not like

we were in danger from looters."

Libby's attitude softened. "I guess."

Shawn pulled aside the gate enough for them to get through, closing it behind them, then continued to Route 1.

When they reached the road, Andy stopped. "Jesus fucking Christ."

They all felt the same way. The area along Route 1 appeared like a battlefield. Not because of the explosion, but because of the mayhem. Dozens of stalled vehicles lined both lanes of the road, doors and trunks open, items scattered along the asphalt. The Thai restaurant across the street had been ransacked, the front door hanging ajar on its hinges, litter scattered around the parking lot. The Market Basket beside the main gate had also been looted. Shattered glass littered the walkway around the entrances. Several shopping carts lay overturned on the asphalt, their remaining contents broken. Though difficult to tell from this distance, a figure lay crumbled near the exit onto the main street, apparently shot by someone who had robbed him of what he had just stolen. Even more eerie, no one was around, not even bodies except for that one.

Shawn remembered an old black-and-white movie he had watched years ago where the main character was the last man on the planet, and this scene reminded him of that movie.

Brad shook his head. "What went on out here?"

"People were fending for themselves," Shawn answered. "Gathering what they needed to keep their families alive."

Libby had his gaze focused on the corpse in the parking lot. "Okay, but to kill someone over food? That's fucked up."

"It's the way the world is now." Brad looked over to Shawn for backup. "We missed it by being stuck inside for five days."

Andy shook his head. "I can't believe we put our lives on the line to save people so they could do this."

"Believe it," said Shawn. "And there's a lot worse waiting out there."

An awkward, disturbed silence passed through the group.

Brad spoke first. "Guys, I'm out of here. I have a long walk back to Portsmouth. Anyone with me?"

"I am," Shawn replied.

"I thought you lived near Concord. That's west of here."

"But I have to take Route 101 to get there."

"Makes sense. Anyone else?"

"I'm in," added Andy.

"Where do you live?" asked Shawn.

"Epping. I guess you and I are travel partners for a bit." Andy turned to Libby. "What about you?"

Libby shook his head. "I live west of here in Kensington. So, I guess this is it."

"Guess so." Shawn stepped up to Libby and extended his hand. "Thanks for all you did here. You should be proud of yourself."

Libby shook his hand. "We were all in this together."

"Good luck."

"Thanks. Same to you." Libby leaned to the side. "Good luck to all of you."

They watched Libby head south along Route 1 until he disappeared in the darkness.

"I hope he makes it," Brad whispered to himself.

"We all do." Shawn turned around. "Let's go."

Shawn and his team headed north.

CHAPTER FIFTY-TWO

KIRSTIE STOOD IN Keith's backyard, more commonly known now as The Stable, petting her new horse, an Andalusian. After being abandoned for so many days, the horses were naturally jittery when Andrew and the others arrived. However, once released from their death sentence, given food and water, and eventually brought to the compound, they began to warm up to the new owners. Especially Kirstie.

After the depressing all-hands meeting, she wandered around the neighborhood for an hour before deciding to come here and be with the horses. Grabbing a handful of hay, she slowly approached the Andalusian and tried to feed him by hand. He backed away at first, but eventually came closer to be fed, and seemed to enjoy it. Kirstie attempted to pet him twice, but the horse shook its head. On the third try, he let her stroke his mane.

By now, the other four horses wanted in on the action and surrounded Kirstie. She spent an hour feeding each one by hand and petting them, often being interrupted by a horse that did not want to wait its turn. Two of the horses had their fill of food and attention and strolled over to the trough for a drink. The third horse, an American Quarter Horse, nudged Kirstie with its nose before leaving. The Andalusian, apparently jealous, came over and rubbed the side of its head along her face and chest.

"You're a good girl."

The horse moved its head to one side and snorted.

"Sorry, good boy."

The horse went back to rubbing against Kirstie and she petted it, thriving on the affection.

Like everyone else at the meeting, Kirstie still found it hard to comprehend their situation. She had lulled herself into a false sense of security being stranded out here in the suburbs. However, everything Andrew said made sense. Because of what had gone on the past two days, she had forgotten about what took place at Walmart and the asshole who mugged Mikayla for the flashlight. Even this quiet neighborhood was no better. Most of the neighbors had raided Dignam's house for weapons and killed him. And when Andrew attempted to unite the neighborhood to give everyone a chance of survival, Joel and Ralph tried to steal everything they had. Despite the unity they had formed over the past few days, she wondered if it would last and if others in the group would off their neighbors to give themselves a better chance of survival.

Was it any wonder she had become a cold-blooded killer in order to survive?

Kirstie worried most about what happened to her mother and uncle, more so her mother. Shawn had been on shift at Seabrook when the solar flare hit and rode this out in a secure building with limited access and, she assumed, enough supplies to last the crew a few days.

Her mother, however, was a different story. If her mother was smart, she would have hunkered down somewhere near Boston. But that meant her mother would now be in the middle of a war zone. However, Kirstie knew her mother better than that. She would head back to their house in Dunbarton to check on Kirstie. And there were a lot more dangerous places between Boston and Dunbarton than her group had encountered locally. Once her mother arrived home and found her not there, then what would she do? Wait for her to show up? Doubtful. She would head out looking for her.

Every scenario Kirstie ran through her mind depressed her

even more.

Sensing Kirstie's anxiety, the horse moved closer and leaned against the teenager to comfort her.

Kirstie hugged the horse. "I'm going to call you Danielle."

"You're going to name a male horse after your mother?"

The question came from Regan who stepped up beside Kirstie.

"Okay. I'll call him Danny."

"That's better." Regan paused a moment before asking, "Worried about your mother?"

"Yes. And Uncle Shawn. And all of us." Kirstie stopped petting the horse and turned to her friend. "Andrew said that out of eight billion people, only a million will survive the first month. What are the odds we'll be amongst those survivors?"

"Point zero four percent."

Kirstie stared at her friend who smiled. "I'm good at math."

"Well, those odds don't make me feel any better."

"We'll get through this."

Kirstie chastised herself for being self-centered. "You must be worried about your family."

"We all are. Abbey is freaking out, though she's hiding it well. And almost everyone here is missing a loved one. Kathy's husband hasn't returned home yet. Andrew and Justin haven't heard from their girlfriends since this began. But there's nothing any of us can do about it. Our only option is to hope for the best and prepare for the worst."

"Easier said than done."

"I know. But it's the only way we're going to survive this." Regan hugged her friend. "Come on. Let's get some rest. We have guard duty in a few hours."

CHAPTER FIFTY-THREE

THE HORSE-DRAWN CART and its escort traveled through
the countryside before turning east onto Route 114 then
veered off onto the Goffstown Rail Trail. Danielle appreciated
the diversion because it took them through a tree-lined walking
trail, keeping them out of the sun for a while.

Despite her initial trepidation about having to do this, Danielle began to feel more comfortable. The National Guardsmen
and police personnel accompanying them were friendly, and
the two driving the carriage chatted amiably with the civilians
at the front. As the sun went down and the temperature cooled,
she leaned against the sideboard and relaxed. Liz sat to her left,
cuddling Kyle, both kids sound asleep. Leaning over, she
wrapped her arms around them.

After a while, the trail ended and emerged into an urban
setting. Most of those inside the carriage became concerned,
chatting nervously amongst themselves. Finally, a middle-aged
woman near the front tapped the driver on the back.

"Where are we?"

The guardsman glanced over his shoulder. "Manchester."

"What?" A father left his children and crawled forward. "I
thought Manchester was dangerous."

"Some parts still are, but we've secured a section of the city
to establish the refugee center. You'll be fine."

The middle-aged woman and father sat back down but, like
everyone else in the carriage, an air of anxiety settled over
them.

Liz stared up, concern in her eyes. "Miss Danielle?"

"I thought you were asleep."

"Only resting. Will we be okay?"

"Of course, dear," she lied and hugged the girl close.

The carriage and its escort crossed over the Merrimack River via the Granite Street Bridge. A few minutes later, it stopped in front of a Residence Inn. The drivers climbed down from the carriage. Before leaving, one of them shifted in his seat to face the civilians.

"Good luck."

Five Guardsmen stepped up to the rear of the carriage. An officer lowered the rear hatch.

"Welcome to the Manchester Refugee Center. I'm Major Barrows. I'm in charge here. Now, if everyone will please get out, we'll get you registered and settled in."

Two guardsmen assisted the civilians out of the carriage and ushered them to a nearby area. Major Barrows helped Liz and Kyle down, then offered a hand to Danielle as she climbed off.

Danielle smiled. "Thank you, major."

"My pleasure, ma'am."

Liz pointed to the Residence Inn. "Is that where we're staying?"

"That's been commandeered as our barracks." The major pointed to the other side of the street. "You'll be lodged there for now."

The civilians turned around. The middle-aged woman gasped while the father with two kids muttered, "No fucking way."

In front of them sat the Southern New Hampshire University Arena. Large-pane windows made up the front façade. Two large posters hung on either side of the centerline promoting upcoming concerts that would never take place. The place looked like a military headquarters. Three parallel strands of barbed wire lined each of the four streets surrounding the structure, with a pair of armed guards stationed every two hundred feet. Dozens of metal trash barrels surrounded the main entrance and the open area off to the right, fires burning in each, providing the only light in the area besides the aurora. Six tables had been set up in a row near the barrels with lines of people in front of each.

The last thing this location appeared to be was a safe refuge.

Major Barrows stepped in front of the group. "If you'll follow me, please. We need to get you checked in."

The officer led them down a side street toward the arena's main entrance. Two guards moved the strands of barbed wire aside, allowing them access. The major stepped to the side.

"Each table is lettered from A to Z. Find the table whose letter begins with your last name and get in line."

"Why that system?" asked the middle-aged woman.

"It's easier to determine if any of your family members are here. That way you can be reunited."

A sense of excitement went through Danielle. With luck, she would get to see Kirstie again.

Danielle headed for the first table, which had a cardboard sign in front of it with A-D written in red marker. An elderly black woman stood at the table, registering with a slightly overweight National Guardsman with a surly expression. Danielle led the kids to the end of the line. The only people were a family of three—a husband and wife plus a ten-year-old girl holding a Labrador puppy.

Liz tugged on Danielle's sleeve. "We shouldn't be in this line."

"Yes, we do. My last name is Costner."

"But ours is Taylor."

"If we have to, we'll check you in at the other table after I'm done. Okay?"

Liz grinned. "Okay."

Kyle gave her a thumbs up.

When the elderly black woman finished, a National Guard

private escorted her to the arena. The surly Guardsman waved his hand.

"Come on, people. Keep it moving."

The family moved forward.

Danielle glanced around, studying the surroundings. The personnel outside the arena were a mixture of the National Guard, State Police, and Manchester Police. In addition to the barbed wire strands surrounding the structure, similar barricades were laid out in four rows in front of the main entrance creating a winding corridor leading inside. And more guards were placed by the entrance than anywhere else, almost as if they intended not to keep people out of the arena but prevent those inside from leaving.

She kept an eye on the Guardsman escorting the elderly black woman. He seemed pleasant enough, talking with her and moving along at the woman's pace, not hurrying her. As they neared the glass doors, a State Trooper unlocked a padlock, removed it from the links in a chain, and unwrapped the chain from around the door handles while two Guardsmen stepped aside and unslung their AR-15s, holding them in the low-ready position. The Statie opened the door, and the elderly woman went inside, the private escorting her to the entrance but going no further. Once clear of the doors, the Statie reattached the chain and locked it in place. Only then did the two Guardsmen lower their weapons.

"NO!"

The cry startled Danielle.

The little girl clutched the puppy tightly and quickly backed away from the table. "I'm not giving up Roxie! You can't make me!"

"Honey," the mother tried to comfort her. "You heard the man. No pets are allowed inside the arena."

"Then I'll stay out here with her!"

Major Barrows strolled up. "What's the problem?"

"I'm not giving up Roxie! If I can't take her with me, I'm

not going!"

The major crouched down and met the girl's gaze. "Ma'am, I understand how you feel, but there's not enough room inside for pets. And you can't stay out here with your family. It's too dangerous."

The girl shook his head violently. "I love her and won't let her go!"

The major stood and sighed, then motioned to a nearby Guardsman who came over and reached for the puppy. The girl screamed and tried to run, but her parents held him in place.

The mother clasped the girl's cheeks. "I know you don't want to, but we have to do this. Please, give them Roxie."

"NO!"

"Enough of this." The father stepped forward, pried the puppy away, and handed it to the Guardsman. Roxie whined and tried to crawl back to the girl, who lunged to get the puppy back, but the father intervened. When the girl continued to struggle, the father slapped her.

For a moment, she stopped struggling, in shock over what had happened. Major Barrows nodded his head and the Guardsman walked away with Roxie. The girl screamed, buried her head into her mother's chest, and sobbed.

"I hate you," she choked.

Major Barrows mouthed "I'm sorry" to the mother then escorted the family to the arena.

"Next," called out the Guardsman at the table.

At first, Danielle did not hear him, still dealing with the shock of what she had witnessed.

"Next!"

Danielle turned to Liz and Kyle, who hugged each other, and led them toward the table.

"Name?"

"Costner. Danielle Costner."

"Spell it."

"C-O-S-T-N-E-R."

He pulled aside a notebook with a C etched on the cover and thumbed through it.

"Do you happen to have a Kirstie or a Shawn Costner here?"

"Hang on." He eventually found the page he was searching for and scanned it. "Sorry. No one here by that name."

Danielle's spirits plummeted.

"Spell your first name."

"D-A-N-I-E-L-L-E."

"And the names of your kids?"

"These aren't my children."

The Guardsman flashed her a suspicious look.

"Our parents never returned home," explained Liz. "Miss Danielle found us and agreed to bring us with her."

"What's your name?"

"I'm Liz, but my full name—"

"You're last name." He practically barked at her.

"Taylor. I'm Elisabeth. This is my brother, Kyle."

The Guardsman leaned back and yelled down to the next to last table in line. "Hey, Rowan. Bring the T book over here."

"Hang on." He thumbed through his notebooks until he found the correct one and came over to the first table. "What's up?"

"These kids have lost their parents. Have we checked any Taylors in the past few days?"

Rowan opened the book and thumbed through the pages. "We checked in a Maleah and Antonino Taylor yesterday. Do you know them?"

Liz pouted and shook her head.

Rowan jotted down the kid's names and waved over the same guardsman who had escorted the elderly black woman.

"The private will take you to the arena. I have your names in the roster, so if your parents show up, we'll reunite you.

Sound good?"

"Yes," said Liz.

"Thank you," added Danielle.

The private led Danielle and the kids to the arena, him and the guards at the entrance following the same procedures as earlier.

"Where do we go once we're inside?" asked Danielle as she stepped through the door.

"There are plenty of cots available. Find yourselves three together and settle in."

"What about food and water?"

"We bring in rations every morning. Now, please." The private motioned with his head for them to go inside.

After Danielle and the kids entered, the Statie closed the doors and chained them up. Only then did the full nightmare of the Hell they had entered strike her.

The stench reached her first, a disgusting combination of shit, piss, body odor, cigarette smoke, and marijuana. Then the heat and humidity. So many people being crammed into one building with no air conditioning or windows turned the interior worse than a sauna, making the July temperature outside seem like a spring evening. The fourteen fifty-five-gallon drums lined up along the exterior edge of the arena floor, a necessary evil that provided the only lighting available, only added to the discomfort. At least someone had thought of opening the skylights to let out the smoke.

As her eyes adjusted to the dim light, Danielle noticed that refugees packed the arena far beyond capacity. The three tiers of bleachers were filled with refugees, and hundreds more filled the floor, the only open space being those close to the fire drums. An arena this size usually held eleven thousand people. Danielle figured at least three times that many were crowded in here. No wonder the guards chained the doors shut.

Liz tugged on Danielle's sleeve and spoke, but the cacophony of crying, moaning, and talking prevented her from hearing the girl. She leaned over.

"What did you say?"

"I said, I don't like it here. I want to leave."

Danielle did not blame her. This place terrified her. "We can't, hon. The guards won't let anyone out."

"I'm scared," mumbled Kyle.

"So am I."

Danielle looked around for a place to settle in. A woman screaming broke through the background noise, startling her.

"No! Leave me alone!"

Finding an empty spot in the corner of the lobby near the windowpanes, she ushered the kids there, placing them in the corner and sitting beside them, positioning herself between them and everyone else in the arena. She knew it was a futile gesture. If anyone came after the kids, she would be powerless to stop them.

Wrapping her left arm around the kids, Danielle knew she needed to find a way out of here as soon as possible.

CHAPTER FIFTY-FOUR

CARBONE SIGHED WITH relief when he staggered into the parking lot of the VFW Hall. He had been on the road since yesterday afternoon and his legs ached so bad he could barely walk. Nor did it help that he had used up his last bottle of water that morning. With luck, he could finagle one from the guys before having to face Stratman.

He stepped inside. A heavy-set guy with tattoos across his arms and face moved in front of Carbone, shoving a .357 Magnum into his face.

"What the fuck do you want?"

"Calm down, French. It's me. Carbone."

"Carbone?" French lowered the pistol. "Where the fuck have you been? And where are the others?"

"They're all dead. We were ambushed at Timberlane. I'm the only one who survived."

"Stratman ain't gonna like that, dude."

"I know, but I also have some good news for him. Where is he?"

"Across the street partying. You better let him know you're back."

"I plan to." Carbone hesitated. "Can I get a bottle of water first?"

"We don't have many left."

"We'll have a shitload of water soon. Come on, French. I can barely talk."

French yelled into the hall. "Cindy, bring me a bottle of water."

"Sure."

A few seconds later, a chubby blonde with glasses came over and handed Carbone a bottle of water, which he drank down in one gulp. Handing the empty bottle back to Cindy, he left the hall and crossed the street to the cigar bar, which had become party central for Stratman's gang. The windows and doors had been left open to get a cross flow of air through the place, and laughter and loud talking emanated from inside. Carbone entered and coughed from the lingering cigar smoke.

Off in the left corner, one of the gang members sat in a comfortable chair, a brunette's head bobbing in his lap. Another member knelt behind her, his pants around his ankles, taking her from behind. Both men finished at the same time. They stood, one of them slapping the brunette on the ass, then two others took their place. SOP for the bitches around here to earn their food and water.

Stratman and several of his men sat around a table near the door, smoking cigars and working on several bottles of whiskey and vodka. Stratman presented an imposing figure: over six feet in height, two hundred and ten pounds of muscle, and a physique developed over years at the prison gym. At first glance, he did not appear menacing, with dark hair and a well-trimmed beard and mustache as well as a perpetual smile. However, behind that friendly demeanor beat the heart of a psycho who would rather gut you like a pig than tolerate any bullshit.

Carbone was building up the courage to go over when Hart, the second in command, noticed him standing at the door.

"Look what the fucking cat dragged in."

Stratman's eyes narrowed and the smile slid off his face. "Where the fuck have you been for the last two days? We thought you ran out on us."

Carbone moved over to the table. "Another gang ambushed us while at Timberlane. I barely made it out alive."

"Made it out or chickened out?"

"I barely survived. But I followed them back to their place, figuring we could get our revenge on them later. These people have set up a survivalist community for themselves. From what I could tell, they've set up systems to gather water and grow their own food. They have plenty of supplies, and horses."

"What about fresh pussy?" asked Anderson, the third in line.

"Plenty of it, including teenagers."

"Fuck, yeah."

Stratman cast Anderson a disapproving glare then turned his attention back to Carbone.

"Where are they?"

"In Atkinson, not far from here. And the best part is, they're set up in a residential neighborhood so there are no defenses. It'll be easy to take them over."

Stratman thought for a few seconds. "How far along are they in setting this all up?"

"Pretty far. They should be up and running in a few days."

Stratman stood, crossed over to Carbone, and puffed on his cigar until the tipped glowed red. Carbone braced himself to be burned. Instead, Stratman broke into a huge grin and wrapped his arm around Carbone's shoulder.

"Join us. What do you want to drink?"

"Bourbon, if you have any."

"We can manage that." Stratman turned to Anderson. "Get this man a bourbon and a cigar."

Anderson stood and circled around by the bar. Stratman motioned for Carbone to take the empty chair. When both men had sat, Stratman took another puff on his cigar.

"Give me all the details. We'll give those assholes a few more days to set up, then we'll take the place for ourselves."

Thank you for reading *A World Gone Dark*, the first book in the *Ravaged Skies* saga and the first in my latest series. I hope you enjoyed reading this novel as much as I did writing it.

If you liked the novel, please use the QR code below to leave a review on Amazon. The more reviews a writer receives, the more exposure his/her book gets on Amazon, which means the more readers who can experience the adventure. It means a lot to us.

If you're interested in the other books in the *Ravaged Skies* shared apocalyptic adventure, use the QR code below to go to our website (ravagedskies.wordpeddlersociety.com) where you can purchase the other books in the saga.

Acknowledgments

A World Gone Dark has been in the planning stages for years. I was fortunate that when I began writing this book, I was invited to join the *Ravaged Skies* shared world project in which fifteen of the best post-apocalypse writers draft their novels based on a single event—a massive solar flare that disables all electronics across the globe. This book is the first in the shared world experience, and I hope it entices you to read the other novels in the series.

The hardest part of drafting this particular book was accurately portraying the events at the Seabrook Nuclear Power Plant following the solar flare. Because employees at these plants are required to sign non-disclosure agreements, I was unable to find anyone willing to review these sections of the book for accuracy. As a result, I based this plotline on the incidents that occurred at Chernobyl in 1986 and Fukushima in 2011. I'm not a nuclear engineer, so getting the details of the meltdown, especially the radiation levels, was one of the most difficult things I have ever written. My apologies for any errors and inaccuracies in this storyline.

The survivalist projects the Atkinson neighborhood undertakes are based on actual examples from *No Grid Survival Projects: How To Produce Everything You Need on Your Property*, the book Kathy procures from the local library. These are the only means someone can use to survive a long-term natural disaster. Hopefully, they will provide inspiration for those thinking about preparing for similar future catastrophes.

A huge debt of gratitude goes to Dan Uebel and Doc Fried,

my beta readers. They tore my manuscript to shreds, finding my inconsistencies and plot flaws. My books would not be as good as they are without them.

I recently started a full-time job as a teacher at a charter academy in Manchester, which severely restraints my time to write. It also means that when I get home, my pets are so happy to see me they want to dominate my time. Fred, AKA Turd Burglar, my stubborn Beagle-Bassett mix, is always with me when I write, and sometimes I spend more time keeping him out of trouble than I do at my computer. My cat Archer has discovered that my plugged-in laptop makes the perfect heating pad, so getting him to move is next to impossible. At night, while editing and managing social media, my other cat, Michonne, stands in front of my desktop computer, demanding attention. They make the writing process difficult, but it doesn't matter. I love them all.

The biggest thanks go to my readers, especially those who have been with me from the beginning. Writing is the fun part of my job. I appreciate all of you who read my books and patiently wait for the next one. I have a lot of stories floating around inside my head, and I am looking forward to sharing them with you.

About the Author

Scott M. Baker was born and raised in Everett, Massachusetts, and spent twenty-three years in northern Virginia working for the Central Intelligence Agency. He has traveled extensively through Europe, Asia, and the Middle East, incorporating many of the locations and cultures in his stories. Scott is now retired and lives outside Salem, New Hampshire, with his dog Fred and two cats who treat him as their human servant.

In addition to the *A World Gone Dark* series, Scott is currently writing the *OSS: Office of Supernatural Services* and *The Chronicles of Paul* sagas, as well as two zombie standalone novellas. Previous works include the *Nurse Alissa vs. the Zombies* series, his most popular zombie saga; his Tatyana paranormal series, which is also extremely popular; *Operation Majestic*, his first science fiction novel described as *Raiders of the Lost Ark* meets *Back to the Future* – with aliens; *Frozen World*, his first non-zombie post-apocalypse novel; the *Shattered World* series, his five-book young adult post-apocalypse thriller; the *Rotter World* trilogy, his first zombie series; *The Vampire Hunters* trilogy, about humans fighting the undead in Washington D.C.; as well as several zombie-themed novellas and anthologies.

Facebook:

facebook.com/groups/397749347486177

Twitter:

twitter.com/vampire_hunters

Instagram:

instagram.com/scottmbakerwriter

TikTok:

tiktok.com/@scottmbakerwriter

Blog:

scottmbakerauthor.blogspot.com

YouTube:

youtube.com/channel/UC5AyCVrEAncr2E0N5XoyUdg/featured

Wyrd Realities Homepage:

www.wyrdrealities.net

You can also sign up for Scott's newsletter, which will be released on the 1st and 15th of every month. He promises not to share your email with anyone or spam the recipients. The newsletter contains advance notices of upcoming releases/events and short stories from the Alissa universe that will not be available to the public. You can sign up by going to the link below.

Newsletter:

mailchi.mp/0b1401f1ddb2/scott-m-baker-writer